A Heart's Journey

To Quench a Thirsty Soul

ALSO BY JANICE N. ADAMS

About My Father's Footsteps

About My Father's Business

"A Twisted State of Mind"
(Contribution to Another Time, Another Place)

EDITED BY JANICE N. ADAMS

A Heart's Journey

About My Father's Footsteps

About My Father's Business

A Heart's Journey

To Quench a Thirsty Soul

Janice N. Adams

JAVISTA BOOKS

New York   London   Toronto

JAVISTA BOOKS
43 Randolph Road, #322
Silver Spring, MD 20904

ISBN-13: 978-0-9814521-0-4
ISBN-10:   0-9814521-0-8

Library of Congress Control Number: 2008937084

First Javista Books trade paperback edition November 2008
10 9 8 7 6 5 4 3 2 1

Cover photographed by Microsoft Corporation
Cover design by Janice N. Adams

Manufactured in the United States of America
This edition is printed on acid-free paper.

This book is dedicated to
Ellen, Nicole, Stephanie, Kim, Darylle, Cindy, and Jill

Acknowledgements

Thank you, God, for blessing me with the talent to write and the gift to entertain people with the stroke of a pen. All that I am, I owe to You.

To my adorable, loving sons, Mario II and Madison, thank you for being such patient people and keeping me on schedule with our activities as I often lost track of time working at the computer. Continue to do your best at any given task. Respect yourself and others. And most importantly, remember to keep God first in all things. I love you infinitely and pray that your dreams come true.

To my Nicholas family, mom, dad, Juan, and Jewel, thank you for the love and support you give me. Mom, thanks for listening to me no matter what time of day or night I called. Dad, thanks for your kind words. Juan, many thanks for your valued input and keeping me focused when I had too many irons in the fire. Jewel, thanks for the interest you expressed.

To my extremely talented cousin, Sharletta Richardson, who God blessed with the gift of music, thank you for your words of wisdom, your strength and purpose that make me admire you. You keep me reaching for the stars and doing my best.

To my extended Nicholas, Smith, and Adams families, thanks for your interest in my writing.

Mad love to my oldest and dearest friends, Ellen Hines, Nicole Miller, Stephanie Jackson, Kim Pugh, Jill Jenkins Bowles, Darylle Smoot, and Cindy Keaton, we are so blessed that after almost forty years of friendship, we are still laughing and talking about all the fun times we had as we continue to make new memories. I thank God for each of you and for all the years you encouraged me to pursue my writing.

Erica Wigley, thanks so much for pushing me to my limits, making me stretch my ideas and keeping me ready for the next level.

Angela "Angie" Charles, thanks for all the times I called to talk through a creative or business idea. Your input is always on point. LaTeshia Paggett and Ebla Ali Ibrahim, I sincerely appreciate your constant stream of encouragement. I pray that we continue to empower each other to achieve our personal and professional goals. I'm truly grateful for each of you.

To my proofreaders, Darylle Smoot and Stephanie Bird, you're awesome. Thank you so very much for enduring the details of editing every draft of the manuscript. What would I do without you? Sandy Smith, Erica Wigley, Angie Charles, and Ms. Lee, thank you for reading the first version and providing your feedback.

A special thank you to Rique Johnson, Shawan Lewis, and Wilma Brockington, three fantastic authors. Rique, we've gone from a casual introduction to doing book signings together, how time flies. Thanks again for promoting my initial work to Strebor Books. Zane and Charmaine Parker, thanks again for the opportunity to publish *A Twisted State of Mind* in Zane's anthology, *Another Time, Another Place*. It was a major milestone and the beginning of my professional writing career. Shawan, thanks for schooling me about the business and providing such great contacts. Wilma, thanks for your kindness and sharing such fantastic tips.

To my readers, thank you for supporting me, and this project. I trust you will enjoy reading *A Heart's Journey* as much as I enjoyed writing it. There's something for everyone in the pages of this story.

There are a number of other people I would like to acknowledge, but if I continue, you would never get to the rest of this book. I'll close by saying that I'm truly blessed to have such a wonderful support system of family and friends. Thanks everyone for believing in me. I pray the future is good to us all.

Peace and Blessings,

Janice

Contents

Prologue

To learn what love is and what love is not can be an overwhelming lesson at times. The burning desire to be loved and respected is the journey of one African-American, young lady, Cierra Sykes. She is an only child, living in an abusive home that has taken its toll. Yet, deep in Cierra's soul, she believes joy exists and she is determined to have it.

Cierra's journey for love and serenity leads her into the arms and interests of different men, Christopher Jackson, the NFL-bound, college sweetheart; Terrance Sullivan, an established industrial engineer; Kyle Dexter, a notorious drug dealer; and Paul Phillips, a refined federal DEA agent.

Each man has his own agenda and role in Cierra's life. Does any one of them fill the void in heart, quenching her thirst for fulfillment, peace, and love? Will her quest drive her to the brink of emotional disaster as she deals with these men and the choices she makes? Cierra's sisterhood is with her throughout her trials and tribulations, but are her friends supportive and helpful, or actually a part of her dilemma and drama? If she's not careful, she will destroy the very essence of her soul.

Spring 1989

March

Morning dew glistened upon the blades of grass as the sun peeked over the horizon. The break of dawn arrived in Richmond, Virginia with chilly northeasterly winds and an overcast sky, causing Cierra Sykes to shiver when she opened her apartment door. She quickly loaded her luggage into her car for a weeklong excursion to the Caribbean. Hastily, she drove to the Richmond International Airport, excited about being in St. Martin with her old college buddies, especially her ex-boyfriend, Christopher Jackson. She couldn't wait to show him what he'd been missing. Traveling to the Caribbean for the first time in her twenty-three years of life was a dream come true.

She parked her car in the long-term parking, dashed to the US Airways terminal, checked-in her luggage, and briskly walked to Gate A23. *Won't be long now.* Her heart raced with anticipation. After enduring a short wait, she and the other passengers boarded the plane. Cierra found her window seat, opened her planner, and settled in for the seven-hour flight. The plane taxied down the runway and within seconds was airborne. *This is going to be a great trip. I can just feel it.* She turned the pages in her planner to the week of March twelfth and read the events scheduled for Rachel Laveau's festive St. Patrick's Day wedding. *I still can't believe Rachel is pregnant and getting married.*

Rachel and Cierra met during their freshmen year at Virginia Polytechnic Institute and State University, better known as Virginia Tech. Rachel, an exotic looking girl from Marigot, St. Martin, stood poised and confident with a five feet eleven inch slender frame. Her hazel eyes and silky, black mane complemented her espresso brown skin while her incredible smile easily competed with Janet Jackson's pearly whites.

At the end of each school year, she lived in New York City for the summer to work various modeling jobs that ranged from catalog print to fashion runway shows. She dreamed of owning a modeling agency and knew that she had to be business savvy in addition to having a pretty face. When Virginia Tech offered her a full, four-year scholarship in business administration, she jumped at the chance to attend the well-known university.

Over the course of their college years, Cierra and Rachel became close friends. Cierra liked Rachel's straight to the point, don't beat around the bush approach to things, and her do what it takes attitude towards life. Rachel often said in her Caribbean accent, *c'est ça* meaning "that's that" and then she would move on to the next thing. Likewise, Rachel appreciated the way Cierra helped her adjust to her new surroundings. Being in a predominately white school in a college town was quite different than living in St. Martin and NYC. She liked Cierra's low tolerance for immaturity and her determined spirit, but mostly, she cherished Cierra's honest nature. As a result of their harmonious personalities, their friendship blended like peaches and cream.

As the plane flew further south, Cierra glanced out of her window to admire the Atlantic Ocean's beautiful, turquoise water. *I'm almost there.* She then returned her attention to her day planner.

Shortly thereafter, the buckle seat belt light came on and the flight attendant made the usual return to your seat announcement. The attendant then announced that the plane would land in San Juan, Puerto Rico for a maintenance matter. A passenger sitting behind Cierra whispered to the person next to him that he overheard that the plane was experiencing engine problems. *That's just great.* Cierra became disappointed that there would be a delay in her direct flight to the tropical island and an added wait to see Chris.

Moments later, the plane landed safely in San Juan. The pilot grounded the aircraft due to mechanical problems, leaving the passengers no choice but to switch planes to the American Airline flight out of the Baltimore Washington International (BWI) Airport located in Baltimore, Maryland. Cierra gathered her carry-on and exited the plane with the other passengers. They walked to Gate Three and approached the check-in desk where the AA staff validated their tickets, assigned new seats on flight 1785, and allowed the passengers to board.

As Cierra walked down the narrow aisle searching for her assigned seat, she heard a familiar voice. *No, this can't be.* But there he was, Christopher Jackson, her former college sweetheart. He was engrossed in a conversation about architecture with the man next to him and did not see her. But as soon as she said, "Excuse me ma'am" to get to her window seat, he stopped in mid sentence and stared at her.

"Uh, sir, you were saying?" asked the gentleman next to Chris.

"Um, nothing. Excuse me a minute," Chris replied. He walked up the aisle and stopped at Cierra's seat.

"Hi Ci," he began.

"Chris? What a coincidence. How are you?" She pretended to be surprised and extended her hand to shake his. He reciprocated the gesture then slowly released her hand allowing a familiar sensation to enter the greeting. Her body tingled from his gentle touch, a touch she remembered oh so well.

"So, you were on the flight that got grounded, uh?" he asked as he squeezed closer to the aisle seat to make room for the passengers still boarding the flight. Cierra sat in her window seat, enjoying the handsome, Hershey chocolate drop standing before her. He may be eye-candy now, but she intended to change that before the trip was over.

"Yeah."

"Well um, look why don't you come sit with me before the flight gets totally full, I'm only five rows behind you." He pointed to his seat. Cierra hesitated in order to watch his reaction. Without thinking twice, Chris devised a simple plan to convince her because he truly wanted to sit and chat with her.

"Excuse me ma'am but would you mind switching seats with me so I can sit with this gorgeous young lady?" he asked the salt and pepper haired lady beside Cierra. The lady looked at Chris then at Cierra and whispered, "He is mighty handsome."

"There's a very nice gentleman sitting in my row who would make a wonderful travel companion for the duration of the flight. I'm sure he'd much rather talk to a beautiful woman like yourself instead of me."

"Oh stop," blushed the lady with a big grin upon her seasoned face. Chris kept pouring on the charm.

"Seriously. Look at you. You look great. Your makeup and hair are perfect, you're wearing a killer outfit and your jewelry is spectacular. Why are you wasting your ensemble sitting here? I'm sure Mr. Jacobson would enjoy it so much more."

The lady blushed through her chocolate colored skin as Chris finalized his intentions.

"Tell you what, I'm gonna tell Stan that I'm switching seats and introduce you. OK?"

"Very well," the lady agreed.

Chris and the lady exchanged seats just in time for the announcement, "All passengers please take your seats and buckle your seat belts. The plane will take off momentarily." Minutes later, the engines roared and the plane taxied down the runway. Chris leaned toward Cierra to look out of the window as the aircraft ascended.

"I love this part," he said.

"What part is that, my lap or the takeoff?"

"Both."

"Yeah right."

"Seriously," Chris replied as he gave her the look she always found hard to resist. Cierra's mind wondered. *Lord, is this a coincidence or fate?*

The two ex-lovers talked about the upcoming wedding and work. Awhile into their exchange of pleasantries, Cierra navigated the dialog right where she intended. Her curious mind wanted to know what Chris had been doing since they last saw each other on her twenty-third birthday, three and a half months ago on December 1, 1988.

"So, Christopher Jackson, how was your Christmas and New

Year?"

"What?" Chris tried to play off her question by acting surprised.

"Did you spend the holidays with your new girlfriend?" asked Cierra, unable to hold her tongue any longer.

"Now see, why do you want to go there? We're sitting here enjoying a nice friendly conversation on our way to a beautiful island, getting ready to have a wonderful time with our friends, and you want to ask me something like that."

"Well?"

"Well what?"

"Forget it. Never mind."

Relieved, Chris changed the subject back to their careers for the remainder of their trip.

Finally, the plane landed safely in St. Martin. Cierra and Chris patiently waited until they could leave the plane. The two walked through the hangar, retrieved their luggage at the turn style, and then shared a taxi to the Cap Caraibes Resort Hotel in Orient Bay where reservations for the wedding party and other wedding guests awaited them.

"Now this is what I'm talkin' about," said Cierra to Chris while holding her butterscotch face to the sun as a mild Caribbean breeze tousled her shoulder length hair. She relished the moment.

"I feel you. No chilly March temperatures here, that's for sure," he replied.

At check in, the male desk clerk informed that Cierra's room, along with the other girls in the bridal party was located on the third floor west terrace, facing the oceanfront. The groom's party, including Chris' room faced inland on the second floor east terrace.

"Ha, ha," Cierra teased. "Us girls got the better view. See you later."

"Whatever," Chris jokingly replied.

With his heavy Caribbean accent, the desk clerk questioned Chris, "Sir, do you play pro-ball with the Redskins too?"

"No. Why?"

"Well, you're built and have such well-defined, arm muscles

like some of the other players who have arrived that are also in the wedding." He eyed Chris up and down as he handed him his room key. Chris felt uneasy about the clerk's compliment and didn't appreciate Cierra snickering as they walked away from the front desk.

"Why are you laughing? That shit ain't even funny, Ci."

"Chris, give it a rest. He's harmless."

The bellhop rolled Cierra's luggage from the front desk to the elevator. She followed the brass cart while waving to Chris, "Bye muscle man."

"That's cold, Ci. You ain't right," replied Chris as he waited for the next bellman with a cart.

When Cierra and the bellhop reached her floor, they heard loud laughter coming from room number thirty-two. With the door propped open, Cierra saw Bridget Murphy, her other Virginia Tech college-buddy, entertaining some of the other hotel guests.

Raised in a strict household, Bridget, a twenty-three year old daughter of a devout, southern Baptist preacher, ignored her upbringing every chance she got. The short, heavyset, hazelnut complexion girl loved being the center of attention, comedy was her hook. She liked making people laugh and could out wit anyone. She often challenged her peers to try, but no one ever could. The best anybody did was joke Bridget about her big breast. She didn't care or hesitate to tell anyone how much the men liked her boobs. Known for fun, everybody liked having Bridget around because there was never a dull moment. But one lesson that Bridget never let slide by the wayside was how her daddy taught her to pray. There lay the common thread and foundation between Cierra and Bridget's friendship. Bridget, of all people, was Cierra's prayer partner during their collegiate days. After they graduated in May 1988 last year, they only talked every blue moon because of conflicting schedules. Leaving messages on each other's answering machines became the norm.

"Bridget, is that you?" asked Cierra surprised to see a much slimmer friend. Bridget let out a loud shriek and raced to the doorway.

"Ci! Girl, it's so good to see you. It's been far too long. We've gotta do a better job about staying in touch."

"I agree. B, you look terrific," said Cierra admiring Bridget's weight loss. Bridget did a diva turn to show off her new figure.

"Girl, I worked so hard to get the weight off. But I must admit, ain't nothing like being able to wear a size fourteen. No more Women Plus sizes for me. I can shop in the Misses department."

"B, I'm so proud of you. Rachel told me that you lost more weight since school, but she didn't tell me that you lost this much and that you turned into a stone cold diva."

"Oh hush. Ci, guess what?"

"What?"

"I got a man. Well, actually two but I like one more than the other," Bridget confessed as she flicked her hand like never mind that. She continued, "Did you and that fine ass Chris ever get back together?"

"That's a long story. Forget about me, I definitely want to hear about your men and all that you've been up to. Let me go put my things in my room and I'll be right back."

"Okay, but hurry 'cause we're about to get our drink on up in here," commented Bridget as she returned to her room.

Cierra waved from the hallway to the other guests then walked down the corridor to her room. She instructed the bellhop to just leave her luggage by the door but the dark cocoa man insisted on placing her bags in the closet and opening her blinds. Cierra thanked him and tried to give him a tip but he refused. She then rushed back to Bridget's room where she enjoyed an afternoon of laughter and drinks with Bridget and the other bridal guests.

A few hours later, Cierra returned to her bamboo and teak furnished hotel room, tossed her suitcase onto the bed and took out what she needed for the Meet and Greet gathering at the Laveau's estate. She wanted to look extra special for Chris. *I need to wear the perfect outfit, not too sexy and not too casual.* She made her selection then stepped into the shower.

There. That should do it. She gave herself a final look over in the full-length closet mirror. She twisted from side to side examining her perfect curvy size six figure in the coral, cotton linen, sleeveless dress that criss-crossed in the back and stopped mid thigh. The sandstone colored strapped sandals matched her sandstone colored earrings and necklace. With her hair pulled back in a braided chignon knot that accented her facial features, Cierra left the room assured that she looked exquisite.

The wedding party congregated in the lobby of the hotel at five p.m. When Cierra walked into the room, all heads turned.

"Damn Ci, who are you trying to hurt in that dress?" asked Bridget aloud when she saw Cierra.

"B, hush. You're drawing attention," Cierra said shyly as she gave a fake smile to the onlookers. But that didn't stop Bridget, "Hey Claudia, look at Ci. Don't she look nice?" Cierra knew trying to get Bridget to stop was hopeless, so she ignored the flattery and scanned the room for Chris but didn't see him.

"Who are you looking for?" Bridget asked.

"Nobody," Cierra insisted as she continued to shift her eyes. Then the elevator doors opened and out walked Chris. Cierra froze like a deer caught in headlights. Bridget turned to see what made her stop.

"Oh, now I get it. Nobody, huh? You little stinker." Bridget grabbed Cierra by the arm. "Come on. Let's go say hi."

Cierra pulled back, "Bridget, please not now. Be cool. I've seen him earlier today already, but I swear he looks even better now."

Chris, wearing a white Calvin Klein tank shirt, khaki shorts, and tan leather sandals, looked like he just stepped out of a GQ magazine. He greeted the guys with the usual high-fives and "What's up man?" while Cierra and Bridget watched from across the room.

"Ci, I think I've died and gone to heaven. Look at the treats in here. Every last one of these Redskins players has a body on him."

"Yeah, I agree." *But Chris is by far the finest to me*, Cierra thought. Within a few minutes, the shuttle bus approached the front entrance, interrupting her silent observation of Chris.

"Ladies first," announced one of the ball players closest to the door.

As the girls departed the lobby to board the shuttle, Cierra caught Chris looking at her out of the corner of her eye. Bridget whispered in her ear, "Ci, he's looking at you."

"I know. Keep walking," said Cierra.

When the guys boarded, the young ladies made all kinds of facial gestures as they watched the handsome, chiseled athletes pass by. When Chris walked down the aisle, the girls drooled at his perfect Hershey physique, but he only had eyes for one special person on the shuttle.

"Hi Ci, you look very nice," he commented as he passed her.

"Hi Chris," she replied liking the fact that he noticed her ensemble. Across the aisle Bridget gave a taunting, "Hiiiii Chris."

Chris did a double take. "B, is that you? What's up? I didn't recognize you. You look great."

"Man, keep it movin'," voiced one of the groomsmen who wanted a window seat.

"I'll see y'all at the spot." He winked at Cierra and proceeded to the back. Cierra and Bridget returned to watching the other hotties board the bus.

After a fifteen-minute ride through the beautiful countryside of St. Martin, the shuttle bus arrived at the estate of Nelson and Elena Laveau, Rachel's parents. The breathtaking view of the estate with its colorful tropical flowers, palm trees, rolling green lawns, and manicured gardens silenced the crew aboard the shuttle as they marveled at the mansion. One of the guys commented in amazement, "Damn, man, check this out. They have another house across the yard." John, the comedian in the group, looked out of his window and said, "Now, you know that ain't nothing but an old slave quarters from way back in the day." The guys all laughed.

"Y'all are so ignorant. That's the guesthouse, fool," Bridget interjected.

"Say what you want. This is some old Kunta Kinte property right here," John responded.

"Whatever. It's still beautiful," Bridget replied.

Mr. and Mrs. Laveau gave a warm welcome to the guests as the wedding party stepped off the shuttle.

"Welcome to our home. Come. We will take you to see Rachel and Damien," said Mr. Laveau. The group walked through the foyer of the house admiring the decorations and unique, one-of-a kind African art. "S'il vous plait. Come t'is way," Mr. Laveau said with a broad smile, showing all his pearly whites. He tried to hurry the group along but they were too busy looking at the collections and moved slowly. Finally, they reached the rear of the house that opened to a huge outdoor patio. When Rachel saw Cierra and Bridget, she immediately jumped up to greet them. Screaming with excitement and joy, they each gave her a hug.

"How's the baby?" Cierra asked, rubbing Rachel's round belly.

"Kicking like crazy. I think he or she will be an athlete like its daddy."

Just then Damien walked over as suave as ever and gave Cierra and Bridget a hug with his smooth, "Hello, ladies. Good to see you."

"Congrats again, big papa," Bridget teased as she looked Damien's muscular body up and down.

"Thanks, B. I see you haven't changed," he laughed and continued, "Ci, did you see Chris?"

"Yes, and don't start."

"Start what?" he asked jokingly.

"You know what."

"Yeah, a'right. I'll catch up with you ladies later."

"Okay," Rachel, Cierra, and Bridget said in unison.

"Mmm mmm. Would you look at that," commented Bridget as she zoomed in on Damien's booty as he walked away. Rachel hit her in the arm to break her obvious stare.

"What Rachel? I can't help it. The brother is fine. One day, I'm gonna have a black prince like him. Wait and see."

"B, you're a nut," Cierra laughed, "I thought you have a man."

"Well, I do, but not like delicious Damien."

The girls laughed at Bridget and watched Damien from afar. He proceeded to greet the guys with their traditional coded handshakes. John with his silly self opened his big mouth, "Yo D, man, tell the truth. This is an old masta's house ain't it?" Damien ignored John but Mr. Laveau over heard him. "Young mon," Mr. Laveau said as he approached John and placed his arm around John's neck. "Come. You and I have much to talk about, oui?" Mr. Laveau led John away from the group. John looked over his shoulder at his group of friends as if to say 'help'. Bridget laughed loudly, "Serves you right, dummy."

The Laveau cookout was a hit with the partygoers. They enjoyed a spread of fresh seafood, grilled vegetables, and sweet, juicy fruit that melted in the mouth like cotton candy. Cierra and Bridget made a point to sample as much of the cuisine as possible and quench their thirst with ice cold daiquiris and frozen Mai Tai's made with authentic Caribbean rum. With their bellies full, heads just right, they rested in two lawn chairs under a shady palm tree and did what they liked to do best, people watch.

"Girl, look at the feet and hands on that brotha. Now that's what I'm talkin' about. That's some Caribbean Mandingo stuff right there," Bridget said raising her hand for a high-five from Cierra. She then set her eyes on another unsuspected prospect. "Ci, do you see that hunk over there in the white shorts and aquamarine Polo shirt?"

Cierra looked in the direction Bridget pointed and replied, "Yeah."

"Well, the good Lord is gonna have to forgive me because I'm gonna have to get with that one before we leave this island."

"B, you need to stop," joked Cierra.

"I try but I can't help myself."

Cierra shook her head and warned, "You better be careful and you know what I mean."

"Ci, please. Girl, I make sure the ding-a-ling is wrapped. And I inspect everything like this before I let a brother near me." Bridget leaned forward as though she was peering through a magnifying glass. Cierra laughed hysterically. "B, you are too much."

"I ain't lying. You gotta look at the goods extra closely these days. Shiiiiit, I examine them like Inspector Gadget." Bridget then leaned back and took a sip of her daiquiri.

"B, you're crazy, I swear. Hey, will you look at that girl over there flirting with the bartender. Her boobs are about to fall out her dress. Oh my damn, they just did."

Cierra and Bridget laughed so hard and loud that they made a small ruckus among themselves. One of the ball players took notice and asked Chris, "Man, what's up with those two?" Chris looked at them, chuckled and said, "No telling." The tipsy two saw him watching, raised their glasses in his direction, and then tapped each other's glass with a small toast.

"Are they your home girls?" the guy inquired.

"No, we went to college together."

"Word?"

"Yeah why?"

"I'd like to meet the one in the coral dress. Can you introduce us?"

Chris paused and cleared his throat. The guy's request bothered him but he ignored his feelings.

"A'right," Chris answered. He walked over to Cierra and Bridget.

"You sweet ladies seem to be enjoying yourselves."

"Yes, we are. What can we do for you?"

"Ci, uh, listen, the guy in the blue shirt sitting at my table would like to meet you." Cierra peeped around Chris. "Are you serious? You have got to be jokin' me. He looks like Bro'man on the Martin Lawrence Show." Bridget fell out laughing.

"B, it ain't that damn funny," said Chris as he looked at the guy. "So, do you want to meet him or not?"

"Hell no. Besides, I'm tired of tied ass brothers. Next time I date, maybe I'll do like you and date someone of a different race and culture. You know, see what it's like to sample the other flavors."

"Amen to that," Bridget said as she raised her glass and took another sip.

"Y'all need to slow down on the daiquiris," suggested Chris as he ignored Cierra's drunken implication of what he did last year at school.

"Why? We don't have no place to go except back to the hotel

and sleep it off. Or, maybe we'll crash here with Rachel. Ain't like we drivin'," Bridget slurred.

"Chris, I'm just not interested, plain and simple."

"Not interested in him or nobody?" Chris asked, fishing for her feelings.

"'Or nobody?' Do you hear this, B?"

"I hear it, girl."

"Chris, who is nobody, you? I wonder, where do you come off asking me something like that?" remarked Cierra in a tone charming enough to lure him in but stern enough to slightly sting him. Chris regretted his comment while Cierra took advantage of the opportunity. She stood and walked around him.

"Well, let me see, Mr. Nobody. Right now you're lookin' mighty sexy." She stepped closer and entered his personal space and spoke into his ear just above a whisper. "Your shorts are hugging your ass just right. Your muscles are hotter than this heat." She then ran her index finger ever so slightly down his face. "And your piercing brown eyes, ohhhh how they make me melt." Chris stood motionless as she nearly planted her lips on his and said, "Yes, Chris, I'm interested in you. Is that what your ego needs to hear?" She then turned to Bridget and laughed, "Oops, did I say that?"

Cierra and Bridget grabbed hands and doubled over with amusement while Cierra returned to her lawn chair.

"You two are hopeless." Chris shook his head and walked away.

"So, what did she say man?" the guy asked Chris when he returned to the table.

"Na man. She's not interested."

"Damn. Look at all these females out here. I gotta find a warm body for the night." The guy's shallow intentions made Chris glad Cierra turned him down.

As the evening grew to an end and the sunset lingered over the ridge, Mr. and Mrs. Laveau summoned everyone to the patio for a toast to Rachel and Damien. The wedding party and other guests cheered for a happy union and prosperity for the couple. Rachel cried and Damien blushed at the sincere wishes. The caterers then packed away the remaining food and dismantled the tables. The shuttle bus arrived to carry the wedding party back to the hotel. Rachel met Cierra and Bridget in the family room as they walked through the house headed to the front entrance.

"Girls," Rachel said as she approached them, "with all the guests here, I didn't get to visit with you guys that much."

"We understand."

"I've missed you guys. Why don't you stay the night? We have everything you need."

"Sure. That'll be cool," Cierra and Bridget agreed without a second thought.

"It'll be like old times at Virginia Tech. And Ci, guess what?"

"What?"

"Chris is staying too."

"Ah sooky now," Bridget replied as she nudged Cierra on the arm.

"It ain't like that, B."

"Yeah right," said Bridget and Rachel simultaneously.

Rachel led her two friends to the kitchen where Mrs. Laveau sat exhausted from the day's activities while the serving staff cleared the clutter. Cierra and Bridget thanked Mrs. Laveau for inviting them and for her hospitality.

"Mrs. Laveau, everything was absolutely delicious. I wish I knew how to cook like this," Cierra said as she looked at the food on the countertop.

"Maybe I'll show you how to make one dish before you go. No?"

"That would be really nice. Something simple that I can handle though," Cierra suggested.

"Of course dear child. You girls go now. Get out zee kitchen. Go. Have fun wit' your company," instructed Mrs. Laveau as she waved the girls away.

"Rachel, your mom is really cool. If that was my mom, all three of us would be in the kitchen cleaning. My dad would say stuff like 'A woman's place is in the home.' And my mom would go for that mess and have me doing all kinds of crazy ass chores. Freaked me out," said Bridget remembering her childhood experiences.

They chuckled as they returned to the family room to watch television but Damien and Chris had already claimed the remote control and insisted on watching a special report on the sports channel about Mike Tyson. They loved to watch Iron Mike's boxing matches. Uninterested in the program, the girls decided to take a tour of the mansion.

Rachel showed them her family's heirlooms dating back to 1840. She cherished her great- great- grandmother's gold locket the most. Cierra looked down at the jade, angel pendant on her gold necklace that her mother made for her sixteenth birthday. She thought how one day she would pass her pendant to a daughter, granddaughter and so on. It was the only piece of jewelry her mother was able to make her. Cierra remembered the day she unwrapped the pretty pink gift box and saw the beautiful pendant inside. She recalled her mother's words, "It's a one of a kind piece. I made it just for you. No matter what happens, there's always one angel watching over you."

The hour grew late and Bridget decided to retire to her room. Cierra and Rachel returned to the family room and watched the last few seconds of the Tyson special with Chris and Damien. Rachel opened the French patio doors, allowing a warm Caribbean breeze to circulate the room. Cierra leaned against the sofa and enjoyed the sound and smell of the nearby ocean. Chris tried not to stare at her, but her beauty always captivated him. Suddenly, Damien broke the silence and announced, "I don't know about you guys, but I'm not ready to turn in for the night."

"Us either," the rest replied.

"How about we enjoy some of this refreshing air," Damien suggested.

"Sounds good to me," Chris agreed, glad that he would be around Cierra longer.

The four exited the house for a midnight walk along the beach. Cierra thought it was the perfect way to end an exciting day. The moon hovered close to the horizon, appearing larger than she remembered it in Richmond. The iridescent glow provided the ideal amount of light to create a romantic canvas. Cierra let down the braided chignon that she sported all day, giving the wind permission to toss her wavy locks. Chris, unable to resist touching her any longer, reached for Cierra's hand and she happily placed her palm inside his. As Rachel and Damien walked ahead, Cierra and Chris lagged behind so their conversation could not be heard.

"So did you enjoy yourself today?" Cierra asked as she watched the waves crest and break against the shoreline.

"Yes, I did," replied Chris absorbing their quiet moment together. "It was obvious that you and Bridget had a good time."

"Yes, we did," laughed Cierra recalling Bridget's outrageous antics. "Did Damien or Rachel take you on a tour of the mansion?"

"Not yet," Chris replied as he stretched his arm across her shoulders, drawing her closer to him.

"It's awesome. I've never seen anything like it. Rachel has been very modest over the years about her home."

She recounted the history of the mansion and described all the different rooms. Intrigued, Chris listened attentively. He liked the way she knew how to hold his attention. Just then, the crest of a wave sent her further into his arms.

"I got you," he said as he helped her regain her balance.

"Thanks," replied Cierra standing only inches from his face. Chris seized the moment and tenderly kissed her velvet lips.

"What was that for?"

"Don't know. It just felt right," Chris answered as they continued walking hand-in-hand. Cierra didn't dare ruin this moment by asking uninvited questions about his new girlfriend, although she wanted to. They saw Rachel and Damien in the distance sandwiched together French kissing. Cierra commented, "They're so happy. I'm glad everything worked out for them."

"Me too," Chris said as he found a small boulder to sit on. He held out his hand for Cierra to join him. They sat and watched the ocean and moon until the earth rotated enough to hang the moon high in the sky. Damien gave a loud whistle and Chris whistled back, a code for "Let's go."

"It's getting pretty late. We should head back. I don't want you to blame me for any dark circles under your eyes in the morning. I can see it now. Bridget, girl, let me tell you. Chris kept me up all night talking my head off."

"I wouldn't say that."

"Oh no? What would you say?" asked Chris as they climbed down the rock.

Cierra looked him in the eye and said, "I would say that Chris and I spent a wonderful time walking along the beach, enjoying each other's company."

"Would you tell her about our kiss?" he asked as he ran his hands along her bare shoulders.

"What? That little peck you gave me earlier?"

"No Ci, this one."

Chris swooped his tongue through Cierra's mouth like a down court pass between Michael Jordan and Scottie Pippen, quick and smooth. The rhythmic motion of their tongues made Cierra's heart flutter and the gentle tugging of her lips made her wet in her panties. The kiss lasted long enough for Rachel and Damien to approach and pass them. When the kiss ended, Cierra whispered, "I love you, Chris." He smiled as he placed his forehead against hers while cupping her face with his hands. A silent, awkward moment surfaced, as he didn't reply to her soft-spoken words. Instead, he suggested, "We should go."

Cierra kicked herself for telling him she loved him. She wanted to bury herself right there in the sand and never look at him again. The walk back to the house seemed twice as long. When they reached the back patio, Chris kissed the back of Cierra's hand and said, "Ci, I had a wonderful time with you. And I still care for you too."

"Goodnight, Chris."

Cierra closed the patio door and watched Chris and Damien walk to the guesthouse. *'I still care.'* Was that good or bad? *Does that mean he still loves me?* Just then Cierra heard Rachel scream from the kitchen and went running.

"Rachel what's wrong?"

"Nothing. Bridget is in here in the dark and almost scared me to death."

"I was thirsty and wanted some water. Where have you two heifers been anyway?" Bridget asked.

"Out with Chris and Damien," Rachel replied exiting the kitchen.

"Mm mm mm," Bridget shook her head. "You naughty girls."

"B, hush and go to bed. See you in the morning," Cierra responded.

Early the next morning, Rachel started getting nervous and anxious about her big day. She woke Cierra out of a deep sleep, concerned about how much her belly grew in the last week. She worried if she would still fit her wedding gown. Cierra reassured her that, for being eight months pregnant, she looked great. Bridget heard them and entered the room and added her two cents.

"Rachel, girl, it just looks like you ate a big ass hamburger, some fries, and a shake."

Rachel's eyes watered.

"Bridget, go get dressed. You're not helping," Cierra instructed. She closed the door behind Bridget and started the pep talk with Rachel all over again. It took some time, but she managed to get Rachel's confidence back up and prepared her for the church rehearsal and rehearsal dinner scheduled for later that day along with the Bridal Shower and Bachelor's parties.

Around nine a.m., the Laveau's chauffeur met Cierra, Bridget, Chris, and Damien at the mansion's front entrance with the family's Lincoln Town car. He then drove them back to the Caraibes Resort. After they arrived at the resort and the chauffeur opened the car door, Cierra and Bridget thanked him for the ride, told Chris and Damien they'd see them later, then made a mad dash to their rooms to prepare for the day's newest activities.

At eleven that morning, Cierra and Bridget met in the lobby.

"Ci, let's go shoot some pool while we wait for the shuttle. I see some of the Redskins players in the billiard room."

They introduced themselves and before long had Mai Tai's in their hands taking bets on players. Skilled in the game but laying low like a lioness watching her prey, Cierra pretended not to know much about the game until the guys started wagering larger sums of money. She waited for the perfect moment to join in then pounced her prey as she won game after game, knocking two and three balls in the pockets at a time. "Eight ball, left corner pocket," Cierra called as she pointed to the pocket with the tip of her pool queue. Bridget heard one of the guys mumbled, "From where she is, that's an impossible shot."

"Hey Ci," Bridget yelled, "this guy thinks you can't make that shot."

"Oh really?" Cierra questioned then turned to face the guy. "How much are you willing to bet?" She bent over to align her pool stick to the correct angle needed to make the shot. She paused, looked at the guy again and said, "How much?"

Rallying together, the room of testosterone encouraged the guy's ego to wager far too much.

"Three hundred dollars," he said as he laid three one hundred dollar bills on the table.

"Done deal," Cierra agreed.

As she concentrated on the position of the balls, the room grew quiet. Just as she aimed to take her shot, the guy interrupted, "Hey, where's your three hundred dead presidents?" Cierra banked the queue ball off the back and watched it travel back up the table, around her opponents striped thirteen ball, and hit the black eight ball into the left corner pocket. She picked his money off the table and replied, "Right here." The room of guys roared, "Ah, damn man, she got you." Cierra and Bridget exited the billiard room with a winner's cheer, "I'm bad. Who's bad? I'm bad. Who's bad? Don't stop, get it, get it, don't stop." They continued their mischievous deeds and schoolgirl fun throughout the afternoon making the most out of day two on their trip.

Four o'clock rolled around and the wedding party caught the shuttle to St. Catherine's Cathedral for the wedding rehearsal. Upon entering the church, Cierra sniffed the wood scent from what seemed to be endless rows of oak pews. The huge magnificent stained glass windows reflected a mixture of jewel hues and tones.

Colorful mosaic tiles shaped into biblical artifacts like the Ten Commandments and Noah's Ark covered the walls like wallpaper. The vibrant carpet and podium colors of red, purple, and gold complemented the polished brass and gold pulpit ornaments. Positioned behind the choir stand among the painted mural, stood the most exquisite limestone statue of Mary holding the baby Jesus. The carved details captivated Cierra.

"May I have everyone over here please?" instructed the wedding coordinator, Tema. She introduced herself, read the itinerary, and voiced her expectations. From that moment on, the ebony skinned, petite lady with silver, short dread locks ran the show. She clapped her hands twice and said with her strong French Caribbean accent, "Let's get started."

Cierra tried to calm Rachel's jitters as best she could while the wedding coordinator situated people in their appropriate places. Cierra and Rachel sat in the front pew watching the wedding activities unfold. Bridget tried to assist Tema stating that the bride needed to walk down the aisle so they could time everything, big mistake. Tema, Ms. Tema as they started to call her shortly after rehearsal commenced, walked over to Bridget while pointing her index finger and said, "You there. What do you know about our traditions?"

Embarrassed, Bridget remarked, "I was-"

"Shhh. Don't say any'ting. I tell you. It's bad luck for zee bride to walk down zee aisle before her wedding day, especially in zee presence of her husband. Bad fortune will come to them if they do dis 'ting."

"But Ms. Tema, I was just-"

"Hush girl. I tell you too much mouth is not attractive."

Bridget respectfully followed her advice. Two hours passed and the wedding ensemble finished the rehearsal on time thanks to the strict and organized direction of Ms. Tema.

Next, the group ventured to the seafood restaurant owned by Mr. and Mrs. Laveau for the rehearsal dinner. Greeting the guests at the entrance, Mr. Laveau announced, "Welcome to The Swordfish. Please, enjoy yourselves. Eat and drink as much as you like. Tonight we celebrate." That was all Cierra and Bridget needed to hear. The young ladies and gentlemen sat at three, very long tables in the main dinning room while the elders sat in the surrounding booths. Soft reggae music played in the background of the quaint, semi-fancy, eating establishment. Cierra walked around the first table trying to decide where to sit among the many white rattan chairs and guests. Chris saw her about to sit and signaled her to sit beside him. Butterflies flew about her stomach as she sat in the chair next to him. Damien and Rachel sat at the head of the table while Bridget made herself comfortable next to the Redskins player Cierra beat playing pool. They all enjoyed a blissful evening.

Toward the end of dinner, Rachel and Damien made an announcement that after dinner two stretch limousines would be parked outside. The first limo would take the ladies to the Laveau estate for the Bridal Shower, and the second would take the gentlemen to the Rio Pub for the bachelor's party. Everyone roared with anticipation. The rehearsal dinner ended and a night of partying took place.

The dawn of St. Patrick's Day, 1989 began with a morning of hangovers but quickly turned into a beautiful wedding day. On the job and in action, Ms. Tema conducted the wedding party like a maestro guiding an orchestra through a complex symphony. Every participant walked and talked to Ms. Tema's tune. Her mood and stern but joyous face set the tone that she expected a superb wedding ceremony at St. Catherine's Cathedral for Rachel and Damien.

The organist and pianist played their rendition of Luther Vandross' "So Amazing" to commence the occasion. The front doors of the cathedral opened and the procession began. Ten groomsmen strolled down the aisle to the altar in their tailored, cream tuxedos accented with sea mist green cummerbunds and bowties to join Damien and his best man, Chris. Cierra, Rachel's maid of honor, and the bridesmaids followed with sea mist green, silk strapless dresses adorned with fresh water pearls. The six-year-old ring bearer timidly made his way to the church altar after which identical four-year-old twin sisters trailed tossing pink and white rose petals along the aisle from their white flower girl baskets. The onlookers cooed at the adorable little mocha princesses. Chris tried to absorb the entrances of the youngsters but was too captivated by Cierra's poise and beauty. Eventually, he caught her eye and gave a familiar expression; *you look so exquisite to me*. She knew the look well and recalled the tingling sensations it would send down her spine and now was no different. She smiled at him then looked away.

The music changed to "The Wedding March" and the guests stood at the first notes of "Here Comes the Bride." Rachel entered the sanctuary in a white satin and silk, strapless Vera Wang gown. The dress complimented Rachel's chic style. She gracefully walked down the aisle with her father. When she reached the altar, she took her place beside Damien.

Emotions throughout the cathedral heightened as Rachel and Damien professed their love in front of the congregation. As the priest instructed them through their wedding vows, Cierra and Chris eyed each other as thoughts of *if only* raced through their minds. The heartfelt words that Rachel and Damien exchanged brought tears to many of the guests. Cierra, prepared with an embroidered hanky, allowed her tears to flow. *This should be Chris and me too.* She wiped away another stream of tears. With her angelic eyes, she intentionally looked at him and for the first time in a long time, he looked as vulnerable as he did the day she left him in New York. His soul understood her heartache and his guilt caused him to lower his head as he wiped away an emotional tear. Bridget let out the loudest boohoo, after which people didn't know whether to laugh or tell her to be quiet.

The ceremony lasted twenty-five minutes just as Ms. Tema planned. The benediction occurred as smoothly as the procession. Ms. Tema then quickly directed the wedding party back inside to pose for the wedding pictures. Congratulations echoed throughout the cathedral as the wedding party started an early celebration. Afterwards, the reception followed on the rear grounds of St. Catherine's. Under the white tents and among the crowd of people, Cierra and Chris managed to find one another.

"Let's go for a walk," Chris suggested as he held Cierra's hand.

"Sounds good to me," Cierra replied wanting to be alone with him.

He led her away from the noisy festivity to a wood bench at the far end of the grounds. There they sat hand-in-hand.

"Weddings have a strange way of making you remember all the love a heart can hold for a person. Ci, you look absolutely beautiful today."

"Thank you, Chris. That's very sweet of you."

He stroked her face then sealed his words with a kiss to the back of her hand. Unsure of what to say, Cierra didn't speak. Chris slid closer to her. Secretly, she hoped for another kiss like the one they shared on the beach the other night, but Chris returned her hand and said, "Ci, you know you will always be a part of me."

Looking at Chris' handsome face and fine physique in that tuxedo and being in the midst of all the romantic settings was more than she could stand. Cierra slid closer to him being careful not to snag her dress on the weathered bench and planted a big juicy kiss on his sexy lips. He parted his mouth and the sensuous kiss she lusted for occurred. Chris smiled as the kiss came to an end. Cierra said nothing. This time she knew not to divulge her feelings even though she wanted to tell him how badly she missed him. Instead, she allowed the playful gestures they often shared over the years reconnect their spirits.

They returned to the wedding celebration hand-in-hand relishing their moment of reconcilement then parted their separate ways to mingle with their friends.

"I'll catch up with you later," Chris informed.

"Okay," Cierra replied feeling light hearted and happy. She walked into the main tent and found Rachel by a seafood platter satisfying a craving.

"Rachel, I thought you were worried about your weight?"

"Girl, please. The wedding is over. Here, have some shrimp."

"No thanks. But speaking of the wedding, are you sure it's okay for you to fly to Hawaii for your honeymoon this far into your pregnancy?" Cierra asked concerned.

"Yeah. Ci, don't worry. The doctor said I'm fine. The baby is not due for another month and a half."

"Girl, that's just too close to your May due date."

"Ci, you worry too much. I'm telling you, I'll be fine. Plus, this is really the only time during the year Damien and I can be together without a bunch of demands on us. I want to make the most of my wedding. I only plan to get married once in my life. Now, can we change the subject? Are you sure you don't want some shrimp?"

"Yes, I'm sure."

Mrs. Laveau soon approached them and asked Rachel to join her to meet some more of her friends. Cierra and Rachel hugged and wished each other well.

"If I don't see you again before I leave, call me when you get back," Cierra instructed Rachel.

"Of course." Rachel waved good-bye.

The reception lasted another hour then Ms. Tema rounded up the wedding party for those who wanted a ride back to the resort. Cierra and Chris rode in the same limousine and made plans to meet later that night.

Around eight-thirty p.m., Bridget appeared at Cierra's door just as Cierra finished touching up her makeup.

"Girlfriend, where are you going in that sexy dress?" Bridget asked as she checked out Cierra's lacy black dress and high heel, strapped sandals.

"I'm meeting Chris in the lounge at nine. How do I look?" Cierra turned slowly to show Bridget the ensemble.

"Fine except one thing."

"What?" Cierra asked as she looked into the full-length, closet door mirror trying to figure out what she missed.

"You need more cleavage," Bridget responded as she made a circular motion with her hands above Cierra's breast.

"What?"

"Look Ci, you have on a low cut v-line dress. You need to push those babies up more. Are you trying to impress the man or what?"

"Yeah. But-"

"But nothing. Fasten your bra to the first hook and tighten your straps. Now, position your breast to sit up more. Trust me, it works. I do it all the time."

Cierra followed her advice and after wiggling and pushing everything into place, low and behold she added inches to her cleavage.

"See told ya," Bridget said with a smile.

"Yeah that does look sexier, uh?"

"Yep. Now you look great. Go get 'em girl."

They exited Cierra's room. Cierra's heart played a Congo beat in her chest as she walked down the long corridor. She pressed the elevator down button while taking deep breaths wondering how would the night end. The elevator door opened and she entered. "Lobby please," she requested of the elderly couple standing next to the controls.

"Who ever he is, he's a lucky man," the elderly gentleman said.

"Pete, behave yourself. Stop flirting with the young lady."

The woman turned to Cierra and apologized, "Excuse my husband. What he means to say is you look mighty nice tonight."

"Ester, you don't need to speak for me. I said exactly what I meant to say," he responded.

The door opened at the second floor and the couple exited. "Have a nice evening, dear," the woman kindly said. Pete winked at Cierra behind his wife's back at which point the wife clubbed him with her purse. Cierra laughed as the doors closed. The couple's performance calmed the butterfly feelings in her stomach.

When Cierra reached the lounge, she saw Chris sitting near the rear of the room. His dark brown eyes glistened and watched her every movement as she approached him like a sleek black panther. He stood up like a gentleman and helped her with the chair. As he sat back down, Chris took a sneak peep at Cierra's cleavage and fumbled over his words to find the perfect compliment, "Ci, you look good! I mean you look absolutely great. I thought you looked stunning today at the wedding but, damn, girl, you look sexy as hell. Woooo!"

Cierra blushed at his adulation and secretly appreciated him liking her ensemble. A waiter approached them, took their drink order, and quickly returned with Cierra's apple martini and Chris' second Heineken.

"Would you like to sit outside where there's less noise?" Chris asked hoping she would say yes.

"Sure," Cierra replied. Surprisingly, they found a couple of lawn chairs by the deep end of the pool in the shadows of some palm trees with no one else nearby. The crystal blue ripples of water reflected on their faces, as they looked at each other under the romantic star lit sky.

"Did you have a nice time here in St. Martin?" Chris asked to initiate the conversation.

"Yes, I did. How about you?" Cierra questioned.

"Yeah, I had a great time. It was great seeing Damien and our old friends."

"Yeah, it really was. I'm so glad Rachel and Damien finally got married. The problems she experienced trying to get everything together like Damien's football schedule, the church, the caterer, et cetera were driving her crazy. What do you think about them becoming parents?" She took a sip of her apple martini.

"I don't know. That's a huge step. I just hope Damien can handle fatherhood, being a husband, and playing pro ball all at the same time. That's gonna be hard but Damien has his head on straight so I'm sure they'll be fine," Chris replied.

"That was almost us too," Cierra remarked, waiting to hear Chris' reply. He remained quiet, thinking back for a moment.

"So, could you see yourself being a daddy now?" Cierra asked, half joking and half serious. Chris nearly choked on his beer. Coughing he replied, "Na Ci, not right now. I can't see that at all. Especially after, well, you know."

"I didn't think that would be such a loaded question for you."

"I mean one day when I find the right young lady, I'm sure I'll eventually settle down, get married and have a family." Cierra repeated his words, "'when I find the right young lady'." Chris knew that he hit a wrong chord in her heart. He cleared his throat and prepared himself for her response. She didn't disappoint him. Looking into his eyes she asked, "So is your new girlfriend the right young lady?" Chris paused, stood, and walked over to her chair.

"May I sit down?"

"Sure."

She moved over allowing her toned thigh to stay as close to him as possible. Chris sat facing her. He held her hand and answered, "Ci, you are without question the most beautiful young lady I've every known and the one I've had the most feelings for. There was a time in my life when I believed you were that right young lady. But so much has happened."

"Chris, I know a lot happened but there is a connection between us and you know it. There's a love that exists that can't be denied and a loss that can't be replaced. You felt it just like I did when we kissed on the beach the other night and you sensed it at the church today. You even knew it when Bridget and I were joking with you at the cookout."

He looked at her face and then at her thighs, "Ci, there's definitely chemistry between us, I ain't gonna lie about that. If you only knew what you do to me sometimes." Cierra smiled inwardly. She knew already. His erection when they kissed at the beach was a dead giveaway. Chris continued, "Ci, I'm truly sorry for my part in all that happened."

"I'm sorry for my part too," Cierra said sincerely as she leaned toward him. "I think about you a lot, Chris." She held his other hand.

"I think about you too," he replied with a genuine smile.

"Chris, I miss being with you."

She touched his exposed muscular thigh in the Bermuda shorts he sported. He said nothing but leaned toward her, placed his hand behind her neck and gestured her towards him. The passionate kiss that followed sent surges through them both. He placed one of Cierra's legs across his lap and ran his hand up her dress and stopped short from one of her hot spots he remembered so well. She moved her leg back and forward across his lap to feel the erection that stretched from the bottom of his zipper to the top of his front pocket. Their palms became clammy as their infectious thoughts heightened with each romantic word, each sensuous touch. *Will he ask me back to his room? Would I go? Is this his love for me, or pure lust?* The words circled through Cierra's mind while Chris' tongue swooped through her mouth and down her neck. She held her head back giving him permission to venture further. He cupped her breast with his hands and kissed the top of her cleavage. They panted and moaned under the palm trees taking advantage of their semi-secluded hideaway.

Cierra unbuttoned Chris' shorts and touched his erection through his boxers. He groaned as she stroked his manhood up, down, and around. He returned the favor by placing two fingers under her tiny panties and separated her labia. His third finger rubbed her clitoris making her uncontrollably moist. Then gently, Chris slid all three of his fingers into Cierra and worked them, giving her the pleasure she wanted and the closeness she needed from him. She leaned forward and took hold of his manhood into the haven of her warm mouth. Her tongue circled about his large penis and he found himself clinging to her, for he too missed their intimacy. Lost in the moment, they stroked each other fulfilling a void that hadn't been occupied in months. With each heavy breath, they inhaled and exhaled to an erotic zone where they climaxed together.

Without a word and only eye contact, Chris repositioned her panties like he found them and wiggled his penis back into his boxers in order to fasten his zipper. Cierra watched him straighten his clothes and wondered what thoughts were going through his mind. He remained quiet and another awkward silent moment intruded the space between them. She spoke first.

"Chris that felt so good."

"Yes, it did." He helped her straighten the diamond heart necklace around her neck. He looked at it closer.

"Is this the necklace I gave you on Valentine's Day our senior year?"

"Yes," Cierra replied. Chris looked at her with longing eyes and smiled. Cierra mustered the courage to ask, "Chris, was this love or lust on your part?" He took a drink of his Heineken and said, "Ci, have I ever loved you without lusting for you? Have I every lusted for you without loving you?"

"Chris, you're answering a question with a question."

"Ci, what do you think?"

"I don't know what to think. That's why I'm asking you."

"You don't know," Chris said in a matter of fact way.

"No, I don't."

"Ci, you have no idea?"

"Chris, you're killing the mood here. Come on, this is my heart we're talking about. I need to know."

"This is my heart too, Ci."

"So, you're not going to answer?" Cierra asked.

"I already did.

Cierra didn't want to ruin their encounter by pressing the issue, so she dropped the subject. Chris knew her well enough not to let her questions upset him. He knew she had a right to a more straightforward answer but his defenses and ego wouldn't allow the words that he wanted to say part his lips. The pool water reflected off Cierra's face as she sat quietly looking somewhat sad. He sensed her mood and knew he unintentionally hurt her feelings. Not wanting to cause her anymore pain, he decided to unveil some of his emotions.

"Ci, I'm sorry. I shouldn't hold out on you about how I feel. I felt what you felt."

"Do you think there will be a chance for us to get back together in the future?" Cierra asked glad that Chris opened up to her.

"Ci, who knows what's in the future for either of us," he replied looking into her angelic eyes that he loved so much.

"You never did answer my question about whether your new "friend" is the right young lady for you. So, answer this, after experiencing the feelings we still have and realizing how special our relationship was, are you still going to date her?"

Chris hesitated because he knew his answer would be hard to explain given what just happened between them but he did what he thought was right.

"Yeah, Ci. We were dating before I came to St. Martin. So, um, yeah, I still plan to date her."

"What's her name?" Cierra questioned.

"Her name is Tonya. Tonya Porter," Chris replied as he watched Cierra carefully for her response.

"Are you happy with her?"

"Uh yeah-, I'm happy."

"Happy like we were happy or better?"

"Damn, Ci, I'm happy, ok? Can we just leave it at that?" Cierra knew right then that he wasn't.

"Chris, I don't mean to upset you."

"I'm not upset."

"I just want you to be happy in life no matter what you do or whom you're with. That's all," Cierra admitted as she touched his shoulder. He placed his hand over top hers.

"I know," he said in a low tone. "I'm sorry. I didn't mean to raise my voice at you."

"No harm, no foul," said Cierra as their foreheads touched together. She sensed Chris' feelings for her still existed.

"Ci, I'll make a deal with you."

"What?"

"Let's just let our friendship be, you know, no pressure. I don't want to lose you as a good friend but at the same time I have to deal with the life I started in Baltimore. Our time in St. Martin has been very special to me. I don't want anything to change that."

Cierra wanted to jump into the pool with excitement. She believed the window of opportunity had finally presented itself. Chris wanted her in his life.

"Sure, Chris. No problem. We'll stay in touch." She smiled and Chris planted a peck on her lips.

"Come on. It's getting late. I'll walk you back to your room," Chris offered.

As they walked hand-in-hand back to Cierra's room, they shared their flight information. Both planned to leave early in the morning. The night was all they had left.

"Well, this is my room," Cierra replied as they approached her door.

"Ci, I had a wonderful time with you this entire week," said Chris as he placed one hand against the wall above her.

"Yeah, me too. So, I'll talk with you back home some time?" she asked as she searched for her card key in her cloche purse. She found the key and watched the little green light activate as she removed the key from the door.

"Yes, but, you don't think I'm letting you go that easy do you?" Chris asked as he lowered his arm. Cierra hardly got another word out before he stole a goodnight kiss. She tried to remain as calm as possible but his erection rested against her pelvis as before. He backed her against the door, kissing her like he would never see her again. Cierra matched his passion.

"Chris," she whispered in his ear.

"Yes, baby?"

Cierra's heart skipped two beats.

"I love you. And I've never loved another guy like I love you," she confessed.

Chris placed her face in the palms of his hands and softly said as he gently kissed her, "Ci, I love you too. Always have. Always will."

Tears instantly cascaded down Cierra's cheeks as she heard the words she longed for all those lonely months.

"Baby, don't cry," said Chris as he wiped her tears away. "I know how you feel."

"Do you Chris? Do you really?"

Chris held her next to his chest and whispered, "Yes, Ci, I do." They gave each other a bear hug. He liked feeling her body next to his and asked, "Can I have one more?" He wanted to wrap his arms around her curvaceous body one last time. Cierra smiled as she squeezed him as tight as she could.

"Mmmm. That felt great," Chris said as he released her body but held onto her hand. Cierra turned and opened the door guiding him towards the room.

"Ci, I better not."

"Are you sure?"

"Um yeah. I'm sure. If I come in, I think you and I both know what would happen."

"You're certain?"

"Yeah," Chris said placing his hands in his pockets to keep from touching her again.

"OK," Cierra replied as she gave a flirtatious look.

"I better go before I change my mind."

Cierra entered the room running her hand through her soft shoulder length curls. Chris stood motionless as second thoughts raced through his head. *Why not spend the night? She's been the love of my life for five years and the only girl I conceived with.* Just as he started to take a step inside Cierra's room, the elevator bell sounded and Bridget and some others exited and began walking down the hall towards them. Chris backed away.

Damn, thought a disappointed Cierra. Chris began small talk with her as Bridget and the other girls got closer.

"So, what time is your flight again?" he inquired looking at Cierra regretfully.

"Nine. So, I'll probably leave the hotel at eight. How about you?"

"I think mine is at ten. So, um, call me when you get home. I just want to make sure you're back safe," he instructed Cierra, as the girls got closer.

"Okay, I will. Take care."

"You too." He kissed the back of her hand, turned, and walked away.

As Bridget and the other girls passed him, Bridget said, "Hiiiiii Christopher. You sly dog."

"See you later, B. It was good seeing you." He tried to lean against the wall to let them pass but Bridget still managed to pinch a piece of his butt.

"Damn it, Bridget."

"Oops. My bad. I just see a fine ass and can't help myself." She and the others laughed. Cierra watched Chris until he stepped onto the elevator. He looked back for a last glimpse. Their eyes locked and they waved bye.

Cierra stood in the doorway to speak to Bridget and company.

Their rambunctious laughter was an instant sign that they were out partying.

"Hi Bridget. I'll see y'all in the morning," said Cierra as she tried to close the door but Bridget stuck her foot in the doorway.

"Oh no heifer, don't 'Hi Bridget' me. Open this door up. I want details. What was Chris doing up here in your room?"

"Bridget, you need some coffee and a breath mint," Cierra joked.

"Damn that. What was fine ass, Hershey's chocolate-drop Christopher Jackson doing in your room?"

"He wasn't in my room. He walked me to my room," Cierra informed.

"What? Walked you to your room. Y'all hear this?" Bridget called out to the other girls who entered their resort rooms. "Ci, what do you mean he walked you to your room? I thought the plan was to bed his scrumptious ass."

"Bridget, I never said that."

"Oh, so what was the purpose of the sexy dress and shit?" Bridget asked with an obvious slur.

"The dress worked it's magic without a doubt," Cierra said with a devilish grin.

"So, heifer what happened? Do I have to stand out here all night and play twenty questions?"

"Something better than sleeping together happened."

"What? What?" Bridget asked anxiously.

"Our souls reconnected and we agreed to stay in touch," Cierra proudly said.

"Souls reconnected? Stay in touch? Is that it? After what you two had all those years?"

"Bridget, you don't understand."

"I guess I don't. So, is he going to stop seeing that little ho?"

"No. But that's ok."

"Lord, help me please! My friend has lost her damn mind. Ci, did y'all do anything tonight at all?"

Cierra thought twice whether to tell Bridget about Chris' seductive moments. She knew Bridget couldn't always hold her tongue when she was tipsy so Cierra only told her a little.

"We kissed."

"You kissed. That's it?"

"Yep," Cierra replied. She didn't want to take any chances on Bridget or anyone else messing up what Chris and she found once again.

In dismay, Bridget threw up her hands and said, "I don't know what to say about you two, and I'm too drunk to think about it right now. I'll catch you in the a.m. and believe me, we will finish this conversation."

Cierra shut her door, jumped on top of the bed and ran in place as fast as she could as thoughts of Chris infiltrated her mind. *Yes, yes, yes. I knew this would be a great trip. This is just what we needed to get back on track.* She wanted to call her home girls, Kelly and Josi and tell them everything but she knew they would be fast asleep. Instead she took a shower, turned on the television, and packed her luggage for the trip home tomorrow. Before she closed her eyes for the night, she kneeled beside her bed and prayed.

> *Lord, this was by far the best evening I've had in St. Martin. I thought the night Chris and I kissed on the beach was going to be the best. But tonight topped that. Steadfast I held to the belief that if Chris and I were meant to be together, You would reunite us. I know he felt the same love that I felt throughout this trip even though he tried to hide it at first. I know his heart secretly desires me just as much as I desire him. Thank you for allowing Chris and I to share this time together in St. Martin. Thank you for giving him the courage to once again tell me that he loves me. Thank you for not taking away our special passion for each other. Thank you for allowing Chris and I to experience a love that most people never get a chance to know. I pray that our friendship will grow and bring us closer. I pray that he realizes that Tonya will never love and care for him the way I do and that she is not the right one for him. I pray for patience Lord, as I know more*

understanding will be needed in the months to come. I know in my heart of hearts that Chris and I are meant to be together but it is still Thy will whether we are or not. I have faith that in the end, Chris and I will be more in love than ever before. Amen.

The next morning, Cierra knocked on Bridget's door to say goodbye before leaving, but Bridget was sound asleep from partying the night before and didn't hear her.

"Oh well, I'll catch her the next time," Cierra said to the bellhop as he rolled her luggage down the hall. At the front desk, she scanned the lobby hoping to see Chris one last time. She asked the clerk whether he saw Chris that morning. The clerk informed her that he left a half hour earlier at seven thirty.

"That's odd. I thought his flight was at ten," Cierra said to the clerk perplexed.

"Girlfriend, all I know is that that fine specimen of a man rushed out of here like a bat out of hell. You know that I try to speak to him and all those other fine athletes every chance I get." The clerked shivered his body, "Whew girl, they just do something to me." Cierra amused at the clerk's antics and flirtatious ways with straight men made her giggle. The clerk leaned on the counter top and retrieved her room key. "Maybe something came up back home and he had to leave sooner."

"Yeah maybe," Cierra said disenchanted. She picked up her carry-on, thanked the clerk for an enjoyable stay and commented, "Oh well, nothing left to do now except return home and hope to catch him there."

"Good luck, girlfriend," the clerk said waving bye.

Cierra's shuttle bus arrived at the airport on time. She entered the terminal for the U.S. bound flight number 214. *No, this can't be.* She approached the tall, dark, handsome man standing in the middle of the terminal with a small bouquet of flowers in one hand and a small wrapped box in the other.

"Chris, what are you doing here?" she asked as they greeted each other with a hug and a peck.

"I thought your flight was at ten," she remarked. His mixed feelings of love and guilt led him to the airport to see her one more time.

"Well, it is, but I wanted to give you these." He handed her the flowers and gift.

"Chris, you didn't need to do this," Cierra commented as she accepted his presents.

"I know I didn't need to. I wanted to."

Cierra inhaled the pleasant smell of the flowers. They reminded her of the beautiful gardens at the Laveau's estate. Then with eyes sparkling, she looked at the box.

"Go ahead. Open it," he said with a smile. He enjoyed watching Cierra's excitement as she unwrapped the gift.

"Do you like it?" he asked hoping that she would.

"Yes, it's beautiful. Where did you get this?" Cierra admired the smooth, white, shell pendant that hung on a gold chain.

"I found the shell that night when we were walking on the beach and had a craftsman make it into a pendant for a necklace."

"I didn't see you pick it up."

"I know. You were too busy telling me about the adventures of you and Bridget. Don't you remember me pitching rocks into the ocean."

"Now that you mention it, yes."

"Well, when I saw this was a nice shell and not a rock, I placed it in my pocket to give to you, but I wanted it to be extra special. So, I took the shell to a jeweler and he cleaned it up and made it into the pendant. Since you still wear the necklace with the heart and your mom's pendant, I decided to buy this chain one inch shorter so you can wear both. Do you like it?"

"Chris, I love it. Thank you." Cierra gave him a bear hug then handed the necklace to him so he could put it around her neck. After he clasped the gold chain, she turned to face him.

"Chris, I don't know what to say except thank you. Thanks for making this a great trip and thanks for the flowers and necklace. This was so thoughtful of you."

"You're welcome. I just wanted to give you something to

remember this trip and our time together," he said while stroking her face.

"You know I won't forget any of it," she said with a wide smile. Just then an announcement for Flight 214 came over the intercom.

"Well, that's me," Cierra said.

"Alright," Chris replied holding her hand.

"We'll stay in touch, right?" Cierra asked reaffirming the rebirth of their friendship.

"Yeah. You're gonna call me tonight so I know you got home safe, right?"

"Yes," Cierra answered, happy that the trip ended on such a wonderful note. "I better get going before I miss my flight," Cierra said picking up her carry-on.

"Okay, I'll talk to you later. Call me around ten." Chris leaned toward her and invoked a short tongue kiss.

"I love you, Chris."

"Love you too, baby."

Cierra boarded the plane and found her seat. She sat with her eyes closed for a moment smelling the flowers and reminiscing about her romantic encounters with Chris.

Lord, thank you for this trip. I feel like I've seen and lived a piece of paradise. I truly enjoyed my first visit to the Caribbean. Your world is so beautiful with its wonderful beaches, crystal-clear water, and vibrant tropical flowers and palm trees. What better place for Rachel and Damien to get married and for Chris and me to reconnect. This trip was absolutely magical. But Lord, I must admit, I don't understand why life has led Chris and I to be apart, especially when our feelings are obviously still there. Help me to make sense out of this journey. My heart is depending on You. Amen.

With a huge sigh, she stared out of the window and grew sorrowful as she thought about how things went so terribly wrong. As the plane ascended into the tranquil sky, the noise of the engines faded and Cierra's mind drifted to a hot, summer day at the beginning of her senior college year in August 1987, a year and a half ago.

Fall 1987

The sun drifted below the horizon in Richmond, Virginia, ending Cierra's day of errands and laundry. She lavished in a long awaited bath of warm, sudsy water, removing the sweat and grime from the sweltering August day. Exhausted, the twenty-one year old rested her head on the back of the white porcelain tub, placed the wet washcloth over her face, and let out a soothing, "Ahhhh." After two calm, deep breaths, her moment of relaxation was short-lived as she felt the urgency to return to her bedroom before her father arrived home. She bathed quickly and hurriedly dressed. *I made it.* She surrounded herself with the crisp, cotton sheets of her full size bed. She stared at the off-white ceiling and pictured in her mind, all the things she needed to pack for her return trip to Virginia Tech the next day to begin her senior year. As she thought of one item after another, an uncontrolled slumber took over. While she drifted, she hoped for a peaceful night's sleep.

At eleven thirty p.m., minutes after Cierra's mind and body found a tranquil place, she heard the deep, baritone voice of the man who continued to ruin her family's structure. Intoxicated, her father, Gregory Sykes, entered the house, vigorously cursing anything that stood in his way. Without a doubt, he matched the August heat with his own searing intensity. Cierra placed a goose-down pillow over her head, but his loud voice penetrated the thickness. *Please Lord, make him shut up and go to bed.* Mr. Sykes was agitated this particular night from losing two hundred dollars while playing poker at the local juke joint called Nippy's.

Nippy's rested at the end of a long dirt road toward the back of the neighborhood just west of where the Sykes resided. The owner turned his small brick house into a three-room circus. Cocktails were sold and served in the dining room, fried fish dinners were cooked for sale in the kitchen, and card games were played for money in the living room. Because the house was nestled away from the main road, the neighbors didn't complain much about the noise.

Stumbling from room to room, Mr. Sykes searched the house for Cierra and her mother still uttering profanities along the way. He opened the guest bedroom door.

"Brenda, you in here? I see your black ass," he bellowed. Cierra's mother trembled and didn't answer. "That's a'right, keep your black ass in here. I don't give a goddamn where you sleep no how." He stumbled to Cierra's bedroom and abruptly opened the door. The broken doorstopper served no purpose as he slammed the door into the wall. Cierra froze and pretended to be asleep.

"Cierra," he yelled. "Wake your ass up and fix me a ham sandwich." His loud voice pierced her head but she remained silent and still.

"Oh you sleep too? The hell with 'cha. I'll fix my own goddamn sandwich. Fuck it," he slurred loudly. "But first, I need to go take a piss."

Cierra's father made his way down the hall to his bedroom where she heard him pee like a racehorse. *Thank goodness this is my last night here.* She then heard him fall on his bed and within moments he slept soundly, snoring as if he didn't have a nose to breathe through.

*   *   *

A large man, Gregory Sykes stood six feet three inches and weighed 240 pounds. He had abused alcohol since his adolescent years as a way to rebel against his parents. Born in 1936 in Charlotte, North Carolina, Gregory was the second of three children. His parents loved him very much, but often overlooked him as they prepared Gregory's older brother for a world outside the home and tended to the needs of his younger sister. Gregory tried to please his parents to get their attention. But when he didn't receive the type of love and affection he expected from them, he sought attention elsewhere. At fifteen, he resorted to hanging with a mischievous group of friends and the heavy drinking began.

Gregory's behavior infuriated his parents, particularly his proud, hardworking, law-abiding father. Many arguments and scuffles occurred between Gregory and his father causing a rift in their relationship. His mother tried to keep the peace between them, but it was pointless. Gregory refused to change his rebellious ways and his father insisted the rules of the household be followed. Not until Gregory turned eighteen and left home for college did his parents get a reprieve.

Over the years, Gregory's stubborn nature rejected the advice and wisdom of his father during the few times they spoke. His father tried to inform him of the damage he was inflicting on himself and others, but Gregory couldn't see any damage. In his mind, how could there possibly be anything wrong when he successfully graduated in the top ten percent of his class from Howard University in Washington, DC with a Bachelor of Science degree in chemistry, and married Brenda Fairchild, his college sweetheart.

After graduating, Gregory landed a great job with the Federal government as a senior chemist and forensic expert with the Federal Bureau of Investigation. However, after twenty-five years with the FBI, he was terminated for reasons associated with his drinking. Even then, he didn't see the negative impact of his alcoholism.

And now at age fifty-eight, a year after his father's death and two years after his mother passed, Gregory still refused to change and seek help. He continued his ill ways, causing unspeakable arguments and fights with Cierra and his wife. Cierra hated living at 1810 Berman Street and couldn't wait to take matters into her own hands.

* * *

Bright and early the next morning, Mr. Sykes went to work without saying a word to Mrs. Sykes or Cierra. A couple hours later, Cierra heard her mother yelling down the hallway from the kitchen of their split-level suburban house.

"Cierra, wake up and start your day. It's a long drive back to

Tech and you need to get on the road."

Cierra grunted and pulled the covers over her head not because of the anticipated drive but simply because she was not a morning person. After the third summons from her mother, Cierra finally planted her feet on the floor. The aroma of scrambled eggs and bacon filled the air as her mother prepared breakfast.

"Cierra, are you up? You should eat a little something before you leave."

"Yes. I'll be there in a minute." Cierra quickly showered, threw on a pair of shorts and a tee shirt and went to the kitchen. As she finished breakfast, her father drove up.

"Lord, why is he home already?" said Mrs. Sykes shaking her head.

Being the manager of a local Food Mart, Mr. Sykes believed that he could come and go as he pleased. In disgust, Cierra looked at him as he walked through the back door. He looked awful with his bloodshot eyes and seemingly uncombed pepper grey hair that could look really nice against his bronze complexion if he kept it groomed. As Cierra gazed at him, she pondered how her mother could stay married to this man for thirty plus years when she deserved so much more.

"Good-morning," Cierra and her mother greeted him.

"Morning," he replied as he passed through the kitchen and headed down the hall to his bathroom. Cierra heard the gush of running water from the faucet and then the clink of glass against the ceramic basin. Her father took a drink, giving indication another long day in the Sykes household was in the making. Cierra was glad that she wouldn't be around later to witness it. This was her last summer day at home. Her future plans didn't include 1810 Berman Street. *All I have is one more school year and I'll be free of this hellhole.*

Moments later Mr. Sykes returned to the kitchen, opened the refrigerator door, and took a sip of lemonade from his favorite mug. As he placed the mug back in the refrigerator, he released a loud belch to show the pleasure of a cool drink in his empty stomach.

"Gregory, why are you home? It's only ten fifteen. Shouldn't you be at the store looking after things?" Mrs. Sykes inquired.

"Brenda, don't bother me. I can come home if I want to." He grabbed three slices of bacon and slapped them between two slices of dry toast. With a mouth full of food, he said, "This is my goddamn house and I'll do as I damn well please. Let the store run itself. Just leave me alone."

Although calmer than the night before, Mr. Sykes obviously displayed behavior that indicated the alcohol had not vacated his body. He straddled between being Dr. Jekyll and Mr. Hyde, a grey area Mrs. Sykes felt she could voice her opinion without much repercussion. Angrily, she stopped washing the dishes and turned to face him.

"Look at you Gregory. You look terrible. Cierra is leaving for her senior year today and this is how she'll remember her last day at home. You're so pathetic."

The insult made Cierra look up from her breakfast. Adrenalin rushed through her body instantly as she prepared to defend her mother. She feared the word *pathetic* would send her father into a rage. But he ignored her mother this time. Cierra returned to eating. *Thank God. I know she's disgusted but why say that? It doesn't matter to me what he does anyway.* Resuming washing the dishes, Mrs. Sykes looked out of the kitchen window and muttered, "It's a crying shame for a grown man to act like this. It just doesn't make good sense. You can lose this job like you did the one at the Bureau if you want to, but I'm not supporting you."

"Oh Brenda, just shut up," said Gregory wiping his mouth with a napkin that he tossed onto the counter. He looked at Cierra with a blank expression and said, "Have a safe trip and good luck in school." Then he exited the kitchen slamming the storm door behind him.

"Whatever," Cierra replied rolling her eyes at him as he descended the back porch. The car roared and the tires spun in the gravel as Mr. Sykes drove out of the driveway to return to work. *Man, what a jerk.* Cierra excused herself from the table and hurriedly finished packing. She wanted to be gone before he returned. She knew he would surely come back drunk and more drama would unfold because even though he didn't respond to *pathetic* that time, it would definitely resurface the next time he saw her mother. He often did his dirty work against his wife while Cierra was miles away in school. Unable to protect her mother, Cierra always had mixed feelings about leaving. Living with an abusive alcoholic was her mother's choice, not hers. Cierra realized early on in her life that she needed to make a path for her own life, one comprised of love and serenity.

After entering Virginia Tech and experiencing the peaceful, collegiate lifestyle, Cierra swore to break all ties with her father. She dreamed of the day when she would have peace, love, and respect in her own home. A home she planned to share with a man who would love and cherish her.

Cierra loaded her luggage in the car. Meanwhile, Mrs. Sykes packed a care-package full of canned goods, pasta, and goodies like potato chips and cookies. Mrs. Sykes felt proud and sad at the same time. Her dream of her daughter finishing college would soon come true, but she would miss having Cierra around to help battle the harshness of her husband, a task that they both endured for years.

Cierra entered the house one last time and announced, "Well mom, this is it." She stretched her arms, fatigued from loading her car, a used blue 1984, 318i BMW. She loved it, especially the sunroof.

"I thought this day would never come. Make sure that you keep up the good grades. And don't party too much. I've worked too hard for you to mess up now," her mother joked but in a serious kind of way. Cierra hugged her mother's short, petite frame and kissed her on the cheek. Mrs. Sykes hugged her back and told her how proud she was.

"Call me when you get there so that I know you made it safely," her mother requested.

"Okay."

Cierra then backed out of the driveway. As she exited the neighborhood, she glanced at the sky.

> *Heavenly Father, I ask that you watch over my mother. Keep her safe and healthy. Please Lord, I beg You, don't let my dad beat her. You must protect her in my absence. Give her the strength and courage to leave him. Allow her to find peace*

somewhere. Lastly, I still pray that You help my father to seek counseling for his alcoholism so that he can stop drinking. I also pray for a safe trip to school. Thank you. Amen.

As Cierra traveled west on Interstate-64, she approached the Blue Ridge Mountains that stretched north and south of Virginia's western boarder. The rocky structures truly captured the essence of Mother Nature. Each one stood like a giant against the tranquil blue sky. Evergreens and sun-scorched plants covered the landscape. As she ventured further west, the highway inclined and coiled like a serpent ascending a tree. The mountains always comforted Cierra and reminded her of God's greatness and creativity.

Leaving I-64 West, she veered onto I-81 South where she drove the remaining two and half hours. She finally saw signs for Blacksburg, the location of Virginia Tech. Her heart raced as thoughts of seeing her beloved Christopher Jackson filled her head. She desired to feel the smoothness of his Hershey chocolate skin, touch his soft lips, and smell his seductive Calvin Klein Obsession cologne. For the four years they dated, she could hardly keep her eyes off of him. Chris had a body of steel from playing football and running track. His dark brown, piercing eyes and pearly white smile brightened every day she saw him. He was an intelligent and handsome African-American young man and one of Virginia Tech's finest student athletes. And although he could sometimes sit on his high horse, be arrogant and allusive, she craved him and couldn't wait to see him and be back to the freedom and serenity of her college lifestyle.

Chris was born and raised in Baltimore, MD in 1965. He grew up on the west side of the city in a large ranch style house near an affluent Jewish community. He lived with his mother, father, and cousin Zack, who came to live with them at a young age and shared the same birth year as Chris.

Chris developed a great passion for football after the first time his father took Zack and him to see the Baltimore Colts in 1972 at Memorial Stadium. Already a tenacious, persistent, and persuasive child, he insisted that his dad teach him how to play the sport. From youth football to high school, he excelled in the sport and proudly held the Team Captain position for the teams he played. By the time Chris reached college in 1984, he had accomplished the prestigious titles of All-Region, All-Met, All-State, and USA Today High School All-American. He ranked among the top ten recruits nationwide for college football. Every major university wanted him because of his excellent Wide Receiver skills. Virginia Tech delighted in the fact that he decided to attend school there.

His dedication and hard work paid off at Virginia Tech as he gained the All-Conference and the Associated Press All-American titles during his junior year. He planned to earn the titles again this year, his senior year.

Fans adored Chris. At press conferences following the Virginia Tech football games, reporters rushed to get his comments. He spoke articulately and eloquently, always captivating his audience. He inserted small jokes at just the right moment to humor his attentive listeners. His teammates admired his accomplishments and down to earth attitude. Only when he had one too many beers at their keg parties did he annoy them with his cocky claim to fame.

Many guys on campus tried to mimic his charisma and charming personality, a plus they believed would win them favors with the young ladies. But while the guys tried to master the perfect come-on, Chris already possessed the ability to flirt without being overly aggressive, attracting the young ladies to him like a magnet.

His academic capabilities impressed professors and recruiters just as much as his athletic talents. While enduring hours of football practice and weight training, he never missed a beat when it came to his studies. He maintained an A-minus average in his undergraduate course work. He believed that young African-Americans should strive to give nothing less than one hundred percent. In his opinion, young men should know how to communicate effectively at all levels and in any given situation, a lesson he learned from his father and mother.

Chris also enjoyed building things. For fun, he loved putting together model airplanes. He confessed that working on the airplanes took his mind off the pressures of school and the hype of football. He displayed several of his favorite models throughout his dorm room. His mother showcased his very first models in the family's curio. Chris' natural talent to build led him to major in architecture at Virginia Tech and he excelled.

Cierra reached the city limits of Blacksburg quicker than she realized. People always joked that if you blinked while driving through Blacksburg, you would miss the town. Virginia Tech was the largest entity in Blacksburg, and one of the largest universities in the state of Virginia. Approximately 25,000 undergraduate students attended the university between 1984 and 1988. Cierra was one of 5,000 minority students accepted into the school. Virginia Tech was nationally accredited for its challenging academics and known for being one of the top 50 research institutions in the United States. Many private businesses and government organizations viewed graduates of Virginia Tech as outstanding achievers. Proud to be a student at the university, Cierra couldn't wait to receive her Bachelor's degree.

The digital clock on the car's dashboard read four ten p.m. Cierra hoped that football practice was over. She zoomed through downtown and arrived at Chris' townhouse that he shared with three other teammates. She quickly parked the Beamer, touched up her makeup, and combed her hair. It seemed like no matter how fast she did these things it took forever to get out of the car. Halfway running, Cierra approached Chris' townhouse and rang the doorbell. She could hear his footsteps as he neared the door. Her heart raced with anticipation. The door opened and there he stood, six feet two inches, one hundred ninety pounds of nothing but pure delight.

"There she is," Chris shouted as he expanded his arms to hug her. She returned the gesture and uttered, "Chris, I missed you so much." The emotional weight of 1810 Berman Street suddenly lifted off her shoulders. They stood in the entranceway caressing each other so tightly that it almost took her breath away. Chris placed Cierra's face in the palm of his hands and kissed her lips and cheeks tenderly. Between his soft kisses, he whispered, "You're so beautiful. I couldn't last another day without you." As he gazed into her feline shaped brown eyes, he reminisced about their first encounter when he passed her on his way to the dining hall one morning. Her perfect hourglass figure, flawless caramel skin, and shoulder-length brown, wavy hair instantly caught his attention. Her mere presence set off a different feeling in him, a feeling his heart hadn't felt before and one he didn't want to let go. Without even uttering a word, she tapped his soul and revoked his player's card.

While standing in the small foyer, they began to kiss each other ferociously like life itself depended on each passionate embrace and each seductive touch. Cierra felt Chris' hands exploring the contour of her body. He placed one hand on her butt and cupped her breast with the other as she touched the hardness in his shorts. Within moments, they lied naked on the living room floor making love more intensely than they ever had. As their bodies intertwined and became one, their voices cried out to the heavens how good they felt. She grabbed his buttocks and pivoted her hips towards him. He locked her in his muscular arms and rested his elbows and knees on the carpet. Then he thrust himself in and out of her. They moaned with ecstasy as they climaxed together. As he removed himself from her inner walls, she felt his warm love potion on her buttocks while beads of sweat trickled from his forehead.

"I'm sorry, baby. I don't mean to drip this on you." He wiped his brow with his hand and complained, "Damn it's hot in here."

"Don't worry about your sweat. You can drip on me anytime. I think it's kinda sexy."

Chris continued to kiss her neck and run his fingers through her wavy locks. She looked at him and stroked his smooth, brown face and said, "I love you, Chris."

"Baby, I love you too. You're my world. You know that right?"

"Yes."

"I didn't hear you. Say it again," he playfully requested while tickling her ribs and kissing her cheeks.

"Yes," she laughed uncontrollably wriggling from side to side. "Chris, we need to get up from here. Suppose your roommates come home and see us like this? I'd be so embarrassed."

"Well let's just move this love affair to my bedroom."

They gathered their clothes then Chris carried her to his room where they made love again and again until exhaustion overcame them. As Chris fell asleep beside Cierra, she stared at him and thought that his welcome back was the warmest greeting a girl could have from a lover. She reminisced about all the wonderful experiences they shared over the years at school. A lot of people envied them because they got along so well and had been together since their freshmen year. Most of Chris' friends didn't have a steady girlfriend and they often teased him calling him hen pecked and pussy whipped because he spent most of his free time with her. She stroked his face, happy that they were together.

> *Heavenly Father, thank you for blessing me with this relationship and bringing Chris into my life. He brings me so much joy in a life filled with years of pain. I pray that we will always be together. Amen.*

The first couple of weeks back at Virginia Tech passed quickly as students returned and the new school year began. Saturday, September twelfth arrived and the first scheduled football game seemed to excite everyone. Chris gave Cierra two fifty yard-line tickets to the one o'clock game. She invited her close friend, Rachel Laveau. Shortly after locating their seats, the stadium became very crowded. The band roared and fans screamed with enthusiasm. Cierra felt her adrenaline flow as she saw Virginia Tech's football team enter the stadium. As the team ran onto the field, Cierra and Rachel stood clapping and yelling.

"Ci, where's Chris? I don't see him."

"Right there, number 83. See him? He's the wide receiver," Cierra pointed.

"Oh yeah, I see him. Girl, he looks good. You're so lucky."

"Lucky? Girl, I pray all the time that Chris and I stay together."

"Well, it must be working 'cause the brother hasn't ventured since the two of you started dating. I would love to have a relationship like that."

Cierra wondered for a brief moment why God answered her prayers about Chris but not about her father. Rachel interrupted her thoughts.

"You know, I still want you and Chris to hook me up with his friend, Damien."

"Rachel, you're a trip."

"I'm serious. If I can get with Damien, I would be the happiest woman on Earth. There's something intriguing about his quiet, serious demeanor that attracts me. And those dimples, oh my God. They just make me melt. Where is he anyway?"

"Right there, number 44. He's a DB," Cierra pointed.

"A what?"

"A defensive back. Rachel, when are you ever going to learn the game?"

"When Damien teaches me," she laughed.

Damien Hall, a transfer student from Temple University, came to Virginia Tech during the fall semester of 1986 to complete his college football program and quickly became one of the team's prominent players. His cognac complexion cloaked his six foot three muscular frame. He had extremely dark midnight eyes and brown hair. His square jaw line made Rachel want to touch his intense face. She only saw him in passing while going to class last year. They always made eye contact but never stopped to talk. This year, she planned to change all of that.

"I tell you Ci, Damien is one of the finest brothers I've ever seen and he's so competitive. Lordy, help me Jesus. Do you see the ass on Damien?"

"Yes, Rachel I see," Cierra responded as she chuckled and checked him out.

"Girl, I may not know the details of the game, but I sure love to see the players in those tight pants," Rachel said while raising her hand for a high-five. She shrieked, "Ain't he fine?"

"Damien is fine without a doubt. From what I hear, he's a serious brother too. He's humble but doesn't stand for no bullshit."

"I can tell that, but you watch. I bet'cha under that tough exterior is a kind, gentle, loving man. He's just waiting for the right woman. I can tell by the way he looked at me last year that he wants to meet me too," said Rachel as she watched him jog towards the huddle.

"You know he's going to be at Chris' party tonight," Cierra informed as she braced herself for Rachel's response.

Rachel jumped to her feet. "What? Ci, why didn't you tell me sooner? You know I have to buy something special to wear."

"Rachel, you're so crazy. Sit down. You're blocking people's view," joked Cierra as she tugged at her tall friend.

"Ci, when I get through with Damien, he's not going to know what hit him, c'est ça."

Rachel and Cierra laughed and cheered for their team. Virginia Tech led its opening game, 7-0 during the first quarter. The team looked really good. They had very few turnovers and made most of their first downs. As the game progressed into the third quarter, Cierra and Rachel continued to scream every time Chris and Damien made their normal spectacular plays. When Cierra turned her head to watch the spirited crowd, she saw Amy McKenzie coming down the stadium steps.

Amy was a Caucasian girl who played on Virginia Tech's volleyball team and participated in the Media Club. She had short blonde hair and blue eyes, was very busty and had a flat behind. She had a reputation among the students, black and white alike, as being one of Virginia Tech's campus sluts. The athletes talked about how she sexed several of them, football, basketball, baseball, it didn't matter. She was an easy booty call. She partied wildly and stayed high on cocaine. Cierra and Rachel couldn't stand her, particularly how she flaunted herself around the football players. As Amy and the one friend she had descended the steps, Cierra nudged Rachel.

"Girl, look who's here."

Rachel looked up and shrieked, "Would you please look at what that floozy has on."

Amy wore a pair of running shorts that allowed her buttocks to hang slightly out of them and a fitted cotton tank top without a bra. Rachel and Cierra just shook their heads. Other people in the stands made faces of disbelief as Amy passed them. Amy's sunburned face made her less than attractive features even more unappealing. Cierra could tell by the look on Amy's face that she had been drinking. The look reminded Cierra of her father, eyes red and glazed, and mouth slightly twisted.

"Cierra look. That hussy is going onto the field with the team," Rachel exclaimed.

They watched Amy show the guard her press pass and he opened the gate to let her through. Amy immediately began taking pictures of the players. Cierra noticed how she particularly took an interest in Chris. Rachel noticed too.

"Cierra, is it my imagination or is Amy all up in your man's face with that damn camera?"

"I see her. She is such a sleaze."

Chris and a few other players involved in the game ignored Amy. However, some coaches and players looked at her hot shorts with lustful eyes.

The exciting game finished with Virginia Tech losing to Clemson 10-22 but that didn't stop the Hokies' spirit. Afterwards, Cierra and Rachel walked to the coliseum that was next to the stadium to meet Chris. The players always came out through the coliseum lower exit. While they waited patiently for him to appear, they critiqued each player that exited the door, giving a thumbs up or down pending how good they looked. Finally, Chris and his roommate, Craig Hawkins, came out.

"Heyyy," Chris and Craig shouted. Both were excited about the team's first game of the season even though they lost. Cierra hugged and kissed Chris and told him how awesome he played. He blushed, only she could make him do that. As they walked to their cars, everyone engaged in small talk.

Craig asked, "Cierra, are you two coming to our party tonight?" Before she could answer, Chris interjected, "I know my baby is going to be there," and sealed his statement with a peck.

"Yeah. We'll be there," Cierra replied.

"I wouldn't miss it for the world," added Rachel. When they reached Cierra's car, Chris kissed her and said that he would call her later. Then Cierra and Rachel headed to the mall to buy Rachel's outfit.

Cierra and Rachel arrived at the party around ten that evening. As they walked through the parking lot, they heard the music blasting and people laughing and talking. Rachel checked herself in almost every car window they passed. She wanted everything to be perfect.

"Ci, how do I look?"

"You look fine, stop worrying. Okay?"

"Do you think this dress is too short? How is my hair? Should I let it down?"

"Rachel, you look terrific. Leave your hair up. It looks sophisticated that way."

"You're sure this is cool?" Rachel asked again stopping to look in the window of yet another car.

"Yes. You're driving me crazy. Now come on. Besides Damien should like you for who you are not for what you're wearing."

"Ci, you say that because you have a man. You know what they say about first impressions. And guys always judge by looks first."

They continued their debate as they walked into the townhouse. The music roared as lots of people danced in the living room. Cierra felt good seeing many of her friends and classmates after being away for the summer. Rachel excused herself to the bathroom for a final check. Just then Cierra heard her comedian friend, Bridget, scream her name.

"Cierra Sykes. Girl, look at your little, narrow ass. I told you before we left for the summer that you'd better put some meat on those bones while you were home so your man will have something to hold onto. I just might be inclined to give him some of this." She slapped her hips and joked, "Lord knows I've got plenty for him."

Laughing, Cierra responded, "B, you're still crazy. You talk that mess, but I see you've lost a pound or two. Wat'cha trying to do? Look like my little narrow ass?"

"Hell no. The doctors told me to lose some weight, change my eating habits and exercise because I was getting high blood pressure and my cholesterol levels were all jacked up. Honey, I never knew I could miss pork and all my favorite foods so much. The doctor had the nerve to ask me if I exercise on a consistent and regular basis. I told that doctor the only exercise I do consistently is make love to my man on a regular basis. Honey, he looked at me as professionally as he could with his uptight ass and said, 'Miss Murphy that is not considered exercise.' I said maybe in your house it's not exercise, but the way my man and I go at it, it's like running a marathon."

"Bridget, you're a trip. You don't have a steady boyfriend," said Cierra.

"Well, he didn't know that. Girl, that doctor didn't know what to say. But on the real Ci, I figured it was either give up the food and start exercising or die young. And I like gettin' my swirl on too much to die young, have mercy. I'm supposed to lose fifty more pounds, but damn if I feel like it. We're gonna have to add this to our prayer list 'cause the last fifty are gonna be a beast."

"B, I know you can do it," Cierra said as she patted her friend on the back. "You're doing great."

"Thanks, Ci that means a lot. Hey, you see Wallace over there?" Looking across the room, Cierra saw the starting linebacker for Virginia Tech standing against the wall sipping his drink.

"Yeah, I see him. Why?"

"Well, honey that hunk of man is going to be Bridget's delight tonight. Watch me work it."

"Watch out now. Don't hurt anybody, B."

"Girlfriend, that's exactly what I intend to do."

"B, if your preacher daddy could see you now."

"Girl, he would fall over his pulpit, yelling, 'Lord Jesus, where did I go wrong?'"

They laughed at the thought of her father having a fit about her flirtatious ways. Then Bridget walked away with an obviously over-exaggerated switch, right into the arms of Wallace.

To escape the smoldering body heat, Cierra made her way through the living room and kitchen. She opened the sliding glass doors and stepped onto the deck. Chris stood beside the keg. He greeted his sweetheart with a small peck and poured her a cup of beer.

"Where's Rachel?" Chris yelled a bit intoxicated.

"Inside. Pour her a cup too."

"Word."

He poured another cup from the keg. Cierra continued, "Don't forget that Rachel wants us to introduce her to Damien."

"Alright. I think he's out here somewhere. I'll find him and bring him inside."

"Okay. We'll be by the kitchen bar." As Cierra turned to walk away, he gently pulled her towards him and whispered in her ear, "After all these folks leave, can I get a little bit of your sweetness tonight?"

"We'll see. I drove tonight. I'd have to take Rachel home then come back."

He looked at her with his dark brown eyes and said, "I'll get Damien to take her home. You just plan on staying here." She smiled and walked away.

Cierra saw Rachel across the room and signaled to her to meet her in the kitchen. When Cierra turned the corner, she saw Amy sitting at the breakfast bar staring at her. Before she could address the audacious look, Rachel walked up to her and inquired about Damien. At the same time, Chris approached them with Damien close behind. Little did Cierra and Rachel know but Damien had also asked Chris to introduce him to the girl that intrigued him last year as they passed each other going to class. Finally, they would have more than just eye contact.

Chris did the normal introduction while Cierra watched Rachel to see her reaction. To her surprise, Rachel stood very calm and collected. Damien said the usual "Nice to meet you" and then he asked Rachel to dance. Rachel practically tossed her cup at Cierra and left without a second thought. Chris held Cierra's hand and led her to the laundry room behind the kitchen. He shut the door and kissed her passionately, running his hands under her skirt.

"Baby, you sure do know how to drive a brotha crazy with your sexy self. You look so damn good and smell so sweet. I wish I could make love to you right now."

"Chris, there's a house full of people out there."

"So, I don't care." He kept kissing her neck and ears.

"Chris, come on let's go back. We have all night for this." Under normal circumstances, Chris' advances would have suited her fine but she didn't want her business in the street per se.

"Alright but you just wait until later." He pinched her butt as they returned to the party. When Chris and Cierra turned the corner, there sat Amy at the bar, watching them. She looked disgusted and abruptly left her seat. Cierra turned to Chris and said, "Amy has a thing for you."

"What do you mean?" he asked.

"You know, she likes you."

"Ci, come off of it."

"Why is she here anyway?" Cierra asked annoyed with her presence.

"Amy knows a lot of the players that's all. She just wanted to hang out like everybody else. So we invited her."

"Oh yeah? Who is 'we'? And why was she all in your face taking pictures today at the game?"

"I barely noticed that she was there. Why are you getting so bent out of shape?"

"Chris, I don't like how she looks at you. I mean look at her, she got mad just now when she saw us together."

"Ci, just because she got up when we came out here doesn't mean anything."

With a look of caution on her face, Cierra replied, "Alright Christopher, don't be naïve or play dumb. You know that ho goes after every athlete she can get her slimy hands on. Don't be a fool."

"Damn, Ci. Did you come here to have a good time or what?"

"Yes, I did but that chick irks me."

"Well hush your pretty little lips, stop worrying about nothing and come on and dance with me."

Chris led Cierra to the dance floor where they joined Rachel, Damien, and others. As Cierra moved to the hip-hop and rap beats she couldn't help but to think about Amy. *I don't know what it is about that girl, but something just isn't right.*

The party finally ended around three in the morning. Cierra looked around but didn't see Amy anywhere. Chris and his roommates cleaned and talked with the few people who remained.

Some pitched in to help while others stood around and talked trash about who did what during the game. Chris boasted as usual about his touchdown. Damien remained cool and humble about his interception. Shortly thereafter, all the remaining guests left. Damien offered to give Rachel a ride that she gladly accepted. Cierra stayed and spent another wonderful night with her man. As she lay next to Chris, she looked out of the window at the starry sky.

> *Lord, I'm so happy. Thank you for today. I had fun at the football game and party tonight. But Lord, I can sense something is up with Amy. She had some nerve today flirting with Chris, right in front of me at that. Whatever no good intentions she may have, I pray You keep them away from Chris and me. I'm trusting You. Amen.*

Winter 1987

The school year progressed and Cierra enjoyed every moment with her friends. But when the 1987 winter break arrived, she had to do what she disliked most. She returned home for the holidays, re-entering a world of verbal and physical abuse. Spending the holiday season refereeing her parents and dodging her intoxicated father was not her idea of goodwill and peace on earth.

To get away for Christmas, she traveled to Baltimore to visit Chris and his family. The Jacksons always welcomed her into their home and for a few days, Cierra felt the harmony of the holidays. Her heart was at ease in the Jackson household. She enjoyed helping Chris' mother prepare the festive dinner and assisting Chris and his father with bringing in the logs for the fireplace; she loved toasting marshmallows. Cierra and Chris made the most of their free time away from school, doing everything from attending concerts to playing touch football in the backyard. Cierra wished she could stay through the New Year but her Baltimore trip ended after a four-day stay. Chris had made plans to travel with Zack to Atlantic City. Although she disagreed with his plans, she knew they weren't married just yet so what could she say?

She traveled back to Richmond with thoughts of Chris making love to her on Christmas night and their conversations about sharing a life together. When she arrived home, she called Kelly and Josi but found out that they too were out of town and wouldn't be back until New Year's Day. Unlike past New Year's Eve celebrations, this one was a disappointment to Cierra. She decided to cut her winter break short and returned to Virginia Tech earlier than anticipated, merely to escape home.

After everyone returned to Tech to start the final semester, Chris and Damien decided to take Cierra and Rachel out on a double date to Bennigan's restaurant. While waiting to be seated, Cierra and Rachel excused themselves. They went to the ladies' room where Rachel excitedly told Cierra how Damien came to New York to visit her at her cousin's house during the Christmas break before she flew home to St. Martin.

"Whaaat?" Cierra asked surprised.

"Yeah, girl. He is the sweetest guy. It was the first time that I've seen him so relaxed. Here at school, he's always so focused and intense. But there's another side to him that's gentle, considerate, and understanding." Rachel gleamed with happiness.

"I guess you were right. So what did you do? Did you go out?"

"Yeah. We went to dinner and to this club in Manhattan, but we didn't stay too long."

"Why not? Sounds like fun."

"Ci, he wanted to be alone and have a serious talk. I thought I was gonna die, but I played cool."

"So, get to the good part," Cierra instructed anxious to hear more.

"We talked about our careers, beliefs regarding religion, marriage, and children. Can you believe that? The brother talked to me about children." Rachel looked like she was right back in the moment with Damien.

"Rachel, this is great, continue."

"He told me about his pro football aspirations and how important getting his degree is. And get this, he even opened up to tell me that he's great in science and math but is struggling with some of his business courses that may become an academic issue for him if he doesn't get a handle on them soon. I told him that I would help him this semester 'cause he's gotta march in May. Ci, we talked about a bunch of stuff. We stayed up almost all night. Then before he left the next afternoon, he asked me if I would like to date more seriously. I played cool and toyed with him like I had to think about it. He got this strange look on his face. Then I said, 'yes'. Girl, he looked so relieved. I thought it was cute."

"I'm impressed," Cierra remarked giving Rachel a nudge on the shoulder.

"Check this out." Rachel reached in her purse and pulled out a small box.

"Oh shit," Cierra exclaimed. Rachel opened the box.

"Look what my indigo prince gave me for Christmas." She showed Cierra the nickel-sized ruby, ladybug brooch accessory.

"Wow Rachel. That's really pretty. Why aren't you wearing it? I'm sure he was expecting to see it on you."

"I don't know. I think I'm nervous. I've never been with someone like this before. You know my past relationships only lasted three weeks tops when I had one."

"Girl, you're trippin'. What happened to 'if I get Damien, I'll be the happiest girl on Earth'?"

Rachel laughed at herself and remarked, "Yeah, I did say something like that, didn't I?"

"Yep," Cierra replied as she witnessed Rachel's Love Jones for Damien. She continued, "Look, you guys have been going out since the first football game back in September. You shouldn't be nervous," Cierra said wondering where did all of Rachel's confidence go.

"I know, but-"

"But nothing. Here, open your coat. We can put the pin on your blazer lapel. He's already seen that you weren't wearing it on your outer coat, so it'll be fine on your blazer." Rachel handed Cierra the brooch and she pinned it to the collar. They looked at the piece of jewelry sparkle in the mirror.

"Rachel, that looks nice on you."

"Yes, it does," replied Rachel admiring the gem.

Cierra looked curiously at Rachel then asked, "Rachel, are you falling for Damien?"

Rachel snapped back from her split daydream and uttered, "Huh?"

"You heard me. Are you falling for Damien 'cause you look like you're in love?"

"Is it that obvious?" Rachel asked as she became self-conscience and looked at herself in the mirror and saw the glow herself. "Ci, I can't lie. I'm falling hard for him. We get along great and he makes me so happy."

"Rachel, love is a wonderful thing and when you find it with the right person, it's euphoric. Damien is obviously diggin' you and thinks you're special. So just go with the flow and enjoy yourself. You make a nice couple."

"Yeah, you're right. Thanks, Ci. You're such a good friend."

They gave each other a sisterly hug. "What did you and Chris do for Christmas? Did he pop the big question?" Rachel asked assuming their time for engagement was at hand. After all, the lovebirds had been together for four years and school would be over shortly.

"I spent Christmas with him and his family in Baltimore. It was really nice. His mom always makes a large Christmas dinner. And no, he didn't ask me to marry him."

"Well, what did he give you?" asked Rachel expecting to hear something more wonderful than her pretty piece of jewelry.

"An off-white, lambs wool sweater and a pair of designer jeans," Cierra replied with disappointment. She thought her gift might be an engagement ring, too, or at least something more romantic and meaningful, particularly at this stage in their relationship.

"Sounds pretty," Rachel complimented.

Cierra wasn't so sure and thought Rachel was just being polite.

"Ci, I always wondered something. When you visit Chris, do his parents suspect that you guys do anything? I mean, how can the two of you be together at such a romantic time of year, stay in the same house, and not touch each other?"

"Chris and I are affectionate in front of his parents. We hold hands and make eye contact, stuff like that. Every once in a while, they've caught us kissing in the kitchen. But they're really cool. They don't say anything."

"And what about the nasty?"

"What?"

"You heard me. Do you make love when you're there?"

"No, girl, not in his parents' house. We go get a hotel room."

"That sounds so exciting. I wonder how my visits with Damien will be," Rachel commented.

Cierra dazed off as she thought about her love making with

Chris on Christmas night. She hoped everything would turn out okay next month because for the first time, they decided to throw caution to the wind and didn't use any protection. She could still visualize his firm hands under her buttocks, the warmth of his breath along side her face and his soft spoken words, "Ci, baby. I can't wait to make you my wife one day. I love you."

"Ci, snap out of it. Chris evidently gave you something more than those clothes to remember," Rachel teased.

"Indeed he did."

"How did you guys bring in the New Year together?" asked Rachel with her continued flow of questions.

"Well, we didn't spend New Year's together," Cierra replied.

"What? You're kidding, right?"

"Nope. He went to Atlantic City with Zack this year."

"And didn't ask you to go?"

"No."

"You don't think that's odd? You guys have always spent New Year's together."

"It made me feel a little uncomfortable. But it's okay. He just wanted to do something different. I can understand that".

"That's why he loves you the way that he does. You trust him and let him be his own person. Not a lot of girls would be so understanding."

"Yeah, I know."

After giving themselves a final look over in the mirror, they returned to the front hostess area.

"Is everything alright?" Chris asked observing how long they lingered in the restroom.

"Everything is fine," Cierra remarked with a mischievous grin. The guys offered to hang the girls' coats. When Damien removed Rachel's wool coat, he noticed his gift on her blazer lapel and his dimples deepened as he smiled at her. Cierra watched Rachel blush as Cupid shot his arrow.

After returning to her apartment from a fun-filled evening with her friends, Cierra quickly prepared for bed. In her cozy flannel pajamas, she snuggled under the covers and whispered.

Lord, thank you for yet another wonderful evening with my friends. It's good to be back in their company. Rachel raised a point that I've been wondering myself. Isn't it time for Chris and I to get engaged? We've talked about marriage plenty of times over the years. Now that we're entering our last semester at Tech, shouldn't we be taking the next step in our relationship? I know my heart is ready for such a commitment. I pray his is too. Amen.

January

Cierra entered her Communications class at the beginning of the January 1988 semester and saw Amy McKenzie, the tarnished girl everyone talked about, sitting in the back of the classroom. Cierra chose a seat against the far right wall. As she sat through the professor's introduction, she sensed Amy gazing at her. She turned to her left and saw the unattractive girl gazing at her. *What the hell is up with this chick?* Amy skipped class the next three days. Then on Friday, she showed up and instead of sitting towards the back, she sat in the empty seat directly behind Cierra.

"Hey," Amy said as she sat sliding her backpack under the desk. Cierra responded with a slight, "Hi." Nothing else was said. The professor began class by assigning group projects that were due April twenty-ninth. He randomly selected the groups and read them aloud, "Group one - Ted, Karen, Bill, and Michelle. Group two - Ann, Brian, Carol, and Kim. Group three - Robert, Cierra, Timothy, and Amy. And Group four - Scott, Ben, Kelly, and Aaron. Cierra's heart went to her feet. *You've gotta be joking. I have to work with this sleaze.* Members of Cierra's group came over to her desk. They exchanged phone numbers and planned their first meeting location and date, the Student Union, Wednesday, January tenth at three p.m.

They all met as planned and began working on the project. Amy surprised Cierra by being very friendly. She didn't appear to be at all as shallow as people had portrayed her. Cierra began to let down her guard and related to Amy as a classmate.

Academically, the semester was off to a great start. Cierra just wished she felt the same way about Chris and her. Due to the frequent snow showers and freezing rain, she didn't visit him as much. Usually, he would drive Craig's 4-wheel drive to see her but during January, Chris displayed a new attitude that baffled Cierra.

"Ci, I can't ask Craig to drive his SUV like that," Chris said abruptly into the phone.

"Why not? You've used it before to come see me. You've driven to the mall and into town. Hell, you've even driven to Roanoke an hour away," a disappointed Cierra stated.

"That's his truck. I have no say," Chris retorted.

"Chris, do you hear yourself?"

"Ci, I just can't do that. Suppose I have an accident. Then what?"

"Chris, Craig has trusted you with the SUV before in this weather. Remember a couple weeks ago you went to get a hair cut on the other side of town? I'm only fifteen minutes from you. You can come now while it's just raining and leave before it starts to freeze," Cierra bargained.

"Ci, I'm sorry. I just can't. Maybe next time."

"Lately, every time I ask you, it's always 'maybe next time'."

Chris said nothing. The silence agitated Cierra. Then she suggested, "Well take the commuter bus."

"I'm not doing that. It'll take forever getting there and then by the time I leave, the roads will be icy."

"Chris, you have an answer for everything lately, don't you?" She didn't agree with his reasoning and ended the conversation.

After denying Cierra's request to come visit her one too many times, she automatically stopped asking. Soon they found themselves in a strained relationship. Cierra often talked to Rachel about her winter blues, and being the good friend that she was, Rachel tried to uplift Cierra's spirits but Chris' behavior made it very difficult.

Cierra didn't quite understand why Chris became so edgy and aloof when the beginning of their senior year had gone so well. Every time she tried to talk about what was happening with their relationship, he got defensive and insisted everything was okay and that he loved her. They continued to date but the infrequency of seeing each other remained consistent. Cierra became more concerned and expressed her worries to him. Chris conveyed his passionate feelings for her when they made love, reassuring her that nothing had changed. Cierra set aside her doubt and believed him. She rationalized his behavior by thinking that perhaps he was just anxious about the NFL draft in April and graduation in May. Whatever was bothering him, she didn't want to add to the matter, so she left the topic alone, stopped asking him "What's wrong?" and decided to give him the space he seemed to need. He appreciated her backing off a bit and felt relieved to address the personal issues he didn't want to share with her.

Cierra decided to pour her energy into her studies even though she had a light course load. She decided to focus mainly on the big presentation for her Communications class due at the end of the semester. Concentrating on the class project helped take her mind off of Chris, but it didn't help settle her spirit.

> *Heavenly Father, I don't understand what's happening with Chris and why he appears to be avoiding me. After all the years that we've been together, why are we having uncertainties now? If he's concerned about the NFL draft or graduation, I pray You calm his anxiety. If it's more than that, I pray that he will share with me what's troubling him. I pray that You help me be more patient with him. But most importantly Lord, I pray my period comes. It's the end of January and my period is a week late. I'm starting to worry. Amen.*

February

On Saturday morning, during the first week of February 1988, Cierra drove to the drugstore at six forty-five a.m. She waited for the clerk to unlock the doors at seven sharp. Once inside, she rushed to the aisle for feminine products and retrieved a home pregnancy test. She placed the box on the checkout counter and paid the clerk while trying not to look embarrassed. Then she hurried home and took her first morning urination on the pregnancy stick. Time seemed to stand still as she anxiously waited for the results. She watched the tiny window on the plastic stick wondering what her fate would be, *baby or no baby*. As quickly as her thoughts jolted through her mind, a plus sign appeared in the tiny, round window. Cierra shook the stick guessing the reading might change, but it didn't. She looked in the mirror. *It's positive. I'm pregnant. Chris and I are gonna be parents.* She delighted in thinking of them as a family. *But how will he react? He's been acting so strange. I hope this doesn't push him over the edge. I have to pick the right time to tell him, maybe next week on Valentine's Day. Yeah, I'll do it then.*

Cierra went into her bedroom and phoned Rachel.

"Ci, this better be good. It's seven thirty Saturday morning."

"Rachel, hush and listen. You gotta promise me you won't say a word to Chris, Damien, Bridget or anybody else." Rachel sat up in the bed.

"What is it, Ci?"

"You've gotta promise me."

"Okay, I promise." Rachel wondered what was she promising blindly.

"Are you sure?" questioned Cierra even though she knew Rachel's word was bond.

"Yes. Come on, tell me, the suspense is killing me," demanded Rachel now sitting with her knees to her chest.

"I'm pregnant," whispered Cierra as if someone else could hear her in her apartment.

"You're what?"

"You heard me. I'm pregnant with Chris' baby," replied Cierra feeling the joy in her own words as she spoke them. Rachel shrieked loudly and ran her feet rapidly under the covers like something was tickling them.

"Ci, that's wonderful. I'm so happy for you. But wait a minute.

Apparently, you haven't told Chris yet 'cause you want me to keep quiet about this, right?"

"Right, I'm gonna wait and tell him on Valentine's Day. It'll be my gift to him."

"That's so romantic," said Rachel as she fell back onto her pillow and daydreamed about a family with Damien. She sat up again more alarmed this time, "Have you told your mom?"

"No. Are you crazy? I just found out. After I talk to Chris, I'll tell her." The mere thought of telling her mother almost ruined her joy. She pushed the thought to the far corner of her mind and continued to smile about her baby.

"Ci, how in the world are you going to keep this a secret from Chris for a week?"

"I don't know but I'm gonna try. I really want to save the news until Valentine's Day. So, please don't tell anyone, especially Damien because you know he'll tell Chris. I'll tell Kelly and Josi soon."

"Okay, I promise. C'est ça," said Rachel. The two continued to talk about baby names and clothes for another hour at which time Chris beeped in on Cierra's call waiting.

"Girl, this is him. I'll talk to you later."

"Good-luck. Let me know what he says. And Ci-,"

"Yeah?"

"Congrats. You'll make a terrific mom."

"Thanks Rachel." Cierra clicked over to Chris.

"So what are you and Rachel talking about first thing in the morning?"

"Nothing, just girl talk. What's up? Why are you calling me so early yourself?"

"I was thinking about you and wanted to hear your voice."

"Oh really. So, now that you've heard me, what else do you want?" Cierra teased.

"You got jokes. Anyway, what are your plans for today?" asked Chris glad to catch her in such a good mood.

Cierra tried to determine the true nature of his call. Was he just calling to say hi and make no attempt to visit like the other times or did he want to get together?

"Why do you ask?" she inquired.

"I was wondering if you wanted to catch a movie later today?"

"Well, I have an exam on Monday and was planning to study today," she replied a little torn inside. She wanted to see him but wasn't sure if she could hide her joy about their baby. She realized holding back her news was going to be harder than she originally thought.

"Baby, I haven't seen you all week," Chris pleaded.

Cierra paused and then answered, "And whose fault is that?"

"Mine. I take full responsibility," answered Chris hoping his honesty would change her mind. "Do you want me to beg?"

"Yes, beg."

"Alright." Chris cleared his throat. "I'm sorry that I haven't managed my time well. I miss you. I have a break and want to spend some time with you."

"Chris, I don't know. I really should study," Cierra said rubbing her stomach and smiling mischievously. Chris was surprised at her rejection and guilt took over his subconscious.

"What's up, Ci? Why are you pushing me away? Is something going on I should know about?"

Her attempt to keep him at bay aroused him in a negative way instead of just dismissing the outing.

"No, Chris. I miss you too. But I have to finish this reading. Tell you what, I'll make a deal with you. If I finish these next four chapters by three, I'll go to the movies with you."

Chris sat quietly for a moment wishing he could just see her and hold her, but he knew how important school was. He understood that just because he had a break didn't mean that she did.

"Alright. Study hard 'cause I really want us to get together today."

"Okay. I'll do my best."

Later that day, Cierra looked at the clock that read three fifteen p.m., when the phone rang.

"Hey, it's me," said Chris.

"Well, who else would it be?"

"So, how's it going?" he asked waiting to hear she was done studying.

"Well, I have one more chapter to do. I don't think I'm gonna be able to make it out today," replied Cierra looking at the reading she purposely stretched in order to occupy her time.

"So, are you saying you need more time or you won't be able to go out at all?" asked Chris in a disappointed tone.

"From the looks of things, not at all," answered Cierra feeling the vibe Chris was sending through the phone.

"Are you sure?"

"Yes, I'm sure, Chris. Maybe next week, okay?"

"Yeah, Ci. Whatever, fine. I'll talk with you later." His abrupt tone incensed her.

"Hold up, Chris. Why are you saying bye like that? I have a test. You know how I study."

He felt bad for his brash response then apologized, "I'm sorry, Ci. I just need to see you; that's all. I understand you need to study, but I just-"

"You just what? What's the fire drill about anyway? Usually, when I'm available, you have something else to do and when I'm not available seems like that's when you want to see me," she recounted.

"Nothing. There's no fire drill. I'll catch up with you later."

"Okay. Are we cool?" asked Cierra giving him an opportunity to express what was on his mind.

"Yeah, everything is everything," he said glad the conversation didn't escalate past that point. Chris hung up the kitchen phone. *What is wrong with me? I love this girl. I need to get my act together.* Just then Craig walked through the front door with Amy and a couple other over zealous fans.

A week passed and Cierra managed to keep her game plan about when to tell Chris her wonderful news. He knocked on her door in the early afternoon on Valentine's Day holding a small box behind his back in one hand and a half dozen, long-stem red roses in the other. Cierra took a final look in the mirror by the front door.

This is it. She opened the apartment door.

"Hi Chris."

"Hey baby."

He walked inside where they embraced and kissed. Cierra didn't notice the gifts he held in his hands as she gave him a powerful French kiss.

"Wow. What's gotten into you? Can I have another one of those?"

Cierra gave him another long, passionate kiss then whispered on his lips, "I have something to tell you."

"Okay. But first, these are for you." He handed her his gifts.

"Thank you, Chris. How sweet of you." She quickly opened the box so she could get to her news. She held up the fourteen karat gold necklace with a heart pendant dangling from the pretty chain.

"Chris, this is really nice. I have been looking at necklaces for awhile."

"I know. That's why I got it. Here, turn around." He clasped the necklace for her. She felt the front of the chain just below her neckline and looked in the mirror. She liked the piece of jewelry. It was perfect. Before Chris could converse about the necklace, Cierra quickly invited him to take a seat on the sofa. She placed the half dozen roses in a vase of water and displayed them on the coffee table. When she sat beside him, Chris touched her hand and asked, "What did you want to tell me?" Cierra addressed the matter as best she knew how.

"Remember our time together at Christmas?" she began.

"Of course I do," Chris remarked relaxing his right arm behind her on the back of the sofa.

"And remember when we made love the day before you bought your condoms?"

"Yeah," his voice went up an octave with curiosity as to where the conversation was headed.

"Well, you know how we've always talked about having a family?"

"Yeah," he leaned forward looking at Cierra lovingly with a smile. She felt a sense of acceptance.

"Well, surprise, surprise, we not only made love Christmas night, but we made a baby. I'm pregnant," she said looking into his dark brown eyes.

"Say that again. You're what?" he asked wanting to hear the words again because even though they sounded a little scary, they felt good and exciting too.

"I'm pregnant with your baby."

Chris sat motionless for a moment while the words resonated with him. Then he stood and mumbled, "I'm gonna be a daddy." Cierra watched silently, waiting for his full reaction. Then the news hit him and he repeated louder, "I'm gonna be a daddy. That's so cool." Before she could speak again, Chris gently pounced on her like a kitten playing with a small toy, knocking her backward onto the sofa. "Baby, that's wonderful." He kissed her repeatedly with fast pecks all over her face and neck. In between his pecks he said, "I love you. I can't wait for you to have our baby. I'm gonna be a good father to our baby just like my dad has been to me."

Cierra cried tears of joy as his excitement touched her heart. They enjoyed the rest of their Valentine's Day discussing the baby and their future plans to be married before the baby was born. That day was one they would always remember, particularly Chris. He rested beside Cierra that night, watching her sleep peacefully and thought *I really gotta get my shit together, quick. I have a family now.*

After Valentine's Day, Cierra and Chris reconnected and their relationship took a turn for the better. While visiting her one sunny afternoon, he apologized for being distant over the past months.

"I've had a lot on my mind, Ci."

"About what?"

"Just about school and the future," he replied. For a second, she thought about how smoothly Damien addressed the topics with Rachel and thought Chris could have done a better job. *I guess everybody is different.* Chris pressed his forehead against Cierra's and whispered, "Baby, I'm so sorry if I hurt you. I didn't want to hurt you." She remained silent absorbing his words. "You're still my baby, right?" He worried that his behavior blemished their relationship. Now more than ever, he wished he could undo the past, but he couldn't. All he could hope for was that the girl he loved and who was the mother of his unborn child would forgive him. Without hesitation, she replied, "Yes." But as she wrapped her arms around his broad shoulders, a precautious thought zipped through her mind, *But why treat me like that then? Why did it take a baby to bring you back to your senses?* Chris felt relieved as her answer soothed his concerns.

"You know I love you more than anything, right?" He held her face in his hands, looking into her feline-shaped, angelic eyes.

"Yes," she softly answered watching his lips as he spoke every word.

"Do you still love me as much as before?" He gave her a peck before she answered. Her heart fluttered like it used to and a warm sensation surged through her body.

"Of course. I never stopped. I figured you were going through some stuff about the NFL and graduation," she informed touching his Hershey face.

"We'll always be together, baby. We may have our ups and downs, but I'll never leave you. I promise. I love you," he said hugging her tightly. He then leaned down, lifted her shirt, and kissed her stomach. "I'll never leave you," he repeated. "You're having my baby, our baby. I'm the happiest man on the planet. I've always wanted us to have a family. Granted I thought it would be later. But I'm cool with this happening now. I've got everything I could ever want, right here with you," said Chris.

"Chris, I accept your apology. Let's just put that stuff behind us," suggested Cierra, happy that Chris acknowledged and regretted his wrong doings and that they were looking ahead.

"Ci, I'm truly sorry," he repeated.

"I know. I forgive you, okay?"

"Thank you, baby."

They began an intense French kiss that led to a passionate makeup love session. Strangely, the series of events strengthened the bond between them. Cierra's mind was once again set in forward motion for a happy life with Chris.

Lord, thank you so much for letting this situation with Chris work out. I'm so glad that he is overjoyed about the baby and is looking forward to us being a family. I hope that whatever was troubling him over these past months is truly done and over. I'm so excited about being a mom and Mrs. Christopher Jackson. But mostly Lord, I pray that our baby is healthy and perfect. Lord, thank you for my joy and blessings. Amen.

Spring 1988

April

Cierra welcomed the end of wintry, grey skies and frigid temperatures as spring 1988 arrived. She loved the newness of the season and the beautiful array of colors that appeared each day when the flowers bloomed. Sparrows chirped outside her bedroom window at dawn, often waking her before the R&B station on her radio alarm clock. During the warmest part of the afternoon, she liked sitting on her balcony to smell the sweet scent of the honeysuckle bushes near by. The serenity was a nice way to study and enjoy Mother Nature.

The night prior to April Fools day, Cierra stayed with Chris. When she arose the following morning to go home and get ready for class, she quickly dressed, kissed Chris, and headed out of the townhouse. The spring morning air and low-lying clouds produced a light layer of fog that hovered above the grass. In the distance, the sun ascended over the mountaintops with rays of yellow, orange, and gold. *I wish I had my camera, what a beautiful morning.* As Cierra approached her car, she saw a yellow piece of paper on the front windshield. *Damn it. Don't tell me I got a ticket.* As she walked closer, she saw that the yellow piece of paper was actually a post-it-note. She pulled the piece of paper from under the windshield wiper and read the typed message. **ROSES ARE RED, VIOLETS ARE BLUE, I SEE WHAT HE IS, WHY DON'T YOU?** *Cute. An April Fool's joke no doubt.* Cierra dismissed the note and left. When she arrived home, she showered and drank a cup of herbal tea to help relieve her morning sickness. At three months pregnant, hot tea was the only remedy that seemed to work.

Two weeks passed and Cierra's morning sickness subsided just like she read about in the many baby books she purchased. She felt healthy and was extremely happy. Life was fine for Chris and her until one morning she found another typed note on her car outside of Chris' townhouse that read ROSES ARE RED, VIOLETS ARE BLUE, THERE IS A SNAKE. DO YOU SEE IT TOO? Cierra ran back to Chris' place and banged on the door. When Chris answered, she stepped inside saying, "Chris this is no joke. Someone is following me and I think they put a damn snake in my car!"

"Cierra, calm down. What are you talking about?" he asked genuinely concern. She held up the second yellow post-it-note and said, "This is what I'm talking about. Two weeks ago, I got a note like this but I thought it was an April Fool's joke from you or Craig and didn't pay it any attention. But I don't think it's a joke anymore." Chris read the note and didn't know what to say.

"Chris, do you know anything about this?"

"No Ci, I don't," Chris replied looking her eye to eye.

"Then why do the notes only come when I'm here?"

Chris again stated that he didn't know. Cierra insisted that he ask his roommates. Chris went door to door and asked each of them, but they also denied knowing anything about the notes. Angry and frightened, Cierra asked Chris to check her car because she hated snakes and was scared of them. Chris obliged her wishes and they went outside to check the car. He looked thoroughly but did not find a snake.

"Are you sure you checked everywhere?" Cierra questioned as she stared at the car.

"Yes, baby, I check everything. I looked in the glove box, under the dashboard, under the seats, everywhere."

"What about in the trunk?"

"Ci, you stood right here and watched me check every inch of the car."

"I know Chris, but I don't want a snake in my car. I can't stand reptiles you know that." Cierra looked horrified.

"Baby, I know," Chris replied looking at the car, hoping his search was accurate and thinking, *damn this is fucked up*. He feared the stress was bad for Cierra and the baby.

"Do you want me to ride home with you?" he offered.

"No, as long as you're sure there's nothing in the car," answered Cierra still worried.

"I'm sure," he replied believing in his thorough search. Cierra cautiously sat in the car. Chris kissed her good-bye, closed her car door and watched her pull away. Once out of sight, he ran inside and made a phone call.

Cierra drove home with knots in her stomach, petrified that perhaps Chris didn't see the disgusting reptile. She pulled into her parking lot and gathered her purse from the passenger seat. Out of the corner of her eye, she thought she saw something move. Cautiously, she turned and faced the back seat. Just then, a black snake appeared from the defrost vent at the base of the rear window. Cierra screamed as she jerked at the locked car door. The snake slithered half its body out of the vent. She screamed louder and pulled at the door harder then fell out of the car as the door opened. She scrambled to her feet, kicked the door shut, and then walked backwards staring at the car. The snake sensed the fresh air and grass through the rear windows Cierra lowered for the drive home then slithered out of the car window and returned to its earthy habitat. Cierra rushed inside and called Chris.

"Chris, it was in my car," she said frantically. "You missed it! The snake was in my car! Who would do a thing like this?"

"Ci, baby, calm down. I'm sorry. I didn't see the snake. I looked everywhere." He truly did, but the cold-blooded creature knew how to hide its coiled body.

"I can't believe this shit is happening," Cierra shouted.

"Ci, please try to calm down. I know you're upset and with good reason, but think about the baby. You gotta remain calm," said Chris desperate to get control of the situation. Cierra's mind shifted to her unborn child. She rubbed her stomach with one hand to relieve the knot she felt.

"I just can't believe someone did this. And why me?" she asked totally baffled.

"I'm coming over," said Chris as he slipped on his shoes.

"Thanks, Chris, but there's no need. I just want to be alone right now," she replied sitting at the kitchen table.

"Baby, please. I want to be there with you," Chris begged.

"I understand. But I need time to think, ok?" The phone became silent. "Chris, are you there?" He spoke with disappointment and anger, "Yeah, Ci, I heard you."

"Chris look, the last thing I need right now is attitude from you."

"Baby, I'm not trying to give you a hard time. I'm just as upset about this as you. I just-"

"You just what?"

"Nothing," Chris replied.

"I hate when you do that."

"When I do what?"

"You start to say something and then don't finish."

"Are you alright?" asked Chris still concerned.

"No, I'm not. I gotta go."

Cierra hung up the phone and walked slowly to her bedroom. She rested on her bed, looked out of the window at her car and thought about who would put a snake in her car and why. She called Rachel to see what she thought.

"I think what I've always told you, you gotta watch your back because people are scandalous," Rachel advised.

Cierra was lost for words and didn't really feel like talking, she just needed to hear Rachel's opinion. Their conversation ended rather quickly then Cierra dozed off, exhausted from the excitement.

That evening Chris called to check on her and found her still shaken by the incident. He offered to come over again, but she still wanted some time to herself. Their conversation didn't last long either. Cierra dialed home. She needed to hear the sound of her mother's voice.

"Hi, Cierra. How's my baby girl?" asked her mother excited that she called. Cierra burst into tears.

"Hi mom," she sobbed.

"Lord, child, what's wrong?" asked Mrs. Sykes alarmed that something terrible had happened. Cierra spoke muffled, "I'm pregnant and somebody is stalking me."

"Cierra, did I hear you right? You're pregnant?" repeated her mother.

"Yes, and somebody is stalking me."

"Stalking you?" Mrs. Sykes tried to grasp the notion. "Well, who on earth would do a thing like that?"

"I don't know," answered Cierra.

"When did you find out you were pregnant?" asked Mrs. Sykes trying to put a timetable on these events.

"February. Chris and I conceived at Christmas."

"February?" Mrs. Sykes calculated in her mind. "Cierra, you're three and a half months pregnant. I guess you plan on keeping this baby then huh?"

"Mom, Chris and I want this baby very much. This is our blood. Why would you insinuate anything else? Of course, we're keeping our baby."

There was a moment of silence on the phone. Mrs. Sykes sat and shook her head, totally caught off guard by Cierra's phone call. Cierra spoke, breaking the awkwardness.

"Mom, don't worry. We'll be fine. We plan to finish school. Chris will likely get drafted to the NFL and I will stay home with the baby for a while and then start working. We plan to be married before the baby is born."

"Married? You're engaged too?" asked her mother more stunned with each word Cierra spoke.

"No. But that's our plan."

She talked to her mother and further explained the entire situation about Chris, the baby, the stalking notes, and the snake. Cierra needed her mother to listen to everything she said, but Mrs. Sykes was stuck on the fact that her daughter was expecting.

"Pregnant. Cierra, what is your dad gonna say?"

"Dad? Mom, you can't tell him. Promise me!" Cierra felt like climbing through the phone if she could to insist that her mother keep her secret.

"Cierra, you're gonna show soon, and he's coming to your graduation next month. How do you think you're gonna hide that?" asked her mother envisioning how awful the trip would be now.

"I'm not showing just yet. And I'm not ready to deal with him," Cierra responded flustered that her mother took the conversation down such an ugly path. Mrs. Sykes didn't answer.

"Mom, promise me!"

"Cierra, what do you want me to say?"

"Fine, mom. Thanks for nothing. I'll talk to you later."

"You take good care of yourself. I know things will work out fine. We'll see you soon," said Mrs. Sykes, thinking how in the world was she going to handle this situation with her husband.

Cierra paced the floor with mixed feelings about their conversation. On one hand, she felt good about telling her mother about the baby. But, on the other hand, she was now concerned whether her mother would tell her dad.

That evening while Cierra and Chris relaxed on the sofa watching TV, Cierra received a phone call from Amy regarding the Communications project. Amy informed Cierra that their group members wanted one more meeting to do a practice run of their presentation and that she suggested everyone meet at her apartment.

"Do you think you can make it?" Amy asked. Cierra's mind was on her stalker and not the class project.

"Huh? I'm sorry, Amy. What did you say?" asked Cierra. Amy repeated herself.

"Oh um, yeah, that's fine," Cierra responded half-heartedly. Chris nudged her arm and asked, "Who's that?" Cierra covered the mouthpiece and answered, "A girl from class." Chris returned to watching TV.

"Cierra, are you okay?" Amy asked wondering what was making her so spacey. Disturbed about the notes she answered, "No, not really."

"What's wrong? You don't sound like your normal self," said Amy.

"I'm fine. It's just that, well, there's this asshole leaving these notes on my car every other week. I'm trying to remain cool about it, but the coward is really starting to piss me off. I want to catch the jerk so my boyfriend can kicked his ass."

Chris sat up and looked at Cierra like she had lost her mind. "What are you doing? Don't tell anybody," he said with his brows frowned.

"Wow. Sounds like someone doesn't like you or your boyfriend," Amy commented.

"That's just it. I haven't done anything to anyone," said Cierra still puzzled and ignoring Chris' wish to remain silent about the ordeal.

"Well, maybe your boyfriend has. Do you have an idea of who it is?" Amy asked out of curiosity.

"Nope. Not a clue," Cierra said angrily.

"What does your boyfriend think?"

"He doesn't know who it is either," said Cierra watching Chris storm out of the room.

"Oh really?"

"You say that like he should," replied Cierra. An awkward moment of silence passed, then Amy said, "Well good luck with that situation. But you need to pull yourself together. We've got this project to do. Be at my place at seven p.m. on Wednesday, April twenty-seventh. Okay?"

"Okay, Amy. I'll see you guys then."

Chris returned to the room just in time to hear Cierra say Amy's name. When she placed the phone down, Chris questioned, "Amy. Amy who?" He looked like he had seen a ghost and was mad about it.

"Why are you getting so worked up, Chris?" asked Cierra surprised by his tone.

"Answer me, Cierra. Amy who?"

"Amy McKenzie. She's in my Communications class. We're on a group project together."

Chris threw his arms up into the air. "You've gotta be shittin' me. Ci, what else have you told that girl?"

"Nothing."

"Does she know you're pregnant?"

"No, Chris. Why?"

"That bitch is crazy, that's why."

"Chris, you're on a tangent. She called me about our class project."

"Just don't talk to that girl about us, okay? If you need to vent, call Rachel, damn. I can't believe this." He flopped back on the sofa and his mind seemed to go to some distant place Cierra couldn't reach. Tension hovered between them for the remainder of the evening.

Later that night, Cierra told Chris that she needed a break from everything and was going home to Richmond until Monday. She wished that she had some other place to go but there was only home. He tried to talk her into staying, but he could tell by the stress on her face that she needed to get away. Reluctantly, he watched her pack.

The next morning, Cierra drove Chris to his townhouse where they sat a moment inside the car while in the parking lot.

"Call me when you get there so I'll know you arrived safely," he instructed as he held her hand.

"I will." Cierra locked her fingers into his.

"Take care of yourself and the baby," Chris requested rubbing her belly.

"You know I will," she promised.

They gave each other a short French kiss then Chris kissed her belly and exited the car. He walked around the car then gestured for her to lower the window. He leaned into the car and said, "Ci, I love you. Always believe that."

"I do, Chris." She sensed sadness in his tone and asked, "Is there something wrong?" He paused then said, "Just that I want you and our baby more than anything. Take it easy at home, okay?" Cierra knew then his point of concern. "Don't worry Chris. It'll be a good visit. I'll hang out with my friends mostly. I won't be around my dad, hardly ever."

"Alright. Call me if you need me."

"Okay. I better get going. Love you."

"Love you back," said Chris as he poked his head through the window for one last kiss. Cierra shifted the car into gear then drove away.

Lord, if You're listening, I pray my mother didn't tell my father about the baby. I pray You let me handle this stalking situation at Tech first then I can deal with my dad. I pray that You give me strength through all of this. And mostly Lord, protect my baby. I pray that none of the stress I'm experiencing impacted the baby's health. Lord, I know there's only one way to end this stalking business and that's for You to bring the truth to light. Thank you. Amen.

Cierra arrived at her parents' house around one fifteen that afternoon. She called Chris as he asked and told him she had a good trip.

"I'm glad you made it home safely. Where's your dad?" he asked concerned.

"I don't know. Nobody is home. I'm getting ready to go visit my friends. I'll call you later, okay?"

"Alright. Take care."

Cierra tried catching up with her friends, but no one was around. That was the disadvantage about an impromptu visit home. To pass time, she went to the mall. After getting some lunch and walking just about the entire mall window-shopping, she decided to return home, thinking her mother should be back. She drove into the gravel driveway and still no one was home. She parked, went inside the house and hoped her mother would return shortly. She went to her room, stretched out across the bed and unintentionally fell asleep. The drive home and trip to the mall zapped her energy as the baby always made her extra tired.

At four p.m., she heard her father enter the house. She didn't hear her mother's voice and suspected she hadn't returned.

"Cierra! Get your ass out here, right now," demanded her intoxicated father.

Damn. Here we go. She grabbed her car keys and put on her shoes in case she had to run out of the house. She entered the kitchen and tried to greet him nicely, hoping it would take the sting out of whatever he was about to say.

"Hi dad. You're home. Where's mom?"

"'Hi dad. Where's mom?' You don't need to worry your ass about that. What you need to worry about is bringing a bastard into this world and finishing school."

"What are you talking about?" She was stunned that her mother had told him her secret and suddenly felt very dizzy.

"What am I talking about?" He walked towards her. Cierra stumbled backward and fell against the refrigerator door. Mr. Sykes raised his hand and slapped her before she could say another word. She moved away from him as he started yelling.

"I'm talkin' about you disrespecting this household, out there screwing around while your mother and I are putting your ass through college. Now look at you. You're knocked-up and ain't got no future. And your dumb ass don't realize that your so called boyfriend is gonna go pro and forget all about you and your bastard."

"Shut up! Just shut up, you're drunk! You don't know what you're talking about. Chris and I love each other and we're getting married. And whatever I am in life with my child, I know I'll be a better parent than you ever were. And furthermore, you never helped me to go to college. I got grants and scholarships on my own, and mom covered the rest. You don't do shit."

He lunged at her and threw her against the far back wall. She got up and fought him back intensely. As the two struggled in the kitchen, Mrs. Sykes arrived home from the store. She opened the back door and yelled, "Gregory, stop it! You're gonna hurt your daughter." She turned to Cierra and asked, "What are you doing home?" Mr. Sykes slapped his wife and said, "Shut up Brenda and stay out of this. You're the reason why she's fuckin' up anyway." Cierra mustered all of her remaining strength and landed a solid round kick right in her father's ribs. She watched him gasp for air as he doubled over from the impact. Cierra faced her mother and shouted, "You betrayed me. How could you tell him? You know how he is. How could you do this to me, mom?" She returned to her bedroom grabbed her belongings then ran out the back door ignoring her mother's plea.

"Cierra, just wait a minute and listen. I didn't know he would react like this."

Cierra slammed her car door and sped out of the driveway. She cried most of the three and half hours back to Virginia Tech. Her stomach stayed in knots throughout the trip. By the time she reached Blacksburg, she started to feel really bad cramps. She arrived at her apartment and ran straight to the bathroom where she vomited. She tried drinking herbal tea but this time it didn't work. She laid on her bed in a fetal position and desperately wanted to call Chris. But how could she explain the fight between her and her dad? Her cramps intensified. "Ooouch," she moaned as she held her arms over her stomach and rocked back and forward. Her phone rang and she could hear her mother's voice message on the answering machine.

"Cierra, honey, I hope you're okay. Please call me when you get my message."

The mere sound of her mother's voice made Cierra cry again. Her cramps were at their peak and suddenly she felt something wet in her panties. Slouched over, she stumbled to the bathroom. Horrified at the spots of blood, she quickly called Chris. He rushed to her apartment in Craig's SUV, helped her to the truck, and drove her straight to the hospital.

"Chris, it hurts so bad," she cried.

"Just hang on baby. We're almost there."

He wanted to ask her why she returned so soon and what happened, but he knew now was not the time. She needed medical attention right away. Neither said what they were thinking that the baby was in jeopardy. By the time they arrived at the emergency room, Cierra was bleeding worse. The doctors took her immediately while Chris was left answering the nurse's questions about Cierra's name, address, date of birth, and anything else he could provide. After waiting fifteen minutes for someone to give him a status update, Chris grew anxious to see her. For the second time, the nurse at the desk told him that someone would be out shortly. He paced the hallway wondering what was happening behind the grey doors marked 'Authorized Personnel Only'. About forty-five minutes later, a doctor approached Chris and told him that they were just finishing a D&C. Unfamiliar with the term, he asked the doctor to explain. The doctor told him that Cierra miscarried and they had to clean her womb of any reminisce. Chris' strong athletic legs wobbled as he listened to the doctor's words.

"She will be able to have more babies in the future," said the doctor trying to shed some light on a sad situation.

"Can I see her?" Chris asked.

"Sure. Right this way."

The doctor led him to Cierra's bedside. The moment they saw each other, heavy heartache draped the room like a wet blanket. The doctor closed the white curtain to give them some privacy.

"Chris, I'm so sorry," Cierra cried.

"Shhh, baby. It's not your fault. It's just too much going on." He stroked her wavy brown tresses away from her face.

"I should have stayed with you," she continued to cry.

"Shhh, don't worry about that. What's important is that you're okay." He gave her a peck.

"The baby's gone," she said in a muffled cry.

"Shhh, I know. We'll have another. Don't worry."

Cierra cried a stream of tears in Chris' arms as he tried to comfort her.

Thirty minutes later, the doctor came back and did a final exam. He told Cierra that she would continue to experience cramping and minor bleeding as a result of the D&C but both should subside in a few days. He scheduled a follow-up visit then told her that she was free to go but needed to take it easy for a few days. She signed the release forms and Chris drove her home. Only the soft sound of Luther Vandross played in the truck as they rode speechless.

They entered Cierra's apartment and Chris helped her to bed. He gave her the medicine the doctor prescribed to help ease the pain. Eventually, the medicine took affect and she began to feel some relief. Chris sat beside her on the bed, watching the transformation. He stroked her velvet, caramel face and said, "Ci, I'm so sorry about all of this. What else can I do for you?"

"Nothing. Just be with me," she sobbed.

"I'm here baby. I'm not going anywhere. You have me forever." He kissed her gently and wiped away her tears. "I'm gonna take a shower then I'll be right back. Ok?"

"Ok," she replied starting to feel a little drowsy from the medicine.

Chris needed a moment to himself to deal with the misfortunes of the day. Stricken with his own guilt and the loss of the baby, he shed his melancholy tears silently in the shower. *What have I done?*

After collecting his composure, Chris rejoined Cierra in the bed. They held and comforted each other, bringing calm to a very disturbing day.

> *Lord, what did I do to deserve losing my baby? I just needed to get away from Tech to clear my mind of this stalker mess. I had no other place to go but home. I wanted to see my mother, but was this the price that I had to pay? Why would You allow my dad to attack me like that causing me to defend myself and over exert myself? I thought You would always protect the baby and me. I should've stayed at Tech with Chris. How will I ever be able to tell him what happened? I'm so angry, hurt, and confused, Lord. I don't understand this journey You are taking my heart on. I pray there's a good reason for all of this. Please let it be known. Amen.*

As the weeks passed, Cierra mourned the loss of her unborn child. She barely ate, didn't get out of bed, and didn't return anyone's phone calls, not her mother, not Rachel, not Bridget, not even her hometown friends. She only talked to Chris who visited her each day and was feeling the same pain as she. He wanted to question her about her visit to Richmond in more detail, but the timing never seemed right. He was curious about whether her parents knew.

April 29, 1988 came so fast that Cierra almost forgot it was presentation day. She raced to her Communications class and arrived just in time for the professor to begin.

"OK class, let's do this. We'll start with Amy's group."

As the group gathered their props, Amy questioned Cierra about her whereabouts miffed that she missed the group's last meeting.

"Cierra, what happened to you? We all agreed to get together for one last practice."

"Something came up and I couldn't make it."

"I left you several voice messages."

"Look, I was busy. Ok? I know my part," snapped Cierra.

Amy backed off and proceeded to the front of the class. The group gave a flawless presentation and earned the professor's praises for their effort. After the last group completed their presentation and class ended, Amy commented to Cierra, "Girl, I'm glad this class is over."

"Yeah, me too," replied Cierra.

"I heard that you date Christopher Jackson. Is that true?" Amy asked as she grabbed her backpack from under the desk.

"Yeah. Why do you ask?" Cierra's adrenalin immediately rushed through her veins.

"Oh, no reason. He's just a really good football player. I didn't know you guys dated that's all. You've mentioned your boyfriend before, but you never mentioned his name. I just found out recently that it was Chris. How long have you been together?" Amy inquired.

"Four years. Why? What's up with the questions?" Cierra stood looking down at Amy still seated. Amy packed her stuff and stood facing Cierra eye to eye and said, "Well, you know I work with the Media Club. We're doing a piece on all the Virginia Tech guys who got drafted into the NFL. He did get drafted in the last round by the Jets, right?"

"Yeah," Cierra replied still trying to figure out the true basis of Amy's inquisition.

"Well, I just want to make sure our write-up does him justice, that's all. Good-luck with your final exams next week," said Amy as she walked out of the classroom.

What came out of Amy's mouth sounded okay and legitimate, but the look on her face communicated that a lie rested behind her sky blue eyes. Cierra walked away with her instincts on high alert. She felt like her world was caving in and she wanted and desperately needed an outlet other than Chris, as he was part of her issue, someone other than Rachel because of her biased opinions, and definitely someone other than her mother who was under her father's spell. She called Bridget. Although Bridget acted like a comedian most of the time, Cierra knew her serious side, a side that Bridget seldom shared with others.

"Hey B," said Cierra sadly.

"Ci, is that you?" asked Bridget as she turned down her radio to hear the caller better. "Girl, what's going on? You sound down."

"I know we haven't chatted in a while," Cierra began.

"Well, how could we? You know I've been busy with my men and all," Bridget joked half serious and half trying to cheer up Cierra.

"B, you can always make me smile."

"Ci, you know how we do. I'm always here. What's going on?" Bridget asked sincerely concerned.

"B, so much. I wouldn't know where to begin. I just need a prayer partner on this," Cierra requested.

"Ok. What are we praying about?" asked Bridget preparing her state of mind.

"Me and Chris."

"Okay, but can you be a little bit more specific?" asked the preacher's kid. Cierra was silent then replied solemnly, "Yeah. Let's just say Chris and I lost something very precious to us and I'm to blame. There's someone trying to tear us apart and I don't know who or why. I need to focus on school and it's becoming increasingly difficult. My relationship with my mom has become strained almost beyond repair. And my dad is the most evil man I've ever known."

"Well, let me ask you this. What do you want?" inquired Bridget still preparing herself for the prayer Cierra requested.

"I want peace and serenity in my life. My heart is with Chris, and I want the life we always dreamed of, but I know God's gonna have His way. So, I need to make sense out of what's happening with Chris and me. Something is up and only God knows what."

"Okay, I know just what you need," said Bridget.

"Lord, we come to You as humble as we know how in this moment of sadness. As young women, we sometimes make decisions or place ourselves in situations that we regret.

There has been a loss of someone special. We ask that You watch over him or her as they were loved and wanted by those who miss them. We sometimes don't understand our mothers' intentions and it hurts when their actions are in conflict with our own. We ask that You give us understanding and the strength to forgive our mothers because not only did they give us life, but they also love us unconditionally. Sometimes Lord, the ones closest to us hurt us the most. As young women, we need our fathers in a constructive way. We pray that You touch our fathers' hearts helping them to realize what a precious gem a daughter is. There are those of us Lord who believe in our soul mates and the power of love. Shield that love from negative outside forces that try to destroy the happiness You place between friends and lovers. Lastly Lord, when the day is dim and the night seems never ending and our tears stream down our faces, may we always come to You for comfort. You are our rock and salvation. Amen."

"Amen," replied Cierra, "that was really nice, Bridget. Thank you. I feel so much better. I know tomorrow will be a brighter day."

"You're welcome my friend. Anytime," replied Bridget.

May

The sun shined brilliantly on the morning of May 10, 1988. A ray of light peered through the mini blinds in Cierra's bedroom. She rested in the bed and listened to the birds' chirping and for the first time in weeks after the loss of her baby, she felt a little better. After praying with Bridget about the miscarriage, her relationship with Chris, and her family, she was now prepared to tell Chris about the fight with her dad.

She walked across the bedroom, opened the mini blinds and looked outside. *Is that the sun reflecting on the car window or something else?* She went to the living area where she could get a better look. *Damn it! Another note.* Cierra quickly put on a pair of sweats and raced outside. *I can't believe this. It's a damn letter this time.* She looked at the envelope tucked under the windshield wiper then around to see if she saw anyone but the parking lot was still and quiet. She didn't see the person across the street parked in a car beside a thick evergreen watching her reaction. Cierra opened the envelope and started reading the contents. She quickly ran inside while the person behind the evergreen laughed. She anxiously called Chris right away to tell him what she found.

"Hello," Chris answered.

"Chris, I got a letter on my car last night. Listen to this." She started reading the hand written letter aloud. As she read it, Cierra started questioning him about the things detailed in the document.

"Chris, what's this about you seeing somebody else?

"Ci, don't read anymore. Somebody wants to hurt you and me and cause us problems."

Cierra didn't listen to him and continued to read. The more she read, the less she believed him.

"Chris, I'm coming over right now so you can see this."

She sped to Chris' townhouse, reading the letter at every red light. Each word seemed to make her adrenaline pump harder. When she arrived at Chris' place, she practically plowed over Craig who answered the door. She raced upstairs to Chris' room and handed him the letter but he rejected it without reading a word and instructed her to throw it into the trash. But she didn't. She wanted to absorb the fact that the letter informed that Chris was cheating on her for quite some time. The five-page letter detailed sexual encounters, places, times and frequency. Disturbingly, some of the occasions mentioned in the letter filled the voids when Chris told Cierra he could not visit her. Cierra didn't want to believe the five-page letter and all its contents but there it was in black and white, everything except a signature. Chris used the fact that the person didn't sign the letter as his basis for explaining the ill document.

"Cierra, look at me," he said with a firm voice. She raised her eyes away from the letter and looked at him. "Whoever is doing this is just trying to fuck with us. We need to stick together, okay? Look, the person is a coward. They wrote all this shit and didn't have the courage to say who they are because they're lying. I'm telling you, just ignore this bullshit. We only have two more weeks left in school. Whoever this is will be out of our lives for good. All we have to do is concentrate on taking our final exams and then after graduation, we're out of here. OK?"

"Chris, what about these parts that describe when you told me you couldn't come over? It says here that you went to see this person." She flipped through the pages again.

"Ci, I don't know. Maybe someone talked to one of my roommates and they said something about my schedule since I depend on them for rides here and there."

Cierra looked into his eyes for a sign of whether he was telling the truth or not. He kneeled in front of her where she sat on the bed and pushed the letter aside.

"Baby, please. Just ignore this. Two more weeks that's all we need to focus on. We're be starting a whole new life in New York. Okay?"

After questioning Chris and hearing his logical answers, she dismissed the accusations once more. "You're right, Chris. Just two more weeks and this will all be over."

"Now you're talkin'. Forget about that damn letter." He felt better that he had convinced her and quickly changed the subject, "What do you want to do today?" he asked trying to please her.

"I really need to study for finals. All four of mine are next week. What's your schedule like?" asked Cierra as she folded the letter and placed it in her pocket.

"Um, I have one this week on Friday and the other three are next week. Hey, um, aren't you going to throw that away?" he asked annoyed that she kept the letter.

"Probably, when I get back home." Secretly, she had no intentions of throwing it away. She planned to keep it with the other notes and read them again. Chris wanted to take the letter out of her hand and shred it, but that wouldn't have been the right thing to do, or would it?

Cierra returned home and did just as she planned. After reading the letter, she made a decision not to let the situation derail her from what she wanted, a peaceful, loving life with Chris. But something deep inside her spirit made her feel like things would never be quite the same. How could they?

> *Lord, this is a horrible mess. I'm almost in disbelief that all this is taking place, especially so close to us finishing school. I know people say that the devil will try to steal your joy. And You know my joy has been with Chris these past four years. I'm confused. I don't know whether to trust him and continue with our plans. Sometimes I wonder if this entire mess is happening because there are things about Chris that I should know? Folks say that whatever is done in the dark will come to light. I continue to pray that You allow the truth about this matter be known to me. Amen.*

During the week of May fifteenth, Cierra completed three final exams and only had one more to take on Thursday. She eagerly awaited graduation the following week. Extremely pleased with her A-minus course work, she couldn't wait to get her Bachelor of Arts diploma. Nothing would stand in the way of that.

Late Wednesday night while studying for her last exam, Cierra's phone rang.

"Hello," she answered turning the pages of her business statistics notebook.

"Hello, Cierra?" The voice sounded familiar.

"Amy?" Cierra asked a little surprised.

"Yeah. It's me. I need to talk to you," Amy requested rather insistently.

"About what?" Cierra couldn't imagine what she wanted. The Communications class they had together ended with the group's presentation two weeks ago. Cierra didn't mind her calling back then because their interaction was class related. And although Amy befriended her with exchanging jokes and small talk about classes, sports, and graduation, Cierra didn't want the alliance to continue beyond the class. Amy's reputation still existed and she stilled dressed the part, Daisy Duke shorts and spaghetti strapped tank tops, sometimes with a bra and sometimes without. She still got high on cocaine and partied wildly, sexing the athletes.

Cierra could tell Amy was drunk or high and tried to politely end the phone call. "Amy, I'm in the middle of studying for an exam and I don't have time to talk right now. Can you call back another day?"

Amy persisted, "I really need to talk to you, Cierra." Her tone became more demanding at which point Cierra didn't want to talk with her. "Amy, I'm sorry but I'm studying. I have to go." Cierra hung up the phone in Amy's face. Before she could settle back to studying, the phone rang again.

"Hello," Cierra said. Amy went right into her purpose for calling.

"Cierra, I'm the one leaving the notes on your car."

"Amy, you're sick!" Cierra hung up again. The phone rang a third time.

"What?" Cierra yelled.

"If I were you, I would listen to what I have to say."

Cierra wanted to return to her studies and not deal with any of this, but curiosity got the best of her.

"Talk Amy and make it quick. I don't have a lot of time."

Amy explained that she put the notes on her car because she wanted Cierra to know how badly Chris messed around on her. Cierra couldn't imagine him cheating on her especially after all of their happy years together. She knew their relationship was strained for a few months, but nothing to warrant disloyalty. She also thought about how each time a note appeared Chris said that he didn't know why someone would do this or who the person was.

Amy proceeded to tell Cierra how she and Chris met, how many times during the week they saw each other, how often and intensely they had sex, and how he helped her cut back on using cocaine. Amy continued to tell Cierra how she fell in love with Chris even though she knew that he would never leave his girlfriend.

"Chris told me from the very beginning that he had a girlfriend that he loved very much. But I didn't care."

The more Amy talked, the more Cierra felt her adrenaline rise like a flash flood. Cierra's head spun with the shock of all that Amy told her. She composed herself and asked Amy questions to try to find holes in her story, but that only made matters worse. Amy told her things about her family that Cierra had only confided in Chris. Cierra saw red as a result of his betrayal. *How dare he!* Amy further mentioned conversations that Cierra had with Chris late at night on the telephone, indicating she laid in bed with him at the times Cierra phoned. Then when Amy told Cierra how hard and long Chris sexed her, Cierra became dizzy and nauseous. In a subdued voice Cierra said, "Amy, I've heard enough." But Amy persisted to tell her more so Cierra asked, "Why did you bother to tell me about you and Chris?"

"Chris used me. I knew he would never love me the way he does you, but I thought he cared about me as a person. And I'd be damned if he thinks he can just screw me like I ain't shit and get away with it. Everybody thinks he's such a fuckin' nice guy, but he ain't shit! I didn't know that you were his girlfriend until I saw a picture of you on his dresser back in April. During our class, you were such a nice person and you had no idea what he was doing. I thought you should know what he's really about. I want you to know that your man is a dog just like all the rest of them. He ain't shit! He thought he could play me and then just dump me when he was done. Well, I've got news for him." Amy cried like her feelings were truly hurt. With a huge lump in her throat Cierra inquired further, "How long have you two been seeing each other?"

"Since the first football game against Clemson in September. At first we were just friends for a while but then we got intimate."

Cierra's heart went to her feet but she continued with her questions, "And when did this affair stop?"

"Not until February of this year when he started pulling away. I wanted us to continue to see each other."

Well, that explains his aloof behavior. "Amy, let me get this straight. You and Chris were seeing each other for five to six months? I don't believe you. He may have banged you a few times this semester, but that's it. I don't believe that he's been seeing you for so long."

Then Amy reminded her of a party the football players had after the East Carolina game in October.

"Chris told you that he had to pick up Craig from the party. Well, it wasn't true. Chris and I made up the lie so he could be with me at my place and spend the night," informed Amy. Cierra remembered that night so well because she practically begged him to let somebody else take Craig home so he could stay with her. But he insisted that he had to pick up Craig and return his SUV. She also remembered how she tried to contact him at home that next morning, but she didn't get an answer until two thirty p.m.

Never in her wildest dreams did Cierra think Chris would lie and betray her trust. She could buy into him out drinking and partying, but sexing Amy? It was more than she cared to handle. Once again, Cierra told Amy that she heard enough and wanted to get off the phone. Amy rattled on but Cierra couldn't comprehend her words because of the anger she felt circulating in her veins. She hung up the phone in Amy's face, grabbed her car keys, and drove to Chris' place.

A few moments after midnight, Cierra rang the doorbell and banged on the front door of Chris' townhouse. Craig opened the door and she marched upstairs and down the hall to Chris' bedroom. Her fury festered and resided in her mind and soul until the moment she saw him. She turned the doorknob waking Chris. He jumped up suddenly and asked, "Ci, what's wrong?" She couldn't restrain the hurt, anger, or betrayal she felt. She lunged at him with her fist and repeatedly hit him with all her might.

"You son of bitch! You've been fucking that whore! How could you do this to me? Damn you," she screamed while throwing punches. Caught off guard, Chris scrambled to catch her fists. Hysteria took over Cierra, and Chris found himself backing towards the bed. Somehow they fell onto the bed but she never stopped throwing punches and cursing him. Within seconds, he used his strength, flipped her over and pinned her wrists to the mattress.

"Cierra, what the hell is wrong with you, uh?" he yelled shaking her fist to the bed.

Scrambling to get loose, she glared at him and bellowed, "You know what's wrong with me. You've been fuckin' Amy that's what the hell is wrong with me. Now get off of me you lying, no good, cheating, dirty, dog! You knew all along who was stalking me. You've been humping that bitch since September. How could you? Now, let me go!" She resisted the strong urge to spit in his face as she continued to struggle to get free but his grip restrained her. Her name-calling cut him to the core, but he said nothing and let her vent.

"Christopher Jackson, you can kiss my ass 'cause you ain't worth the breath I use to say your name. As far as I'm concerned, you can continue to go fuck your skank whore 'cause I don't want shit to do with you anymore. Now get the hell off of me, you selfish asshole!"

In the moonlight that beamed through the mini-blinds, Chris witnessed hurt in Cierra's eyes like he had never seen before. He saw more hurt than when she spoke of her family and more hurt than unanswered prayers. When she stopped fighting and looked at his face, tears streamed down her cheeks as she looked into his brown eyes and saw eyes that lied to her face, eyes that lied without a second thought, betraying eyes that led to his deceitful soul. She felt her body cave and began crying uncontrollably. "Chris, I trusted you. How could you do this?"

He tried to find the right words to calm her. "Cierra, baby, listen to me. I love you. No matter what you've heard, nothing will ever change that. You're my girl." Sitting on the bed, she sobbed, "You promised to always be faithful to me. We promised to always be faithful to each other. I never cheated on you, Chris, not once. Why did you do it? Why? I don't understand that. I thought we were happy. Now I know why your ass was flippin' out during the winter. I can't believe you did this and with Amy of all damn people. What were you thinking?"

"Baby, nothing happened between Amy and me," Chris persisted. The words burned in Cierra's ears like fire.

"You're a damn lie, Chris. I know everything about you two!"

"What are you talking about, Cierra?" He walked across his room and turned on his desk lamp, continuing to maintain his innocence, playing dumb about the whole thing.

"You know what, Chris? It's bad enough that you did this dirty shit. But for you to sit here with the audacity to act innocent and continue to lie to my face is incredible. I have no respect for you anymore, none!"

He still tried to convince her that Amy was crazy and just out to hurt them because he wouldn't be with her like she wanted. Cierra had enough of his deceit and said, "Oh really? Well how about this?" She disclosed her extensive conversation with Amy. When she finished, Chris looked like he had seen a ghost. He sat on the bed lost for words thinking, *This wasn't supposed to turn out like this. That bitch will pay.*

Cierra collected herself, sat beside him and calmly said, "Chris, I only want one thing from you and that is for you to look me in the eye and tell me whether or not it's true. Can you give me that much respect? Can you be honest at least once with me and tell me in your own words whether or not it's true?"

Unsure of what she might say or do, Chris cowardly replied, "Ci, I don't want to lose you."

"Chris, tell me whether it's true?"

"Baby, please. I love you."

"Chris, tell me, is it true?" her voice escalated.

He said nothing. She looked at him and did not see the glow that usually greeted her or the spark his eyes revealed when silent passion existed between them. She only saw sadness and guilt. The room became still, only the hum of the air conditioner could be heard. His silence made her cry again.

"Chris, you can't even look at me and be honest with me right now in this very moment."

He wiped her tears away as his piercing brown eyes dulled and watered. His lips parted but no words or sounds came out. He brushed his tears away, looked at Cierra and said, "Yes, Ci, it's true. But I always loved you. I never stopped loving you." Her reflexes took over and before she realized it, she smacked his face so hard that it burned the palm of her hand. He would now have a raised, red imprint like the ones her father gave her in childhood.

"How dare you say you love me when you're out here humpin' that slutty bitch! And you think that by saying 'but I always loved you' makes this shit ok? Forget you Christopher Jackson!"

"Cierra, baby, please forgive me. I'm so sorry. I never meant to hurt you. I made a huge mistake and I'm willing to do anything to correct it. I'm so sorry. I just got caught up in something I shouldn't have.

"Yeah, I bet you're sorry, sorry that your ass got caught. If Amy and I didn't have that class together, I never would have known. She felt compelled to tell me because I was nice to her during class."

"Ci, please. What can I do to make this right?" He kneeled in front of her, but his gesture meant nothing to her.

"Chris, I'm sitting here thinking about all the times we were together throughout this school year and how you played me. You lied to my face like it was nothing. Tell me, what did you see in her that made you so willing to risk everything we established?"

"Nothing baby. She had nothing," he answered trying to hold Cierra's hands but she jerked them away from him.

"Nothing? That's interesting. So for nothing, you let our four good years and future escape you. Come on Chris, you can do better than that. Was it her big breast, was it because she was an easy fuck? Perhaps it was because she's white. That seems to be a common theme with the black players. Come on, tell me, you ain't got shit to lose now."

Chris didn't like the turn of events but conceded to try to get back in Cierra's good graces. "Baby, I'll admit that I got curious about being with a white girl. My roommates and other players do it and they teased me because I stayed true to you all these years. Amy has always flirted with me over the years, but I never paid her any attention. Then during the fall of '87, she came to me to help her with some personal problems. And that's how it started. We were just friends at first then other stuff started happening. I only wanted to experiment outside of our race once to see what it's like. But she took matters to a whole other level and I got caught up. I swear that's what happened."

"So, when I was pregnant, you were banging this bitch?"

"Yes and no," he answered.

"What the hell kind of answer is that, Chris, 'yes and no'?"

Chris looked at her intense eyes and knew he had to divulge the timeline of his affair and hoped it wouldn't make matters worse.

"I was seeing Amy pretty steady from September until February," Chris tearfully admitted.

"Basically, up until I told you that I was pregnant, you were screwing this bitch regularly?"

Chris grinded his teeth, disgusted with himself as he admitted, "Yes. Then when I cut her off, she started acting psycho. In March, she kept calling me upset because she wanted us to continue to see each other, but I didn't. Then she started calling and hanging up. Then in April she started the notes."

Tears streamed down Cierra's cheeks. Her head ached with a migraine but she continued, "I need to ask you something Chris and please be honest with me. Did you really go with Zack to Atlantic City for New Year's Eve like you told me you did?"

"No. Amy met me in Washington, DC to hang out," he regretfully replied.

"Chris, please tell me you used condoms with this girl."

He didn't answer.

"Chris! You didn't? How careless can you be?" Cierra felt sick on the stomach. He looked at her realizing just how reckless he had been and shamefully said, "Most of the time."

"Most of the time? Are you out of your damn mind? You put us both at risk. What the hell is wrong with you? That skank has been with everybody. Damn, I can't believe this!" She paced the floor.

"Baby, we're fine," he said trying to bring Cierra's attention back.

"What do you mean?" Cierra asked wondering what else he was hiding.

"In February, I had a checkup to make sure I was clean. My tests came back negative for everything."

"You got tested and didn't even give me a hint that I should be? Well, thank God that I did get pregnant 'cause they check you for everything. Lord, thank you for sparing me," she said aloud looking up at the ceiling with raised hands.

Chris didn't know what else to say. He had messed up so badly, he had no words. But Cierra did.

"Chris, you could have told Amy no, but you didn't because you liked what you were doing. She told me about all the ways and how hard you fucked her. What else could she offer you? Nothing. You had nothing else in common. Were you planning on introducing her to your parents, sharing a life with her?"

"No. No, Ci. I didn't want anything with her," he answered realizing how horrible his actions were.

"So basically, you risked everything we had, including our health because you were curious about anal sex and some white pussy. Man, I never knew you could be so shallow and stupid. I hope it was worth it to you. I hope she gave you the fuck of your life."

"Ci, she meant nothing to me. You mean everything to me, and you're right. I was stupid, very stupid. But please don't let this come between us. I promise I'll never cheat again. I swear this was the one and only time something like this has happened. It won't happen again, I swear." His eyes watered with shame and regret.

Cierra's heart was broken and burdened with sadness.

"You know Chris, this hurts like hell. But you know what? I'm glad that I found out before it was too late. Now I see your true colors. I see the deceitful person you really are."

Suddenly, Chris jumped up, opened his closet, and quickly threw on a pair of jeans and sneakers.

"Where are you going?" Cierra asked amazed that he would walk out on her.

"I'll be right back." He hurried out of the door.

"What do you mean you'll be right back?" Cierra blared after him.

Chris left the room in his jeans and bare chest. Cierra heard him run down the stairs and out of the front door. She sat on the bed in total disbelief waiting for him to return. *I can't believe he just ran out of here. He's unreal.*

When Chris got outside, he saw Amy and her friend running to Amy's car. He chased them and caught Amy by the hair as she tried to get into the car. She broke loose but her windows were down. He reached through the open pane, grabbed her hair again, and tightly held her blonde mane. Amy pressed the button to close the window, but Chris wouldn't let go. As the window closed, he banged Amy's head against the glass yelling, "You whore! You fucked up everything! I'll kill your ass, you bitch!" Amy's friend ordered her to drive away. She did, but Chris ran with the car still holding onto her hair, banging her head and cursing. Suddenly, the window cracked and cut Amy's temple. She drove faster until Chris couldn't keep up with the speed of the car. When he let go, he noticed the cracked car window. He stood in the middle of the street about two blocks from his townhouse, huffing from the fast sprint.

"Shit, shit, shit!"

His loud yell echoed among the buildings causing some neighbors to turn on their house lights and peek out of their windows. To Cierra's surprise, Chris suddenly bolted through the bedroom door and fell onto the floor with his knees to his chest and head between his hands. Cierra glared at him.

"Christopher, what the hell is wrong with you?"

"I think I hurt her," he repeated over and over.

"Who are you talking about?"

"I didn't mean to hurt her."

"Chris, who the hell are you talking about?"

"Amy," he replied as he sobbed.

"Amy? Chris, what happened?"

He told Cierra how he heard girl voices outside his window so he went to check it out. He then rehashed the encounter with Amy at the car.

"You did what? How stupid can you be? You assaulted her. I guarantee you that she's gonna press charges. Chris, you're screwed." Cierra thought about the ramifications of his actions. "Chris, if she presses charges, your name is gonna be all over the local news and your rep that you worked so hard for is going to be nothing. I can see it now, 'Prominent black Virginia Tech football player brutally assaults a white female co-ed.' There goes your golden career." Mortified, she sat on the bed, shaking her head from side to side looking at the person she thought she knew so well.

"Ci, she messed up everything for you and me," said Chris as he moved to the bed and sat beside her. "All the stress she caused you, I know it's why you lost the baby. I hated her for that and I wanted her to pay." His comment caught Cierra off guard. She was not ready to dive into another heavy conversation about the fight with her dad being the real reason she miscarried. She skipped around the issue and focused on Chris and Amy.

"She didn't mess things up. Chris, you did. How can you blame all this stuff on her? I guess it's her fault that you took your dick out of your pants and put it in her. You know what, later for this." Cierra stood up to exit the bedroom but Chris stepped in front of her.

"Ci, baby, please don't go. I need you." Cierra stepped to the side and ordered him to get out of her way but he insisted, "Please Ci, don't go. I think Amy is really going to the police. She said she's going to press charges."

"Serves you right. Where the hell do you get off grabbing and hitting a female anyway? I don't know who you are."

"Don't say that. You do know me, Ci."

"No. I don't. First you betray me and now you're beating females. The guy I loved and cherished would never do something like that. The guy who I thought loved and cherished me wouldn't have lied to me like this and played me. I can't believe I trusted you completely. What a fool I was."

She again tried to move towards the door but Chris blocked her. Cierra's voice went up two octaves, "Chris, move!" She pushed him in his chest, reached around and opened the door. He followed her down the hall, pleading with her to stay. While at the top of the stairs, Chris reached for her hand and tried to pull her towards him. He desperately wanted to hug her to let her know he meant every word he said but she jerked her hand away and lost her balance. Chris tried to grab Cierra's shirt to stop her from falling, but she tumbled backwards down the stairs to the bottom.

"Damn it," Chris exclaimed as he raced down the steps after her. "Baby, are you alright? I'm so sorry. I'm sorry for all this."

"I hate you, Chris. This is all your fault!" She rubbed at her left foot that was injured. Chris climbed over her tumbled body and stood in front of her.

"Baby, let me help you up."

"Get away from me," she cried out. He tried to help her up but she pulled away and screamed at him again. Using the banister for support, she pulled herself up and hobbled on one foot to the front door. Chris followed.

"Ci, come here. You're hurt. Let me take care of your foot."

"Leave me alone. Just leave me the hell alone." She cried so hard that she could barely see where she walked. She then made her way to the car. Chris continued to follow her to make sure she was ok. She got into the car and shut the door.

"Call me when you get home," Chris pleaded but Cierra sped away before she heard him finish his sentence.

She returned to her apartment about three a.m. with a swollen foot that now looked like a huge sausage. She immediately put an icepack on the injury and elevated her foot. She couldn't focus on studying anymore and knew it was pointless to try to study for her scheduled eight a.m. exam that morning. She lied on her bed with the ice pack on her foot, looked at the ceiling and wondered why Chris did these things. He repeatedly called her home until she finally answered the phone. They tried to talk about the matter at hand but between the loud shouts, neither one heard what the other said. Chris knew that he didn't want to lose his love, but Cierra felt that he betrayed her in the worse kind of way. After they hung up, she prayed.

> *Heavenly Father, I lie here in disbelief that Chris betrayed me so. Never did I think he would do this to me. Even when I had my small suspicions that he was up to something, I never thought it would turn out to be this and with Amy of all people. Lord, I'm just so thankful that I didn't get any diseases from this incident. Thank you again for Your mercy. I've been faithful and good to Chris over the years, and I thought that he loved me solely. Lord, I shed these tears with You because I don't understand my heart's journey. All my life, I've been praying to You for peace and love in my world. I truly thought You had answered my prayers with the love I found with Chris, but now that's a*

lie. I guess this is what people mean when they say 'The Lord giveth and the Lord taketh away.' I have nothing now. I don't have a good relationship with my family, I miscarried my baby, and now Chris and I are torn apart at the seam. Why is this happening? Please be with me and stop the hurt that I'm feeling. I pray that you are with me as I take my exam today. I will need your strength to help me through this for I cannot handle this situation alone. Thank you. Amen.

Summer 1988

After completing her last exam, Cierra drove to her apartment and called Rachel.

"Hey Rachel, it's me," said Cierra.

"Girl, where have you been? I haven't heard from you in weeks. I left you several messages."

"I know. Forgive me. So much has happened in such a short period of time that I don't really know where to start."

"Start at the beginning," said Rachel trying to help her through what appeared to be a difficult conversation. She sensed that whatever was disturbing Cierra was major because Cierra always knew how to express herself and now she was at a loss for words.

"Okay, here goes," said Cierra. She told Rachel about the miscarriage, but chose not to tell her about the fight with her dad. Then she told her about Chris and Amy and that she broke up with him as a result. Rachel's mouth fell to the floor.

"Ci, I'm very sorry about the baby. I know how badly you wanted it," said Rachel compassionately.

"Thanks, Rachel."

"Girl, didn't I tell you these hoes are scandalous. How much of this are you blaming on Chris 'cause you know how these heifers throw themselves at the players. Damien tells me about all kinds of stuff those groupies do to get with the players. It's a shame and the guys are stupid enough to fall for it. That's why Damien stays to himself most of the time. He says the fellas invite too much temptation around. And with the roommates Chris has, he didn't stand a chance. Sooner or later something would've happened. I'm just sorry it was Amy McKenzie of all people."

"So, what are you saying Rachel? That it was okay for him to mess around on me?" asked Cierra agitated with Rachel's statements.

"No. Hell no. I think he should've been stronger than that and tell his roommates to kiss his ass and tell Amy to go jump off a cliff. I'm just saying it's hard for them to turn down pussy when it's being thrown right in their faces. You know most guys at this age think with their second head anyway. They do some really dumb stuff. C'est ça."

"So, it wouldn't matter to you if Damien did something like this?"

"Hell yes, it would matter. That's why I tell him whatever he's doing, I don't ever want to know and he better not ever bring anything home, if you know what I mean."

"Yeah, but Damien is one of those strong silent types. He would've told those guys to buzz off," said Cierra liking that trait about Damien.

"Yeah, probably, but he still has a Johnson. There's no guarantee that I'm all the woman he needs. I'm just shocked because you and Chris never had those kinds of concerns. You two have been so into each other since freshman year," said Rachel still trying to put her head around the notion of Chris cheating with Amy.

"Well, all that's changed now," said Cierra assured that things would never be the same.

"Yeah, I guess you're right about that. Well Ci, what do you want? Do you want Chris back or not? From what you've told me, his apology sounds sincere."

"I don't know. It's like I love him and hate him at the same time. I honestly don't know what to do. I'm praying on it."

"Well, that's the best thing to do."

"Did Damien hint at any of this?" asked Cierra curious if Chris mentioned anything to him.

"No, not as far as I know. He never said anything to me. Why?"

"Just wondering who did Chris tell, if anyone. I know his roommates knew because Amy frequented there during their affair. And according to her, they openly showed each other affection in front of them by holding hands and kissing."

"That's so jacked up," remarked Rachel wishing there was more she could do for her friend.

"Well, I better go. I just wanted to call you and talk this through a little bit and let you know what's happening with Chris and me," said Cierra sadly.

"Okay. Again, I'm very sorry about the baby. I can't imagine what that's like. Give you and Chris some time. Things will work themselves out."

"Yeah, maybe. I'll chat with you later."

"OK, au revoir."

Cierra and Chris spent every spare moment trying to reconcile but they made little to no progress. He became more worried and concerned about losing his relationship with her. He tried every way he knew how to regain her trust. He spent all of his free time with her. Searching for the quick fix, he bought her flowers, cards, and her favorite perfume but nothing filled her hurt and emptiness. Didn't he understand that regaining someone's trust takes time?

Aside from speaking, Chris' roommates said very little the few times Cierra visited him. Craig, however, told her that he was sorry to hear about what happened. She found that hard to believe since he and the other roommates knew about Chris and Amy from the start.

The final exam week concluded and graduation arrived on Saturday. Somehow in the midst of her heartache Cierra prepared for her family's arrival.

As the birds sang their early morning songs, Cierra heard a knock at her door. She took a deep breath and opened the door.

"Why there's my graduate," her mom shrilled.

"Hi, mom. How are you?" They exchanged hugs as Cierra's mother and father entered her apartment. Cierra ignored her father.

"How ya doin', Cierra?" he asked intentionally to get her attention.

"Fine," she said abruptly.

"I see you've taken good care of yourself. Your place is nice," said Mrs. Sykes looking around. Not really interested in much her mother had to say, Cierra responded, "Thanks."

Cierra walked away unnerved by their presence, more so her dad's than her mom. From the opposite end of the room, she studied her father to see if she saw any traces of his drinking. He seemed sober. Her parents rested for a while as they sat in the living room and watched television. Cierra gathered her commencement cap and gown took one last check in the mirror, walked down the hall and said, "Okay, I'm ready."

Cierra drove her own car to Lane Stadium while her parents followed. The stadium crawled with the Class of 1988 graduates. Cierra walked her parents to the section of the stadium where parents, visitors, spectators sat and explained to them that after the doctorate and master degree ceremonies, each undergraduate school would disassemble and relocate to various buildings to distribute the undergraduate degrees. She told them where to meet her then left to join her classmates.

Cierra found Section L without any problem. As she walked up the incline through the narrow tunnel, she felt her heart pounding harder with excitement. She stood at the top of the opening that gave a bird's eye view of Lane Stadium and looked from side to side. She marveled at the vast number of graduates and wished that more faces of color sat among them, a couple hundred African-American students weren't nearly enough in a graduating class of over four thousand.

She descended the stadium steps while looking at classmates popping bottles of champagne, a treat from the beer they consumed most of their college days. She then heard Rachel calling her name. She looked around and saw Damien and her standing on the bleachers fanning their arms wildly, signaling her to come sit with them. As she made her way to them, she saw Chris on the other side of Damien trying to make eye contact with her. She hesitated at first and then thought about the promise she made to herself. *Nobody, not even Chris, is going to ruin my graduation. Forget him. Just pretend like he's not even there.* Ignoring his attempt to get her attention, she made her way to Rachel.

"Hey girl. How are you?" Rachel asked as she greeted Cierra with her standard hello, one air kiss on each cheek.

"I'm fine. How are you? You've been MIA this week."

"Well, with Damien leaving for the Redskins training camp tomorrow, I wanted to spend all my free time with him. I've called you a few times, but never got an answer. How are things with you and Chris?"

Cierra peeped around her to see if he was listening, then whispered, "I don't know what I want. A part of me says, forget his ass and move on, and another part says you still love him and you've invested so much, why not forgive and forget?"

"Well, just follow your heart. I'm sure you of all people will make the right decision. I do know that he's very sorry and wants to get back together. He came by Damien's one day when I was there, and girl, he was a mess. He was asking Damien, what should he do? The brother damn near broke down and cried," said Rachel.

"He did that in front of you?" Cierra asked surprised that Chris would do such a thing.

"No girl, I was in the back. He didn't know I was there. I snuck down the hall and listened from the kitchen while they were in the living room." They laughed at Rachel's I-Spy work. "Ci, don't say anything, but Amy pressed charges. The police came to Chris' house early this morning and arrested him. He tried to bargain with them saying that he would go to the station voluntarily. But you know the police weren't gonna pass up arresting a black, Virginia Tech football player for assault and battery of a white female."

"What? You're kidding me. How did you find out?" Cierra asked.

"Girl, he called Damien because he couldn't find Coach Bradley. He asked Damien to locate the coach because he couldn't make any more phone calls," Rachel informed.

"What else?" Cierra asked curious to find out as much as she could about the arrest.

"He was booked, finger printed and all. That's all Damien would tell me. I know he knows more, I can tell," said Rachel wishing she had more scoop to share with Cierra. She continued, "Ci, he's lost without you."

"Yeah, maybe. But look, let's talk about this some other time. Right now, it's time to celebrate!"

"Word, girl. Hey Damien, pass the champagne," Rachel yelled as she walked around Cierra leaving Chris and her near each other.

"Hi, Ci. I'm glad they spotted you. I was afraid we wouldn't be together today for graduation, but here you are."

He smiled and looked at her lovingly. Cierra looked at him and wished she could turn back the hands of time. She wanted to respond but she didn't know what to say, so she just smiled. Chris slid closer to her and without saying a word, took her hand in his, raised it and kissed the back of her hand. The touch of his velvet lips sent chills down her spine and the smell of his Calvin Klein Obsession cologne drove her crazy. His brown eyes met hers.

"Cierra, baby, I'm so proud of you. You're a very smart young lady and I love you."

Cierra felt the lump in her throat grow larger and her eyes watered, but she managed to hold onto her emotions.

"I'm proud of you too, Chris. I'm sure life will be good to you. You have a lot to look forward to, especially playing pro ball with the New York Jets."

"Later this evening, we're having a cookout at my place for the fellas who were picked in the draft. Why don't you come over? It would mean a lot to me."

Cierra could care less about the cookout. She wanted to know about the assault charges but knew she couldn't say anything because she promised Rachel that she wouldn't.

"I'll see. My folks are here," she responded.

Chris didn't let up, "So, bring them too. A lot of the players' parents are in town. There's enough food and drink for everybody."

"I'll see," she responded again.

Chris didn't know that Cierra was trying to spare him from being around the person she held accountable for her miscarriage.

As the doctorate and graduate programs came to an end, the group of friends and other students joked, laughed, and took pictures. Time never seemed to stand still when they gathered. Soon they split and went to their separate undergraduate ceremonies, Chris to the School of Architecture, Damien to the School of Engineering, and Rachel and Cierra to the School of Business. In the mass of people, they all managed to find their parents and headed on their way.

The hot sun beamed down on Cierra and her family as they walked from Lane stadium to Pamplin Hall, the academic business building. Mr. Sykes fussed because he wanted to drive instead of walking across the Drill Field but parking was bad everywhere. Cierra wanted to walk with Rachel and her family, but by the time Mrs. Sykes convinced her husband to listen to Cierra, Rachel and her family were far ahead.

After another hour of speeches and marches, Cierra and her classmates received their long awaited diplomas. Sounds of joy rang out across campus as excited students concluded their college years. At the end of the ceremony, Cierra extended Chris' cookout invitation to her parents. Mrs. Sykes graciously accepted while Mr. Sykes sucked his teeth in disgust.

Upon the Sykes' arrival, Chris did all he could to make their visit enjoyable. But, Cierra noticed that he seemed preoccupied with something else. She instantly asked him to join her outside on the front away from everyone.

"Chris, what is going on with you? You're not behaving like your normal self."

Chris paced a bit then looked at her with worried eyes and said, "The police came to the house earlier this morning and arrested me."

"What! Are you serious?" She acted surprised.

"I'm dead serious. Amy filed assault charges against me," said Chris in an apprehensive tone regretting that he put his hands on her.

"So, what are you going to do?" Cierra questioned glad that he decided to share what happened but more delighted that he would be held accountable for his actions.

"I finally got in contact with Coach Bradley. He said that he would get an attorney. Also, I asked around and found out that the girl with Amy the night of the incident was the daughter of the Offensive Coordinator. Coach Bradley is hoping he can get the other coach to step in and convince the girls to drop the charges. He doesn't want any bad publicity for the team."

"Well, I hope this works out for you," Cierra replied pretending to be uninterested.

"That's it? Just like that, you just don't care anymore?"

"Chris, I do care but what do you want me to say? You have no one to blame but yourself."

Chris placed his hands in his shorts pockets, took a deep breath, and paced the sidewalk pavement. Cierra sensed how badly Chris wished he could undo his mistake but the damage was done. An awkward pause filled the space between them. Then out of genuine concern for his future, Cierra asked, "So, what are your next steps?"

"I have to meet Coach Bradley at the courthouse tomorrow morning at eight."

Cierra felt like she was still in a bad dream and couldn't wake up. She gave Chris a small hug to reassure him that everything would work out. Then she excused herself to return to her parents.

In the midst of the music and laughter, one of Chris' roommates stepped to the middle of the living room to toast the players who made the NFL draft. Cheers and best wishes followed for Chris, Damien, and a couple of other guys. Then Damien stepped to the middle of the floor for what they all thought to be another toast.

"I would like everyone's attention please," Damien requested, "you know a year ago, I never would have thought that I would be standing here today about to say these words. But there is a very special person in my life that I need to say something to. She has seen me through some tough times this year and has always been there for me. Well, tomorrow I leave to start another part of my life and I wouldn't feel complete if she was not by my side. Rachel, would you please come here?"

Rachel looked puzzled but gracefully joined Damien. He faced her and continued, "You and I have become so close that to be separated for any amount of time just doesn't seem right to me." He fell to one knee and the entire room gasped as he continued, "So, I was thinking that if a man and a woman are meant to be together, then they should be together completely. He reached in his shorts pocket and took out a small white box, opened the unsuspected surprise, and displayed a sparkling two-carat diamond marquis. "Rachel Laveau, my beautiful Caribbean queen, would you do me the honor of being my wife; will you marry me?"

"Yes, Damien, yes!" Rachel bellowed without hesitation. Tears rushed down her face dragging along her mascara. Damien placed the dazzling solitaire on her left ring finger. She raised him from his bent knee then gave him an ever so passionate kiss. The room cheered. Rachel pranced about the room showing all the women her ring. When Rachel approached Cierra, she gave her one of the biggest hugs that Cierra ever received.

"Thanks Cierra. If it weren't for Chris and you, I may never have gotten a chance to meet Damien."

"Rachel, as excited as you were back then, you would have made it a point to say something to him eventually. Chris and I just helped the process. I'm very happy for the two of you. Now let me see that rock."

Rachel displayed her hand and before she could comment, Bridget blurted, "Well, we know where Damien spent his signing bonus."

"For real," Cierra joked as she admired the stone.

"Ci, your day will come soon too. Things will get back on track with you and Chris. Wait and see," said Rachel optimistically.

"I don't know about all that," remarked Bridget, "if you ask me, he must be doing cocaine with that crazy ass Amy 'cause that fool lost his damn mind. I heard he threw her out of a car. Did y'all know that?" inquired Bridget.

"B, he didn't throw her out of a car. And where did you hear that from?" Cierra asked amazed how rumors were spreading already. She couldn't wait to leave Tech and all the bullshit behind.

"I have my sources but if you say it didn't go down like that then I guess my source is wrong."

Rachel and Bridget's comments made Cierra feel sad as the thoughts of how far off course Chris and her were, filled her head. Her melancholy heart pounded distressful rhythms as she fought to hold back her tears. Rachel sensed her sorrow and tried to change the subject.

"So, I guess I'll be moving to Washington, D.C. huh?"

"Yeah, sounds like it," said Cierra.

"Just be careful. I hear the ratio of women to men is ten to one,"

Bridget cautioned.

"Damien is a fine catch, Rachel. So, watch your back. Don't let anyone come between you," Cierra advised.

"Thanks girls. You've always looked out for me."

Cierra and Chris' eyes met as they congratulated Damien and Rachel. Chris tilted his head and signaled Cierra to meet him outside on the front, so she did. While outside, they exchanged best wishes for Rachel and Damien and reminiscence and laughed about the first night the two of them met at Chris' party. As much as Cierra wanted to forget, she remembered Amy telling her that that night began her affair with Chris. Distraught with those thoughts, her facial expressions changed. Chris noticed and quickly started the conversation he really called her outside to have.

"You know Ci, there's something that I want to ask you. And I want you to think about it seriously and take as long as you like to answer."

As she scanned his square jaw line and admired his broad chest, she couldn't help but to wonder what was he about to say.

"I was wondering if you would join me in New York. You know that I leave for the Jets' training camp tomorrow at three p.m. and I don't want to leave with us like this." She placed her finger on his lips and tried to stop him from talking further, but he pulled her close to his chest and caressed her in his arms. "Cierra, I need you."

"Chris, I don't know what to say. After everything that has happened, I made plans to return home."

"What's at home Ci that you can't find in New York? We need to be together not apart. Sometimes I think you don't even want to try and get back together."

"Chris, I just don't know what I want. I need some time to sort things out."

"You mean to tell me that you would rather move back home with your dad and mom than to come with the man you love? I don't get that at all, Ci."

"Chris, you don't have to wait for me. You can go on with your life."

"Oh, so now you don't care if I see somebody? Well, I'm not

giving up on us that easy. I made one big mistake and have been paying the price for it. We're all human Cierra including you."

"What do you mean by that?"

Chris frowned and turned away as if to think of what else to say. He continued, "Ci, look, I want us to work things out. I want us together plain and simple. I'm sorry for what happened with Amy. I got caught up in something I had no business. But what do you want me to do? I can't take it back as much as I wish I could, I can't. I never meant to hurt you. Baby, I'm sorry."

Cierra wanted to believe his apology but something inside her still could not accept it, possibly because of the hurt or maybe just from pride. Whatever she felt, she knew she needed to follow her gut instinct.

"Chris, let me think about it okay?"

"Baby, that's fine. I know you're not ready right now. Once I arrive in New York, I'll call you to give you my address and phone number perhaps by then you will feel differently."

"Okay," she agreed. Chris kissed her forehead and hugged her while he whispered, "I love you, Cierra," in her ear. A warm, tingling sensation fluttered down her spine as his calm words soothed her troubled soul. She smiled at him knowing that his words were sincere but her broken heart just couldn't trust them.

"Chris, I think I should go now. I don't want my dad around the alcohol much longer."

"I understand. Will you think about what I said?"

"Yes."

"Seriously because I mean every word."

"I know, Chris."

She ended their conversation with a kiss to his cheek and they returned to the celebration. She found her father outside with some of the players having a beer. She told him that her mom and her needed to finish packing her clothes and they were ready to leave. He finished his beer then the family left.

Cierra's parents came to her apartment early the next day with a U-Haul rental truck to take her belongings home. Caught up in the excitement of graduation and the ordeal with Chris, Cierra forgot about loading the truck. She wondered whom she could get to help move her furniture and boxes, and even more importantly who would drive the Sykes' family car to Richmond because her dad had to drive the U-Haul, she was driving her own car, and Mrs. Sykes didn't like driving through the mountains.

"I told you to have this shit worked out before we got here," Mr. Sykes angrily said to his wife and Cierra.

"Dad, I'm sorry. I just forgot with exams and all."

"You forgot because your head is wrapped up in that damn boy."

"Gregory, please don't start."

"Shut the hell up, Brenda. You're just as stupid as she is. That's where she gets it from."

"I'll find someone. Don't worry," said Cierra.

"I ain't worried 'cause I can carry my black ass home and leave you and your shit right here. How in the hell can you forget?" Mr. Sykes walked out onto the balcony.

"Mom, why can't you just drive the car? We can be done with this situation right now."

"I'm not driving on the highway with all those big tractor-trailers. They make me nervous. I thought perhaps Chris could drive."

"Chris can't drive because he's leaving for the Jets' training camp today. Why can't you just drive? I'll be right behind you."

"I'm sorry Cierra but I'm not driving."

"Fine!"

She slammed the apartment door behind her and walked down a flight of stairs to ask her neighbor, Tony, who was also from Richmond and who didn't have a car. She thought it would be a good way to help him get home too. Tony agreed and appreciated the offer, especially since his parents wouldn't be able to pick him up until the following weekend.

"Cool. This way I can get home sooner. Thanks, Cierra."

"No, thank you, Tony. You are a life saver for real."

Since they had to now load Tony's things too, he suggested that two more guys would make the moving job much easier. Cierra called Chris, partially to test him to see if he would help her on such short notice and partially because she wanted to see him again before she left. When she asked him to help, he immediately accepted and said that he and Craig would be at her place after he returned from the courthouse. Cierra entered onto the balcony to give her father an update.

"Dad, Tony agreed to drive the car and mom will ride with me. Chris and Craig are coming to help Tony and you load the truck."

"I'm not loading a goddamn thing. You got everything in here. You can take everything out. And, I don't want that fuck up around here."

"Who are you talking about?"

"Chris, that's who. I don't want that son of bitch around me."

"Well, he's coming whether you like it or not. And he's not a fuck up. He's very smart and has a bright future."

"Umph. And you got the damn funny bunny driving my car."

"What's with you? Tony is a very nice person and he's doing us a favor by driving the car to Richmond. He's a good friend and the best neighbor I've had my three years off campus. You see him every year and every time, you have something negative to say about him. I'm sick of it. He's a good guy."

"Guy, my ass. Ain't nothing manly about him."

"Why don't you stop judging people? How can you judge anybody with all the problems you have? Have you looked in a mirror lately?" Disgusted with her father's small-minded opinions, she left him sitting on the balcony. Whatever he thought about Tony didn't matter to her.

About two hours later, Chris and Craig arrived. When Mr. Sykes saw them park, he grabbed his car keys and headed out of the door.

"Gregory, where are you going? Aren't you gonna help?" asked Mrs. Sykes surprised that he would leave.

"Nope. Y'all can handle it. I'm going to the store."

Cierra suspected the liquor store was what he meant. "How can you make that kind of run and we have to drive all the way home? You talk about Chris being a fuck up, who's the fuck up now?"

"You watch your damn mouth! Who do you think you're talking

to? I'm your father."

"Don't remind me."

"Gregory and Cierra, please stop," begged Mrs. Sykes.

"I will leave your black ass right here," Mr. Sykes threatened.

"Whatever."

"Please you two, let's just finish and go home," pleaded Mrs. Sykes, nervous that the disagreement would escalate.

Chris and Craig heard the yelling from the parking lot. Chris shook his head. *I still can't believe she would rather deal with this mess instead of being with me in New York.* They knocked on the door. Mr. Sykes opened the door and brushed passed them. He barely spoke to Craig and gave Chris a hateful look then he walked down the three flights of stairs. Chris wondered if he knew about the baby and that was the reason for his mean glare. He wanted to ask Cierra more about what happened during her visit to Richmond when she was pregnant but now was not the time or place.

Tony, Chris, and Craig loaded the truck around ten that morning and finished by noon. Mr. Sykes returned in time to find the three of them leaning against the living room wall breathing hard and wiping the sweat from their brows.

"Are you boys done?" Mr. Sykes asked while standing in the doorway.

"Yes, sir."

"Well, let's hit the road."

"Wait, dad, I want to make sure everything is out of the apartment. Tony, you should double check yours too."

"Well, I'm not hanging around here. I'll see you in Richmond. Tony, here are the keys. Don't let anything happen to my car."

"No sir. I'll drive very carefully."

"I know you will. As a matter of fact, I want you to drive in front of me so I can see everything you do."

"Yes, sir."

"Well, what'cha standing there for? Get the lead out your ass. Let's go."

Cierra gave Tony a hug. "Sorry my dad won't let you double check your apartment."

"Girlfriend, don't worry. I got everything."

"I'll take you to your parents' house when I get there."

"Girl, are you crazy? I'm gonna have my dad and brother there with my daddy's truck when we pull up. We are going to unload my stuff and head out of Dodge. Your pops is a trip. I ain't hanging around him any longer than need be."

"I feel you. Thanks, again Tony for doing this. I owe you."

"Maybe we can hang out in the Fan district sometimes."

"Sounds like fun."

"Smooches." He gave Cierra a kiss on each cheek then walked down the stairs to the parking lot. Cierra waved bye as he and her father drove away.

Cierra looked around the apartment to make sure that she didn't miss anything. Out of the corner of her eye, she saw Chris staring at her but she pretended not to see him looking.

"Well, it looks like you got everything," she announced to her mother, Chris, and Craig as she stood in the middle of the living room thinking about the memories she had there with her friends. She felt a little strange knowing that this was it, there was no coming back to Virginia Tech. Mrs. Sykes suspected her daughter needed a few minutes alone with her college sweetheart. She asked Craig to walk her to Cierra's car. When they exited the apartment, Chris closed the door behind them.

"Chris, what are you doing?" Cierra asked as he circled around her. She took a few steps backward and bumped into the door. He raised his arms and placed his palms on the door, locking Cierra between them. Looking in her eyes, Chris whispered, "Do you really think that I would let you leave without a kiss?" Not sure how to reply, Cierra asked, "Judging by your mood today, I assume things went okay at the courthouse this morning?" Chris seemed disinterested in the conversation, "Yeah. Amy dropped the charges."

He began to kiss and suck Cierra on her neck. She panted but said nothing. He then nibbled at her ears breathing his warm desiring breath about the side of her face. She gasped from her inner need to have him. He kissed her cheek and her brows wrinkled. Cierra's heart raced with anticipation of feeling his lips against hers. It had been over a week since they last kissed and she craved him. Slowly, Chris lowered his arms, wrapped them around Cierra, and caressed her tenderly. His lips followed the contour of her pretty face then rested gently atop her desiring lips. Chris parted his mouth then kissed her caringly making the kiss and his display of affection one of his best ever. He looked into her feline shaped eyes and pleaded, "I love you, Cierra. Please join me in New York. My life won't be the same without you. And I know you really don't want to go home to that environment."

"Chris, I love you too. And you're right, it's going to be very difficult to return home. But I just can't make any promises about us right now. I have a lot to think about. But please believe me, I do wish you the very best with the Jets."

He stared at her wishing there was something he could do or say to make her change her mind, but there wasn't. He kissed her lips one last time then opened the door. He walked Cierra to her car where her mom patiently waited. In a gentlemanly fashion, he opened the car door. Cierra's eyes watered as the unfulfilled dreams of them in New York together flashed through her mind. Chris held her hand as she climbed into the car and placed a peck on the back of it as he winked at her. When the door shut, the finality of her decision sent a hurtful surge through them both.

"Cierra, are you ok?" her mother asked.

"Yeah. I'll be fine." She watched Chris walk towards Craig's SUV looking as if the world rested upon his shoulders. She started the engine then drove away.

> *Heavenly Father, I always believed that everything happens for a reason. I may not understand what Your reason is sometimes, but I'm willing to follow Your lead. So, I leave this situation in Your hands and if You decide to keep Chris and I together, then so be it. If You have other plans for him and me then I must have faith that You know what's best and I'll have to deal with what is to come. Amen.*

Clueless to her daughter's heartbreak, Mrs. Sykes talked about everything Cierra didn't want to hear during their ride home to Richmond. She inquired about Cierra and Chris' career plans, when would they get engaged, Rachel's wedding, and why did she decide not to go with Chris to New York. She definitely took advantage of their long drive. Finally, Cierra couldn't take another word. She stopped her mom in mid-sentence and told her that she broke up with Chris.

"Well, why in heaven's sake did you do that? He's such a nice young man. Plus, you have a baby on the way. Why would you break up with the father of your child?"

"Had a baby on the way. Thanks to you, mom, I don't have my baby anymore. I lost it due to a ruptured placenta caused by the fight dad and I had," said Cierra angrily as she tried to focus on driving. Shocked, Mrs. Sykes replied, "Cierra, I'm terribly sorry. I certainly didn't want that to happen." She instantly regretted telling her husband. She knew there was no greater pain than to lose a wanted child.

"What were you thinking? Why did you to tell him anyway?" Cierra asked heatedly.

"He is your father. I thought he had a right to know and you were starting to show."

"But mom, he's not a normal, rational man. When will you ever get that? And, I wasn't showing." A lump grew in Cierra's throat as she tried to hold back her tears.

"Cierra, I hope you believe me, I'm truly sorry."

"Just save it. There's nothing you can do to bring back my baby. And certainly saying you're sorry won't," Cierra hissed.

Mrs. Sykes took offense to her daughter's sharp words. "Well, Cierra, you knew your condition. You didn't have to fight your father."

"What? Mom, he attacked me. I was defending myself! Just don't say another word. The more you talk, the more I despise you sitting here."

Mrs. Sykes gasped for air, stunned by her daughter's feelings. They sat quietly a few moments, each wondering what else did the other have to say because there was certainly more to discuss. Mrs. Sykes broke the silence, "Well, I don't get it. If you wanted his baby, why did you break up with him?"

"Long story short, I found out he was cheating on me most of this school year."

"Oh, child that ain't nothing. Probably just a little phase he went through. I don't know too many men that don't cheat at some point or another."

"Mom, he cheated on me with one of the sluttiest girls on campus."

"How do you know she's a loose girl?"

"Are you kidding me? Everyone knows she's a big slut. Secondly, the crazy bitch stalked me. To make matters worse, she gets high on cocaine and drinks. And lastly, she's one of those groupie white chicks who go after the athletic brothers. I don't have anything against interracial dating or couples, but it's this undercurrent trend among the black athletes and certain white girls who just have their claws in for them. Why is it that out of all the available black girls on campus, the black guys want to go out with these certain groups of white girls? I'm not the first one this has happened to. I just didn't think it would happen to Chris and me. These guys sport the white girls like they're some kind of prize trophy then treat the black girls like they aren't good enough to be with them. Some of the guys say that black girls are too demanding and controlling. They don't see that perhaps a sista just wants to be respected. The sad thing about it all is that most of the white girls who they're with, don't understand their culture or the struggles they face in society as black men. And let me tell you this, when we've gone to the white keg parties, the very same white girls hanging and kissing all over the black athletes in the dormitory or at the black parties are avoiding them like the plague in front of their white friends or they just casually talk to them like they're nothing special to them at all. Now you tell me, how is this suppose to be ok?"

"My goodness, I didn't know it was like that. You young people have much more complex relationships to deal with than my generation did coming up." Mrs. Sykes thought for a minute and then said, "Well Cierra, maybe Chris liked her. Something had to be there to make him do this."

Cierra looked crossly at her mother and nearly sprung out of her seat. "I don't believe you! Mom, he hurt me and you sound like you are defending him."

"Cierra, watch the road," Mrs. Sykes instructed, concerned Cierra would have an accident not paying attention.

"I'm watching the damn road," she retorted.

"Cierra, I know he hurt you. I guess I just don't know what to say. All I know is men will be men."

Cierra shook her head. "Mom, what kind of mess are you saying? Do you hear yourself? Damn, dad has really made you a victim."

Anger flowed through Cierra like a turbulent river. She then dared to say what she wanted to say for years. "You're the kind of woman that'll let a man walk all over you. Look at how badly dad treats you and you choose to stay. You go to work everyday at the hospital and make enough money as the manager of Hospital Admissions to live on your own comfortably. And not only that, but you make awesome stone jewelry. Look at this jade angel." She held up the pendent her mother made her. "You can't find things like this in the stores. I've been trying for years to get you to sell your jewelry instead of making it as a mere hobby. Everybody who sees it wants to buy it. But no, you choose not to move. You want to stay in an abusive relationship and see possible entrepreneurship go right down the damn toilet for a drunk ass, cheating husband. Only a weak woman would do that. 'Men will be men'. What kind of shit is that? Like it's okay."

"You watch your mouth young lady. I'm still your mother, just 'cause you graduated from college doesn't mean that you can talk to me any way you want to."

"See what I mean? You can sit here and tell me not to talk to you like this, but you won't say that to dad and he talks to you a whole lot worse."

"Look, I was raised in a different time. Things were different for women back then. And as for your father, he was a very bright man." She tried to explain her rationale as she looked out of the window at the livestock grazing on the hillsides of Interstate 81.

"Mom, you're only fifty-six years old. Things couldn't have been that different. As for dad, you looked at him for his potential and not for what he was 'cause he was a drunk then just like he is now. Papa Sykes told me about dad's youth. I don't know how it escaped you."

Mrs. Sykes continued to defend her life choices. "Gregory was very smart in school, finishing in the top ten percent of his class."

"You just refuse to take off your blinders," said Cierra wishing her mom thought differently. She continued to push the matter, "I don't want to end up like you, unhappy, lonely, and living in a make believe world."

"Watch your mouth Cierra and stop looking at me like that. I know what I'm doing."

"Do you, mom? Do you realize what you've been doing? What kind of role model have you been for me? Do you even know who you are?"

"What kind of question is that? Of course I know who I am," said Mrs. Sykes disturbed by Cierra's question. She stared at the passing white lines in the middle of the highway, each one took her back to a far distant place in her past.

*　*　*

Born in Hampton, Virginia, Brenda Harris entered the world as a preemie in May 1932. Because of her small frame, Brenda's parents were very protective of her. She was the only child to a construction-working father and a mother who worked as a grocery store cashier. The family lived on a meager income but was a happy unit. Brenda loved her parents and especially being "daddy's little girl". There wasn't anything he wouldn't do for her.

As Brenda grew up, her parents remained overly protective, never allowing her to test all the advice they gave her. They didn't want her dating with as they put it, "over zealous boys." To preoccupy herself, Brenda learned how to make fabulous jewelry. She enjoyed working with stones and precious gems. With her business sense and craft skills, she desired to own her own jewelry boutique someday. She saw college as her golden ticket. With her savings and a federal grant, Brenda had enough money to attend Howard University.

She met Gregory Sykes at a dance during her freshman year at HU. She was attracted to the bright-witted, spirited young man. His country-boy, down-home nature made her comfortable. He asked her out on a date and from that day, their worlds entwined like a rancher's bull rope. She dreamed of the life they could have together, she with her own jewelry business, and Gregory working as a top forensic specialist.

On the first holiday break, she invited Gregory to meet her parents. They only met him that one time and disapproved of him.

"Brenda, I'm not too sure about this young fella. I don't like the look in his eyes," her father told her.

When Brenda returned home that summer, her father died of a heart attack on the job while pouring a concrete foundation. Suddenly, daddy's little girl was without a father figure. She and her mother did the best they could to maintain a normal Harris household. But stricken with grief over the loss of her loving husband, Mrs. Harris took ill and died of a stroke a year later. As fate had its way, the bank forced the sell of the Harris' Hampton home and Brenda went to live with her aunt in Washington, DC.

As a result of the financial burden, Brenda didn't return to Howard University for her junior and senior year. Instead, she got a job at George Washington Hospital as a receptionist in the Administration Office. Despite not returning to HU, Gregory and Brenda continued to date.

Each time Gregory appeared at her doorstep to take her out, Brenda watched his red, glassy eyes and thought about her parents' skepticism of him. But she pushed their words aside. *It must just be all the studying he's doing because his grades are great.* Couldn't she see that they were not eyes of exertion but eyes of consumption? She asked him many times to take her to the campus parties but he refused her requests saying he wanted to spend time with just the two of them. She thought his gesture was sweet. *He wants me all to himself.* Couldn't she see the beginning signs of control and isolation? When he graduated and asked Brenda to marry him, Brenda discussed the matter with her aunt and her aunt gave her blessing.

Within the first two years of her marriage, she realized the nature of her parents' concern. The first year she spent trying to convince Gregory she could work at the hospital, go back to school, and pursue her jewelry business. But after his abrasive slap across her mouth and his comment, "I don't want to hear nothing else about school and no goddamn jewelry," she never raised the subject again. When he became suspicious of her phone calls to her girlfriends, accusing her of using her girlfriends as excuses to meet other men, he ripped the telephone cord out of the wall and whipped her with it. She no longer called her friends.

During the second year of their marriage, after one too many encounters with Gregory, Brenda decided to leave him. But unprepared how to deal with a person like Gregory, Brenda naively left her new apartment deposit receipt in her top dresser drawer. Gregory saw the evidence of her effort to leave him and went into a rage. It was the first time he beat her into submission and shame. She didn't leave the house for a few days because of her swollen eyes and bruised arms and legs. When the swelling subsided and the bruising was less pronounced, she visited her doctor for a check up to make sure she was okay. But the doctor's news that she was two months pregnant made her far from okay. Her life had taken a wrong turn and somehow went down an unexpected road that changed her life forever.

* * *

Where did my life go, Mrs. Sykes thought. Cierra had no idea her mother's dreams were as broken as the white lines on the highway. After their discussion, Mrs. Sykes drifted off to sleep. Cierra turned up her radio to listen to Anita Baker and continued the journey home.

1810 Berman Street was only ten minutes away. Cierra drove slower, regretting the fact that she was returning to her parents' house. Living away gave her the happiness and peace that she needed in her life but now that had changed. She stopped in front of the driveway, looked at the split-level house, and wondered if she made the right decision. She drove slowly into the gravel driveway and parked the car behind the U-Haul truck her dad drove. She gently shook her mom to wake her. "Mom, we're home."

After a long day of traveling, unloading the U-Haul at the self-storage, and checking on Tony to make sure everything went fine upon his arrival, Cierra finally went to her bedroom to rest. She lied facing the ceiling, thinking about the events of last week and how Chris and her dreams were far from what they envisioned. Her heart grew heavy and a tear rolled down the corner of her eye.

> *Lord, I hurt so badly. Why have I ended up right back in the place I've always wanted to get away from? I don't know if I've made the right choice to move back home. I really wish I was with Chris in New York, but I don't know how to be in a relationship with him anymore. I'm certain of one thing, living here is going to be hell. I pray that this time around, You intervene more with my family and shield my mother and me from my father's abuse. We desperately need Your help. I pray You empower my mother to walk away from this mess once and for all. Amen.*

Cierra reached to the edge of the desk in her bedroom to answer the phone on its fourth ring.

"Hello," she said, hoping that the person on the other end of the receiver would be Chris.

"Hey girl. I thought you would be home this weekend. What's up?"

"Kelly? Girl, how did you know I was home?" asked Cierra

happy and surprised to hear from one of her home-girls.

"I just got home from Boston U yesterday. I passed your house on my way to the store and saw your car and the U-Haul. So, I thought I'd give you a call when I got back. How was graduation?" Kelly inquired.

"OK, and yours?" replied Cierra, wishing the last few months had never happened.

"Off the hook. Girl, we celebrated like there was no tomorrow. Have you heard from Josi?" Kelly asked while organizing her Delta Sigma Theta sorority papers scattered on the kitchen table.

"No, but she should be home 'cause Virginia Union got out a week before we did," said Cierra as she rested comfortably on the pillows propped against her headboard.

Kelly Logan and Josette "Josi" Fouquet were two of Cierra's closest and dearest friends. They grew up together from the early age of eight years old in the same suburban neighborhood in Richmond, Virginia. The three were more like sisters than friends. Their respect for each other and sisterly love kept their bond tight even when they disagreed and argued with each other.

Kelly, the sophisticated cool one, loved being "top dog". There was no room for failure in any task she undertook. The Magna Cum Laude graduate of Boston University looked forward to beginning her stockbroker career with Merrill-Lynch in the upcoming weeks.

Regardless of Kelly's hectic and demanding lifestyle of academics, career, and DST functions, she always made time for her girls, Cierra and Josi. She was down for whatever event they planned to attend but her constant forty-five minute tardiness drove Cierra crazy. Kelly's "I'm so sorry I'm late" excuses became status quo over the years. After arriving late to a Prince concert, Cierra made a point to tell her that events started forty-five minutes earlier just to ensure she would be on time. That seemed to work, even now.

A kind hearted young lady, Kelly stood five feet eight inches tall and wore the perfect size eight. Kelly's cocoa brown complexion with red undertones and high check bones exhibited her American-Indian heritage. She had her Cherokee grandmother's deep-set midnight eyes and long thick black hair that she often sported in micro braids. Only the crescent moon birthmark on Kelly's neck made her a little self-conscience because too many people thought it was a botched tattoo. For that reason, she wore her hair down most of the time giving her a Pocahontas look.

Josi, a butterscotch Southern Bell, had the most inquisitive chestnut brown eyes. She moved to Virginia as a young child when her father won a new contract with Phillip Morris, a large tobacco company. Unsure about her new surroundings, Josi talked constantly about her previous home in an affluent Louisiana suburb. Her French accent was difficult for Cierra and Kelly to understand at first, but within a month's time, they grew accustomed to the foreign speaking girl. Shortly, they began to understand Josi, and the novelty of her accent and constant whining wore thin.

Day after day, Josi spoke of her grandpère's large house and other well-to-do families of high social status. She talked about how her grandmère told her that light skin blacks had better social chances than dark skin blacks, something that a cocoa brown Kelly hated to hear. When young Cierra asked her mother what was Josi talking about, Mrs. Sykes explained, "Josi is what some folks call color-struck." Josi's grandmother had a mindset of a generation that experienced extreme racial hardships and as a result formulated her opinions about black people's complexions. Unfortunately, she taught her opinions to Josi at a young impressionable age. Cierra's caramel complexion didn't bother Josi, but Kelly was a different story. Had it not been for the fact that Cierra and Kelly were the only two girls in the neighborhood her age, Josi probably wouldn't have bothered making friends with Kelly.

One summer day, during their youth, Cierra and Kelly had enough of Josi's smug talk. They took it upon themselves to break the snooty girl of her monotonous deep-south stories. At dusk, they purposely led Josi deep into the woods and abandoned her. Cierra and Kelly ran swiftly towards the edge of the thicket, following their secret trails, leaving Josi alone in unfamiliar territory. Just before the clearing, they hid behind a large oak tree and watched Josi run past desperately trying to find them. Shortly, they heard Josi break down and cry, "OK, I'm sorry. Please don't leave me here. I won't ever talk about people's color ever again. I promise. Come get me. Si vous plait."

"You'd think she wouldn't follow us into the woods after we threatened to do this," snickered Cierra.

"I know," said Kelly laughing at their disciplinary measure.

They made Josi promise not to talk about light and dark-skinned blacks, not to compare their neighborhood houses to *la maison de grandpère* anymore, and not to act like she was better than them. After breaking her, Cierra and Kelly got along fine with Josi. She grew use to her surroundings and experienced one of the best summers of her life.

Now at age twenty-two, Josi grew up to be the quietest and tallest of the three. She stood five feet nine inches and had a body frame like a super model. Her deep southern roots resided in her, but she mastered when and how to use them. At family gatherings, she returned to her grandmother's teachings to blend in with *la famille*. But with Cierra and Kelly, she remained close, loyal, and warm hearted.

"Well Ci, let me get off this phone. I have to go to a DST meeting at seven tonight. Give Josi a call and see if she's up for company tomorrow. Maybe we can all get together and go out 'cause we all need to celebrate graduating."

"Sounds good to me." Cierra hung up then phoned Josi as planned.

That next night the stars sparkled in the dark sky like a showcase of loose diamonds and the warm air felt incredible. The three amigos left home in a great mood ready to celebrate graduation. Cierra, the designated driver, parked her car a couple blocks away from the Underground Club on East Cary Street in Shockoe Slip, a well-known historic part of the city. As they walked down the sidewalk, they checked their outfits in the large, glass windows of the restaurants and specialty shops. As they approached the club, the girls saw that the line extended out of the door and halfway down the block.

After standing in line for about twenty minutes, the bouncers finally let them inside. The girls descended the long narrow steps that led to the sub terrain club. The music of LL Cool J blasted, people danced, and the den noise filled the air as everyone talked at once. The girls made their way through the crowded room to their favorite booth to the left of the dance floor, but someone already claimed the red, cushioned circular seat. They continued further towards the back and found a table for four across from the bar. As they settled in, it didn't take but a moment for young suitors to approach them. Cierra and Kelly immediately accepted the young men's invitations to dance. Josi, on the other hand, sat with her legs crossed, lit a cigarette and gave a polite "No thank you."

The song ended and Cierra returned to the table while Kelly continued to dance.

"Josi, you need to put that cancer stick down and get your groove on. Check it out. Here comes a hunk now. I'll watch your purse. Go ahead have some fun," Cierra instructed her friend. The guy approached their table, extended his hand and asked Josi, "Would you like to dance?"

"Sure, why not," Josi replied as she scooted her chair away from the table.

Cierra ordered a round of Miller Lite from the waiter. As she looked down into her purse to get her money to pay the waiter, a deep voice said, "I got this one." She looked up and saw a very handsome young man standing in front of her. The waiter placed the cold brewskies on the table and winked at Cierra.

"May I sit down?" the gentleman asked.

"Sure," Cierra replied, enjoying the interest of the good-looking guy and his charming mannerism. He sat and started a wonderful conversation. He introduced himself as Terrance Sullivan. He grew up in Cierra's hometown but moved to Washington, DC after graduating from Hampton University five years ago in 1983. With a B.S. degree in Industrial Engineering, he was now pursuing his graduate degree at Georgetown University while working fulltime as a senior engineer for Ross Industries, Inc. in DC.

Cierra liked the attention of the twenty-seven year-old professional. He stood about six feet three inches, weighed about two hundred pounds, and had a well-built body as his years of playing sports paid off. Cierra could tell when he smiled that he had a cap on his left front tooth that he later explained he chipped while playing baseball at a family reunion a year ago. Terrance's walnut brown eyes sparkled as he talked with Cierra. He didn't mean to stare, but he couldn't help himself. Smitten with her beauty, he secretly desired to kiss Cierra's rosy lips. He gazed at her heart shaped face and slightly slanted, feline shaped, brown eyes.

"You look like a caramel version of the singer Sade with your hoop earrings and hair pulled back like that. Damn, you fine," Terrance proclaimed.

"Thanks," Cierra blushed.

"I know you're watching your girlfriends' things, but do you mind if we dance when they come back?"

"Okay sure."

The music changed to something slow causing Kelly and Josi to return to the table. Cierra introduced them to Terrance and he politely greeted them. Then he stood, extended his hand and asked Cierra, "May I have this dance?"

Josi and Kelly looked at each other with their mouths wide open. As Terrance led Cierra to the dance floor Josi tugged at Cierra's skirt to get her attention. Cierra fanned her hand away and continued to walk with him.

"What was that all about?" asked Terrance observing Josi's attempt. Feeling a little more relaxed from the drinks, she explained to him how she recently broke up with Chris.

"Please don't say anything around my friends. I haven't told them yet," Cierra requested of Terrance.

He smiled and looked past her and said, "Oh, so that's why they're looking at me so funny right now."

Cierra turned and looked at her friends. They quickly pretended to be engaged in conversation. The friendly slow dance ended and the music changed to an upbeat tempo and Cierra and Terrance danced to a few more songs. Kelly entered the dance floor near them and whispered in Cierra's ear, "You have some explaining to do." Cierra smiled and continued dancing while ignoring her because for the first time since the news of Chris and Amy, she felt good. After a few dances, Terrance walked Cierra back to her table and told her he wanted to talk to her more before she left. She agreed. The girls laughed and partied for a few more hours then left at three a.m. so they could be somewhat rested to attend church in the morning.

While exiting the club, young men hovered and tried their best to talk to the girls as they walked through the crowd. Outside, Terrance waited for Cierra near the entrance. When she walked by him, he reached for her hand and said, "Hey pretty lady, I wanted to know if I can call you sometimes. Maybe we can get together and go to a movie or something the next time I'm in town."

Cierra smiled and replied, "That sounds nice but right now, I'm not really interested in dating. However, you can give me your number and I'll call you." Her response caught him off guard because he was accustomed to girls wanting to date him and giving him their phone numbers with no questions asked. He liked her refreshing approach that intrigued him all the more. He jotted his home and mobile phone numbers on a small piece of paper and gave them to her. She tucked the note-sized paper in her purse and told him, "It was nice meeting you."

"Do you mind if I walk you to your car?" Terrance wasn't quite ready to let Cierra out of his sight and wanted to spend more time with her. Josi and Kelly walked in front of them trying to ease drop on their conversation. When they all arrived at the car, Cierra pressed the car door remote on her keychain, allowing Josi and

Kelly to get in. Terrance stood to the side and asked Cierra, "So, you gonna call me right?"

"Of course," Cierra replied smiling inwardly.

"Um, do you know when?"

"Soon."

She got into her car and started the engine. Terrance shut the door and waved. He kicked himself for sounding desperate, that wasn't like him but something about her made him act out of character.

Inside the car, Josi blurted from the back seat, "Girl, who was that? He's cute."

"What I want to know is, what's up with you and Chris 'cause you didn't seem to mind this guy's attention?" Kelly asked while letting down the front passenger window.

"His name is Terrance and I'll tell you later."

"Oh no Miss Thang. You need to tell us now," Kelly insisted.

"Can you wait until we get to Josi's house? Trust me the story will keep."

"Ahhh, sooky sooky now. I can't wait to hear this," Kelly replied bouncing up and down in her seat like a happy child.

"Did you guys have a good time tonight?" Cierra asked to change the topic.

"Yeah. I'm glad you talked me into coming," Josi responded.

"Josi, what you need to do is stop waiting to see what your ex-boyfriend is going to do. You don't go out, you don't date. Meanwhile, he is having the time of his life, dating who ever he pleases. You need to move on with your life," Kelly advised.

"Kelly, if you don't mind, please keep your thoughts to yourself. I think you've had one too many drinks tonight," Josi replied as she filed her already manicured fingernails. But Kelly didn't let up. She added, "Your problem is that you always live in a hopeless romantic world like you're Scarlet O'Hara and he's suppose to want to be with you simply because you're of the Fouquet family. Girl, you need to get over yourself, find a new man and move on.

"Kelly stop. Give her a break," Cierra interjected as she drove up East Main Street.

"Love is overrated anyway. Men are so immature and don't know what they want. If they can't do anything better for me than I'm doing for myself, what good are they? I haven't found one yet good enough for me. That's why I don't date anyone special. I have more important things to do. I date around," Kelly stated in a matter of fact way.

"Sounds like the makings of a lil' ho to me. And my ex is not doing all those things."

"Oh yeah? Then why did you call me crying 'cause you saw some girl's car at his house a month ago when you went creeping by his crib at one in the morning."

"Josi, you did what?" Cierra questioned shocked at Josi's late night activity.

"Oh Ci, I didn't tell you about that? A month ago, Josi started spying on her ex," Kelly informed while laughing hysterically. Josi didn't see the humor in any of it and huffed, "Ça ne faire rien."

"It does matter to you," Cierra and Kelly replied in unison.

When the girls arrived at Josi's house, she invited Cierra and Kelly in for a much needed dose of caffeine to help balance the consumed alcohol. The three friends gathered in the kitchen, kicked off their high heels, and sat for a couple hours of girl talk. Cierra told them about her situation with Chris and Amy, but chose not to tell them how she miscarried the baby.

As they discussed Chris, Kelly quickly announced, "See, didn't I tell you. Men don't know what they want. They're just stupid and immature."

"Ci, don't listen to her. You and Chris belong together. It was only a mistake. I think you should give him a second chance and don't call Terrance," Josi advised while sipping her homemade mocha latte.

"You would think something like that, Josi. You always give useless, unrealistic advice. Chris deceived her for almost the entire school year. I say kick his ass to the curb, call Terrance, and move on," Kelly voted.

"You guys, forget about it. You're driving me nuts. Let's talk about something else," Cierra requested after growing tired of Kelly and Josi's quarrelling. When Cierra returned home and settled in her bed for the night, she prayed.

Lord, thank you for a wonderful outing with my friends. I enjoyed everything except their bickering. Usually, they don't bother me and sometimes their debates can be quite comical. But tonight, they got on my nerves. They're like oil and water. Nonetheless, it felt good to get out for a moment and leave my heartache behind. What should I make of this guy, Terrance that I met tonight? Why have You introduced him to me? I guess that remains to be seen. Amen.

Daybreak came with the ringing of the phone and Cierra springing to answer it before the loud noise woke her parents.

"Hey baby, how are you?" Chris asked happy to hear Cierra's voice on the other end.

"'Hey baby,'" she mocked, unmoved by Chris' enthusiasm. "Chris, it's been two weeks since I've heard from you. I thought you were going to call me when you got settled."

"Ci, I meant to call you sooner but everything is happening so fast here. We have early meetings and long practices. Every time I'm just about to call you, someone wants me to do something or go somewhere. I'm truly sorry it took two weeks to call you. Do you forgive me?"

Cierra skipped answering his plea and asked, "So how is The Big Apple?"

"Ci, you would love it. You could shop for days. Anything you want, you can get. You wouldn't believe it. I mean the clothing district is the bomb. And the restaurants are great. You can get any kind of cuisine you like."

"Sounds like you've been getting around. How are the clubs?"

Chris answered before he realized she set him up, "Oh the clubs are cool but we don't really hang out. We have to be back in the rooms by a certain time."

"But you've been to some right?"

"Yeah, once. Why?"

"I'll tell you why. You can make time to go out with your teammates but you can't pick up the phone and call me."

"Ci, come on now, you know it's not like that."

"No, Chris that's exactly how it is." Her voice quivered from the disappointment.

"Look Ci, I wasn't just calling to say hi. I was calling to let you know the coach is giving us a break. In two weeks, we only have a team meeting on Saturday morning and a light practice afterward. We should be done by ten a.m. So, I thought it would be a good weekend to ask you to come visit. I admit that I screwed up with contacting you but you were always on my mind. So what do you say? Will you come?" He hoped his slip-up didn't upset her and make her turn him down. He really missed her and wanted to see and hold her.

"Chris, I don't know. Where will I stay?"

"At a hotel in Manhattan. The players can't have visitors in our dorms. Why are you hesitating? I thought you would be happy." He worried that he blew his chance.

"How will I get there?" she asked.

"You can fly into LaGuardia and I'll pick you up. I plan to pay for your ticket and hotel. Look Ci, whatever you want, I'll do. I just need to see you, that's all. Is that so bad?"

"No, you just caught me off guard. Okay, I'll come."

"Now that's my baby. I'll make your roundtrip travel reservations for June eleventh and twelfth. I'll give you the confirmation number by Wednesday. Alright?"

"That's fine."

"Cool. I love you, Ci."

"You too."

"Word. Well, I have to get ready for practice. I'll talk to you later."

"OK." When their conversation ended, she grabbed her favorite pillow and fell back onto the bed and thought about going to the Bronx Zoo and shopping in NYC.

Cierra occupied her two weeks with job hunting. She submitted her resume to a number of local investment and insurance companies. She desired to work in Marketing as an Assistant Product Manager. During the two weeks, she did not receive the job callbacks she hoped for so she went to New York to visit Chris as they planned.

Early Saturday morning on June eleventh, she parked in the overnight garage at Richmond International Airport then walked to the terminal to board the plane. As she thought about seeing Chris, she felt excited, anxious, and nervous all at the same time. She found her seat, and settled in for the small journey up the East Coast.

About one hour later, the plane landed in Washington, D.C. for a layover. The stewardess announced, "Ladies and gentlemen this is Washington National Airport located in our Nation's Capital, Washington, DC. Please be advised that this is an hour layover. You may exit the plane and enjoy the shops or stretch your legs. However, the plane will depart at eleven a.m. sharp. So, please allow yourself enough time to return to the plane. Thank you and enjoy."

Cierra exited the plane to stretch her legs and breathe some fresh air but the temptation to buy something cute took over and she scurried to the shops. She walked into a women's boutique and immediately noticed a cute, black lace chemise she wanted for her re-union with Chris. She paid for her merchandise and noticed the clock on the wall read ten twenty-five. *I have time for a quick phone call to Rachel. She would kill me if I came to town and didn't call her.* She located the nearest payphone.

"Hello," answered Rachel while drying dishes from a late breakfast.

"Hey girl. How are you?"

"Hi, Ci. This is a nice surprise. Where are you? I hear a lot of noise in the background."

Cierra explained her New York trip to see Chris. Rachel delighted in the notion that they were working things out. In turn, Rachel informed her best friend about living in the D.C. metro area and how well Damien was playing with the Redskins. She then explained how the availability of the church, reception hall, and caterer all had scheduling conflicts hindering Damien and her from setting an actual wedding date.

"Well that's not good."

"Tell me about it. I'm about to lose my mind. C'est ça."

Noticing that the time was ten forty-five and she only had fifteen minutes to reach the plane, Cierra abruptly interrupted her friend and ended the conversation. They wished each other well and Cierra made a mad dash to the plane.

"Excuse me, excuse me," she said as she ran through the airport. Right after she boarded the plane, the stewardess closed the aircraft's door. *Man, that was close.* She stood at her seat and fumbled with the shopping bag placing it into her carry-on. The elderly woman sitting across from her who was doing needlepoint smiled at Cierra when part of the black lace chemise poked out of the bag. Embarrassed, Cierra quickly stuffed it back into the bag and smiled at the woman.

"I remember those days," said the woman and continued stitching. Cierra smiled and they laughed together. The woman and Cierra chatted about the woman's life that covered four husbands and seven children. Amused by the woman's story, Cierra lost track of time. Before she realized it, the plane landed at LaGuardia airport. Cierra said farewell to the woman traveling to Connecticut to visit one of her daughters and exited the aircraft.

She made her way through the crowded airport and found the signs that led to the main entrance. As Cierra approached the doors, she saw Chris standing there. She walked slowly toward him admiring him from afar. Her heartbeat became hard and irregular while butterflies flew about her stomach. She realized she missed him more than she thought. Chris spotted her in the midst of a group of people and approached her.

"You made it. How was your trip?" he asked overjoyed as he kissed her soft lips.

"Fine," she replied as she embraced him with a bear hug.

"Baby, I've missed you something awful," Chris said as he took her bags. He gestured which way to go as they engaged in small talk. At the main entrance, a well-built guy walked toward them, extended his hand to Cierra and said, "So, you must be the little lady Chris is always talking about."

Cierra shook his hand and gave a friendly, "Hello" while looking at Chris disappointed that their first moments together would be shared with one of his teammates. Chris understood her expression and quickly introduced his teammate, Wesley "Shake" Jefferson.

"So, how did you get the nickname Shake?" Cierra inquired.

"Because I shake 'em and bake 'em when I take the rock down the field."

"Oh, so you're one of the running backs."

"You got it."

As the trio caught the shuttle to the short-term parking lot, Cierra decided to make the best of the situation.

"Chris, what do you have planned for the day?"

"First, we'll go to the hotel to check in and drop off your luggage. Then you can ride with me to take Shake to his mother's house in Brooklyn. After that the rest of the day is up to you. We can do whatever you like."

"Can we check out the Bronx zoo?"

"Sure. Whatever you like."

"She looked forward to dropping off Shake. The three exited the shuttle and walked down Row E3. Chris pulled out his remote key ring and unlocked the doors of his ride. The taillights of a shiny new black 1989 Nissan Pathfinder lit.

"Chris, is this you?" Cierra asked surprised to see the sleek SUV.

"Yeah, baby. Do you like it?" he asked as he placed her bags in the back.

"It's nice. Look at these rims. When did you get this?"

"Actually, I ordered it when I received my signing bonus and it just came a few days ago."

He opened her door and she climbed inside smelling the new car scent. The plush leather seats felt cool and comfortable next to her body. She looked around and admired the interior as Chris included every optional package possible.

"This is a serious chick mobile you have here. Now I see how you managed to hang out at the club and all. I bet you get mad attention from the girls, huh?"

"Ci, you know you're the only girl for me," Chris responded as he put the SUV in drive.

They reached the Waldorf Astoria Hotel about thirty minutes later. Chris gave the SUV keys to the valet attendant then all three of them went inside. Shake decided to get a beer at the bar while Chris and Cierra checked in. Cierra walked around the lobby admiring the art deco of the grand hotel. Chris summoned her as the bellhop walked to the elevator with her luggage loaded on a brass cart.

"The Belmoire Suite please," Chris requested of the bellhop.

"Very well, sir."

Cierra's mouth fell open. Chris winked at her then continued to look up at the elevator numbers as they passed each floor until it reached its destination.

"Right this way please," the bellhop instructed as he led them down a long corridor then left around a corner. Chris opened the door of the Belmoire allowing the bellhop to carry in Cierra's luggage. She entered and marveled at the spacious suite. She kicked her sandals off and walked across the cool marble floor gasping at the luxury that surrounded her. Chris watched her from the door as he tipped the bellhop. When the door closed, Cierra ran to him, jumped into his strong arms, and sealed her appreciation of his efforts with a sweet kiss.

"Chris, this is beautiful. What made you think to do this? How much did this cost?" she rambled as she looked out of the window at the city's vast skyline.

Chris embraced her from behind and kissed her shoulder. Cierra tilted her head toward him and said, "Look at this view. It's incredible." Chris kissed her neck and responded, "Nothing is too good for my baby. You deserve the best and now that I have this Jets contract, I can give you the best. I'm so glad to see you, Ci."

"It's good to see you too." She looked into his longing eyes while stroking his face then parted her lips to share a long awaited kiss. Suddenly, the phone rang. Chris answered to hear Shake on the other end.

"Yo, Chris, I don't mean to interrupt, but man, I need to get to my mom's by one."

"Alright, Shake, keep your shirt on. We're coming."

Chris and Cierra locked the penthouse door and returned to the lobby. As the three traveled from Manhattan to Brooklyn, Cierra enjoyed seeing the urban sights. Chris purposely took the scenic route even though it made Shake uneasy as he often reminded Chris of the time. At twelve forty-five, Chris pulled up to the front of a Brooklyn brownstone. Shake exited the SUV.

"Alright man, thanks for the ride. I'll holla at you later," said Shake as he opened the vehicle door.

"Cool. Is Pete still picking you up?" Chris asked as they talked through the window.

"Yeah. I'm set. It was nice meeting you, Cierra."

"You too," she responded as she waved.

Shake walked up the steps of the brownstone then disappeared behind the front doors. Chris looked at Cierra and asked, "Where to?"

"The zoo."

"Alright."

Chris turned up his stereo to the thumping sounds of Public Enemy and they proceeded to the Bronx Zoo. They walked hand-in-hand looking at the exotic animals. Cierra found the chimpanzees most amusing of all while Chris took an interest in the tigers. After a few hours at the zoo, they went to Central Park for a picnic that consisted of a street vendor's famous NYC hotdog, chips, and soft drink. They watched children playing, lovers courting, runners jogging and cyclists biking. Cierra felt light hearted and wished they could be happy like this forever. Chris caught the attention of a panhandler and bought Cierra a bundle of roses. Cierra thanked Chris but joked how the flowers probably wouldn't last the rest of the day.

"It's the thought that counts," Chris commented as he looked at her out of the corner of his eye feeling that she didn't appreciate his gesture. She knew she was wrong for her remark and quickly changed the subject.

"Have you heard from Damien?" she asked.

"Yeah, I called him a few days ago," Chris informed while taking the last sip from his soda can then tossing it into a waste bin. He continued, "I can't believe he's getting married."

"At some point, I would imagine that most guys want to settle down," remarked Cierra taking a seat on a park bench.

"Don't get me wrong, love is cool. I'm just saying for him to do it now when he's just joining the NFL is a major step," Chris replied intentionally to see how Cierra would respond. He would do the same if she let him.

"Well, it's obvious that marriage isn't on your mind," said Cierra standing to leave.

"You don't know what's on my mind," replied Chris in a joking manner.

"You're right, I don't. But what I do see is you playing big spender."

"You don't like where you're staying? We can change that you know." Chris stood and gently embraced Cierra close to his chest. She tried to stay focused on her thoughts as she explained, "What I'm saying is you should be careful how you spend your money. And yes, I like the suite you got, but it wasn't necessary."

"You can be so ungrateful. I do something nice to show you how special you are to me and this is what I get?" He released her then backed away. Cierra held his hand to get his full attention.

"Chris, it's not that I'm ungrateful. I appreciate what you've done, seriously. But you and I both know pro ball is a gamble even after players are drafted. The league will trade you or cut you at the drop of a hat. I just think until things are more settled, you should save the money you're making, that's all."

"You sound like you don't think I'm gonna make it here. I got drafted, Cierra. I'm not a walk-on or free agent. Damn! Do you have any faith in me anymore about anything I do?"

"Yes. Chris, I believe you're a great player and I have always supported your efforts and dreams. I just want you to be cautious, that's all."

"Ci, don't worry. I've got everything under control, really I do," Chris assured her.

Cierra looked at him with raised eyebrows and said, "OK. I won't say another word about it."

On the way back to Manhattan they stopped at the Studio Museum of Harlem. They admired the exhibits for a couple of hours then returned to the Waldorf Astoria Hotel. Upon entering the Belmoire suite, Chris carried Cierra across the threshold whispering to her that one-day this would be for real. She hugged his neck glad that his mind was still on a committed union between them. He then carried her to the master bedroom where red and white roses in every shape vase imaginable awaited her. The flowers adorned the mahogany dresser, marble top nightstands, Ebanista writer's desk, and Victorian vanity. Chris tossed Cierra onto the bed and pounced on top of her as he jokingly referenced her earlier comment about the panhandler's flowers, "I think these roses will last all day and all night. What'cha think?"

She caught the joke and laughed even though she felt a little guilty about her remark. After a few moments of cuddling, Cierra prepared to take a lavish bath in the oversized Jacuzzi to wash away the grime of the day. The tub filled quickly as she poured in the aromatherapy jasmine scented bath gel she found on the marble countertop. She then slid into the warm, sudsy water. Chris decided to get some wine and join her. He stripped down to his smooth flawless Hershey brown skin and stood at the bathroom entrance with an ice bucket of chilled wine in one hand and two wineglasses in the other. Cierra's mouth fell to the floor when she looked up and saw him standing in the doorway, butt naked watching her. He requested if he could join her and she agreed.

He stepped into the tub with oohs and ahhhs as his body adjusted to the hot water. He turned on the jets and the bubbles rose above the rim. He raised his wineglass for a toast, "To us, Ci." She wrapped her arm around his like couples do at wedding receptions and repeated his toast. As the smooth melody of Luther Vandross' "Any Love" and other R&B soulful songs played in the background, they relaxed in the soothing bath while drinking two bottles of Moet.

They reminisced about their relationship over the past four years and how wonderful it was. Chris pulled Cierra close to him and positioned her over his lap. As she straddled his legs, his desire to have her found its way inside her womanhood. Cierra wrapped her arms around Chris' neck and rode the waves of emotions that followed. She missed their passion and wanted to enjoy the intimate reunion with her best friend and lover, but those raging thoughts of Chris' affair with Amy filled her head. She held onto Chris as he moaned with ecstasy. She kissed the side of his neck and ran her hands through his hair and down his muscular back. Her touch excited him more. He grabbed her buttocks with one last invigorating grip then released his love potion inside of her. Cierra sobbed quietly as their encounter came to an end. Chris felt her body quivering and pulled her away a bit so he could see her face.

"Cierra, baby, what's wrong?"

Overwhelmed with emotion, she couldn't answer. She just shook her head.

"Come on now, talk to me. Why are you crying?" Chris asked again genuinely concerned about her emotional wellbeing.

"I'm sorry," she answered.

"Sorry for what?" Chris asked as he wiped her tears away. "You have nothing to be sorry for."

"I wanted this moment to be special, especially since it's our first time back together, but I can't stop thinking about how you were with Amy. I feel like she had you like this and you touched her like you're touching me." She cried harder. Chris stepped out of the Jacuzzi and grabbed the two white cotton robes hanging by the shower.

"Baby, come here," he instructed as he held up her robe. Cierra put on the robe then sat on the bed with him. Chris held her hands and kissed them. He looked at Cierra's hurtful eyes and said, "Amy never had me like this. I love you and have only loved you. I made one horrible mistake and I'm so sorry for it. You have to believe me when I tell you, you are the only one I've ever given my heart to."

"Chris, it hurts me to my soul."

"Ci, what can I do to make it right for us again?" he questioned as he brushed her hair away from her face. Cierra shrugged her shoulders and answered, "I don't know." Chris placed his arm around her and kissed the tear that ran down her cheek. He moved closer and softly whispered in her ear, "Baby, I'm so sorry. I never meant to hurt you, I swear." His eyes filled with water and a tear streamed down to his chiseled jaw. Cierra knew Chris meant what he said.

They tried to comfort each other's pain as they sat for an hour hugging and talking their way through all that happened during the last ten months, his affair with Amy, her stalking Cierra, and Cierra's miscarriage of their baby. At the end of the hour, Chris tried to lighten the mood by suggesting that they go out to see more of the Big Apple. Cierra agreed, hoping the change of pace would improve her spirit. They dressed in their chic outfits and headed to The Shark Bar for dinner. After an enjoyable time at the restaurant, the two spent several hours dancing at The Roof Top. They returned to the Belmoire tired and tipsy. They quickly undressed and crashed into the California king size bed layered with pillows and Egyptian cotton sheets. Chris wanted to be intimate with Cierra again but knew she needed more time to prepare her heart, mind, and soul. Instead, he navigated her body to his chest and there she slept for the night.

The next morning, the sound of rain against the window woke Cierra. She turned onto her side, stared at the falling raindrops as they cascaded down the glass panes and thought about her relationship with Chris. Her soul filled with hurtful memories from their senior year at Virginia Tech. She rolled over and looked at him and thought about how he must have laid in Amy's bed from September to February, before he knew she was pregnant. Her heart raced with anger and her breathing became heavy and shallow. Chris sensed her staring at him and opened one eye.

"Ci, why are you up so early?"

She didn't answer. Chris reached over to snuggle with her but she moved away from him. He reached for her again and she pushed his arm away.

"Chris, I can't do this."

"Ci, what are you talking about?"

"I can't pretend that all this is okay."

"Damn Ci, you're starting this mess all over again?"

"I can't do this," Cierra repeated as she tossed back the covers and got out of the bed. Chris jumped up and followed her to the bathroom where she started gathering her things.

"Ci, slow your roll. What are you doing?"

"What does it look like? I'm packing."

"Why?" Chris asked nervously.

"Because, you may be over what happened but I'm not. The truth is I'm still pissed with you."

Cierra threw her toiletries into the small carry-on bag. Then she went to the other room and packed her clothes. Chris tried to stop Cierra but her mission to leave exceeded his desire for her to stay.

"I'm begging you not to go. Please don't go like this. Let's talk."

"I'm all talked out Chris. I have nothing left to say except there's nothing for you here with me."

"What? Damn it, Ci. How can you say that after the night we just had?"

"Chris, our night started by me crying on your shoulder, remember?"

"Ci, we can get through this together," he pleaded as he cornered her in the closet, "Listen, all we need is some time. Everything will be okay."

"Yeah, but during that time, I don't think I can be with you, Chris. It hurts too much. Don't you understand that? You betrayed me and ruined the trust I had in you."

"Ci, I'm willing to do anything to gain your trust back. Please don't do this to us."

"Chris, you already did this to us."

Cierra finished packing, quickly dressed then called LaGuardia airport to find out the schedule for the next flight home.

"My plane leaves in two hours," she informed.

"I don't believe this shit," Chris yelled.

While Cierra sat on the sofa in the den with her packed suitcase beside her, Chris left the room to shower and dress. He contemplated taking his time so she would miss her flight, but he knew that would only escalate the matter. A half-hour went by then he returned to the den dressed in his Calvin Klein jeans and white cotton Polo shirt. He sat beside Cierra and calmly asked, "Are you sure you want to do this?"

"Yes," she replied.

"Is there anything I can do to convince you to stay and give us a chance?"

Cierra slowly shook her head from side to side; her decision was final.

"Guess I'll have to cancel the second night here."

"I suppose. You can do what you need."

"What I need is you."

Cierra said nothing. Chris' eyes watered as he stood and reached for her suitcase. He walked to the entrance and opened the door. Cierra stood, took a deep breath, looked around the elegant room then walked through the door.

As Chris drove to the airport, dead silence occupied his new Pathfinder. He didn't want their relationship to end but he couldn't think of what else to say or do. He wanted the drive to last longer but they arrived at LaGuardia rather quickly. Much to Chris' surprise, Cierra insisted that he drop her off at the drive up, curbside.

"Ci, I can go with you inside, just let me park and we can take the shuttle."

"No Chris, this is fine."

"Ci, come on now. This isn't right. Let me go with you."

"I'm fine, Chris. Just pull up to the curb," said Cierra a little annoyed by his persistent requests.

"Fine," Chris said angrily, parking the SUV and turning on his flashers to help her with her luggage. Cierra exited the vehicle and gathered her suitcase.

"May I at least have a hug and kiss?" Chris asked with open arms. Without words, Cierra hugged him and planted a soft peck on the side of his cheek.

"Ci, it's like that now?" His eyes watered as he realized the extent of her heartache.

"Chris, I'll call you when I get home so you'll know I arrived safely.

"That's fine. I'll be back at the camp. Make sure you call me, okay?"

"I will." She turned, picked up her luggage, and walked into the lobby of the airport. After boarding the plane, she stared out of the window.

Lord, I pray I'm making the right decision. I thought I was ready to be with Chris, but I'm not. When I think about how he only stopped seeing Amy because I was pregnant with his child, I feel incensed. It's good that he did, but I wonder how long would he have continued to lie to my face about them, and how long would he have continued to put our health at risk messing around with her? I get so angry about it all. I can't even tell what's real and what's not anymore. When he holds me, what's the truth and what's a lie? If he had sex with Amy all the different ways she said, he was enjoying it and that makes me sick to my stomach. I wish I could just put this whole ordeal behind me, forgive him, and be happy again. But this has cut me to the core and I ache to the depths of my soul. I pray Lord that You are with me as I take on life's journey without him. I don't hate him, but I hate what he did. I pray that You keep him safe as he continues his football career. But mostly, I pray You mend my broken heart. Amen.

Cierra entered her parents' house late in the afternoon on that Sunday. She tried to sneak pass her mother but Mrs. Sykes stopped her in the kitchen to inquire why was she back from New York so soon. When Cierra faced her, her mother could tell she had been crying.

"Ci, is everything okay?"

"Yeah, I'm fine."

"Well, what happened? I thought you would be back early tomorrow morning."

"I decided not to get back together with Chris."

"Why?"

"Mom, can we not talk about this? Please no more questions, OK?"

"I hope you aren't doing anything you'll regret. And I hope this is not about that thing that happened at school."

"'That thing'. Obviously, you still don't understand."

She ran down the hallway to her room and dove across the bed. The emotional knot in her stomach took away her strength to face her mother another moment. A sense of loneliness came over her because her mother could not understand the depth of her sorrow. How could she, when she had endured far more from her husband? Shortly thereafter, Cierra composed herself as best as she could and phoned Chris as promised.

"Hi, Chris."

"Hey, baby. You made it home safe I see."

"Yeah. The trip was fine."

"I still wish you were here."

"Chris, don't start."

"I'm not. I just miss you. That's all. I'll um-, I'll holla at you later then."

"Okay. Thanks for understanding."

She closed her eyes and drifted into a much-needed nap. A few hours later, she woke then unpacked and joined her parents downstairs for dinner. She stood at the stove putting smothered chicken, potatoes, and collard greens on her plate when she heard her father ask her mother, "Brenda, what the hell is wrong with Cierra?"

"Gregory, just leave it alone."

"Cierra, why you 'round here mopin'? You act like you just lost your best friend or somethin'," Mr. Sykes commented.

Cierra glared at him and replied, "Sometimes you really get on my last nerve."

"Watch your mouth. Don't make me get up from this table," Mr. Sykes responded as he put a fork full of collards in his mouth. Cierra rolled her eyes at him and returned to her room with her dinner plate. She turned on the T.V. and watched a rerun of the Cosby Show.

On Tuesday, two days after returning from NYC, Cierra interviewed with Health First Insurance Company (HFIC). Impressed with her academic credentials, professionalism, and communication skills, HFIC made her a job offer during the interview. Her new position as Assistant Product Manager would begin in three weeks on the Tuesday after the July fourth weekend.

When Cierra arrived home, she called Kelly and Josi to share her exciting news. During their three-way call, they congratulated her and discussed celebrating the milestone.

"Welcome to corporate America. Did you get a cubical or an office?" Kelly asked.

"A cube, everyone has one except the manager," Cierra replied.

"A cube, an office, who cares? You got the job, Ci. That's all that matters," Josi commented.

"Agreed," said Cierra.

"Let's all get together and celebrate at the Underground on the Fourth," Kelly suggested.

"That'll work. We can celebrate my new job and Independence Day," Cierra said still at awe that she got the job.

"Works for me," Josi agreed.

"What are you going to do over the next three weeks?" Kelly asked.

"Girl, please. I need to shop for some business clothes," replied Cierra as she thought about how she needed to update her wardrobe.

"I heard that. Call me when you go," requested Kelly.

"Will do," said Cierra ending the call.

During the next few weeks, Cierra did exactly what she said

she needed to do to prepare for her new job. She shopped for the pants suits, blouses, and shoes that she needed. She felt good about her new opportunity and looked forward to her first day on the job and her first paycheck. Thoughts of Chris were at the far corner of her mind until he called her early Sunday morning on July third.

The crux of Chris' call was a plea to get back together. The more he tried to rationalize with Cierra, the more upset she became. The conversation escalated to a screaming match.

"Chris, don't you understand? There is nothing here for you anymore. I don't want to be with you."

"Cierra, you're not being fair or logical. We belong together and I'm not gonna let you go that easy."

"Chris, please just let me be."

"I can't. I want us together, baby. You're my world."

Pausing between each syllable, Cierra replied, "Not anymore!"

Chris cried uncontrollably.

"I'm leaving," he muffled between his sobs.

"What did you say?"

"I'm leaving."

"Leaving what?" Cierra became more concerned.

"Leaving camp."

"Chris, you're talking crazy. You can't do that. Last week you told me that you're one step from making the second string, wide receiver position. You can't just walk out. What about your contract? You will be penalized and fined. But most importantly, you dreamed of this your whole life. Don't throw it away," Cierra pleaded.

"Please be with me, Ci. I don't care about anything else. All I need is you. If I don't have you, I don't have anything."

"Chris, I can't promise you anything. Just please don't throw your dreams away."

Chris hung up and the phone went dead. Cierra stood with her hand over her mouth shocked at Chris' intentions. She felt helpless. She tried calling him back, but there was no answer. She called his parents and explained what he told her and asked them to try to convince him to stay at camp if he called them. Mrs. Jackson promised to let her know if she heard from him.

Later that morning, Chris drove south on I-95, angry and disheartened. *How in the hell can they cut me? That damn Offensive Coordinator had it in for me from the jumpstart 'cause I was better than his favorite bitch ass lead man. I was faster, read the plays better, and caught more passes, every damn thing! Fuckin' coach talking about 'You're good but not quite what we need.' Bullshit! Damn that! I know I'm good! I've worked for this all my life. How the hell can one damn coach ruin this for me just like that? I could hurt that son of a bitch.* His eyes watered as he tried to focus on the highway but his mind kept racing. *How in the world am I supposed to explain this to Cierra? I can't believe this ill shit is happening to me. I don't have ball. I don't have my girl. I don't have anything. Damn this, I know what I'll do. I'll go talk to Damien and see what he says. Maybe he can help me get a spot with the Redskins. I know my skills are solid.*

After a few hours, he reached the Washington, DC metropolitan area. He veered onto the Beltway then eventually merged onto Route 267 West and headed toward Reston, VA to see Damien. He calmed down but was still in disbelief. His Sunday trip wasn't planned but was a desperate measure to save the life he wanted. He parked the Pathfinder in the driveway, walked up the steps to Damien and Rachel's townhouse, and rang the doorbell.

July

On Monday afternoon, July fourth, Cierra heard someone at her parents' front door. She set aside her bowl of salad and peeped out of the living room window. She saw the black Pathfinder parked in the driveway. Her heart went to her feet and her lunch took an unpleasant turn in her stomach. She slowly walked to the front door and opened it.

"Chris, what are you doing here?"

"May I come in?"

She opened the door all the way to allow him to pass through.

"Please tell me that the coach gave you permission to leave," she said cautiously as she prepared herself for his comment. He looked at her with worried eyes and thought for a second whether to tell her the truth. *Damn, how can I tell her that I didn't make the team and that there would be no five-year contract?* He decided to only share his feelings about her, hoping that it would make a positive impact.

"No, he didn't. I packed everything and didn't report to practice."

"Are you nuts?" Cierra became upset. "Chris, I pleaded with you not to do this."

"Ci, this is how much you mean to me. I want to be with you."

"But Chris I'm not ready to be with you. I can't believe you quit. You will never get a chance to play pro ball now." Shaking her head, Cierra flopped in the living room chair across from where Chris stood further realizing the extent of his actions.

"Forget about pro ball, none of that matters to me anymore. Don't you get it?"

Cierra continued to shake her head. "Have you talked with your parents?"

"No, why?"

"I called them and told them that you planned to do this. Your mom was pretty disturbed by it."

"Why the hell did you do that?" Chris asked agitated that now he would have to face his mother too.

"Because I hoped that someone could talk some sense into you."

"Speaking of parents, where are yours?" Chris asked as he looked around and noticed their absence.

"Mom is at the grocery store and dad went fishing."

Perfect. He approached Cierra for a hug but she rejected his advance.

"Chris, I know what you're thinking, and you can forget about it. As a matter of fact, I think you should go."

"Ci, what are you talking about? You don't even want me to hold you or visit?"

Before she could answer, Mrs. Sykes pulled into the driveway.

Cierra threw up both hands. "That's just great! Now I have to hear her mouth too."

Chris exited the back door to help Mrs. Sykes with the groceries like he always did when in town visiting. Mrs. Sykes' shocked expression said everything but she didn't dare ask any questions while in his presence. The three of them assembled in the kitchen as Cierra put away the groceries and Mrs. Sykes started dinner.

"Chris, are you joining us for dinner this evening?" Mrs. Sykes asked as she pulled out her cookware from the cabinets. Cierra looked at him anticipating his response.

"No thank you. I'm going over to my cousin Zack's house across town for the night."

"Well, you're more than welcome."

"I appreciate the offer but I don't think I should stay."

"Well maybe next time." Mrs. Sykes looked up and saw Cierra and Chris staring at each other and felt the tension.

"I guess I should get going now," he remarked as he walked toward Mrs. Sykes and gave her a hug.

"Chris, you take care of yourself, you hear? Everything will be fine." She patted his back.

Cierra walked Chris to the front door where they said their farewells.

"So, can I at least call you sometimes?" Chris asked.

"Sure, Chris. Understand that I don't hate you. I just hate what you did and I need time to heal."

This didn't go how I expected, he thought as he looked at her soft lips. He wanted to kiss her so badly but knew now wasn't the time.

"Okay. I'll talk to you soon," he said as he settled for a small hug.

Cierra watched him walk to his SUV and then waved as he drove out of the driveway. When she returned to the kitchen, her mother stood in the middle of the floor with both hands on her hip.

"Cierra Sykes, that boy loves you and if you don't see that you're as blind as a bat."

"Mom, I know but this is not about him. It's about me and how

I feel. He made the mistake so he has to pay whatever consequence comes about this.

"Besides, I'm going out with the girls tonight to celebrate my new job."

"Lord, have mercy. You have Chris here begging you back and you're going out with the girls to some club. I don't know what to say about you sometimes." Mrs. Sykes returned to attending her dinner while Cierra went to her room to pick out her outfit for the evening.

A little while later Mr. Sykes came home. He brought in a cooler full of fish then went back outside to hose down the boat to remove the salt water. Cierra came downstairs to get her mother's opinion about her different outfits. She finally settled on wearing a white mini skirt, black rayon tank top and black, strapped sandals.

An hour later, Cierra heard a horn blow outside. She peeped out of the window and saw Kelly in her white Maxima. Cierra kissed her mom on the cheek and told her not to wait up for her. Mr. Sykes had already crashed in bed from his day of fishing.

"Is Josi going?" Mrs. Sykes asked.

"Yeah."

"Well, you girls be careful."

"We will," Cierra replied, as she closed the front door.

Cierra and Kelly picked up Josi and the three ventured to the Underground ready to engage in a good time. When they arrived at the front entrance, surprisingly, Terrance and his friends were there.

"Cierra? What's up?" Terrance inquired happy to see her again.

"Hi Terrance."

"Why didn't you call a brotha?" he playfully questioned wondering why she never phoned him.

"I planned to but it's just that I've been really busy. You see, I got a job with HFIC and needed to prepare for it."

"Word? That's impressive."

"Thanks. Please believe me, I seriously wasn't trying to blow you off," Cierra explained.

"A'right. I believe you. Starting a new job is exciting and all."

"How long have you been in town?" Cierra asked curious about his stay.

"I just arrived today but will be here through the holiday weekend," Terrance informed secretly wishing he could spend some time with her during his visit. But he didn't dare disclose how he felt, especially after she didn't call him.

"I see," Cierra commented admiring the tall, handsome fellow.

"Well, ladies, shall we?" Terrance displayed the palm of his hand in the direction of the stairs and motioned for Cierra, Kelly, and Josi to move toward the steps that descended to the lower level.

The group of friends immediately got into the music as Keith Sweat's "Don't Stop Your Love" pumped from the speakers. Terrance grabbed Cierra by the hand and stepped onto the dance floor. Kelly and Josi continued through the crowded dimly lit room to find a table. The black strobe lights came on and Cierra laughed at how funny the people looked as everything white magnified. She looked at her own black tank top and wished she wore a light color because the black lights showed every piece of white lint on the garment. Terrance didn't pay the strobe lights any attention and danced around Cierra doing his own special version of the Wop and Run Joe. Cierra laughed at his intentional distorted dance steps.

The lights changed and the regular multi-colored lights circled about the dance floor. Kelly and Josi soon returned to the dance floor with a couple of guys and began getting their groove on as well. As the music played, the party-goers chanted, "The roof, the roof, the roof is on fire! We don't need no water! Let the motherfucker burn! Burn motherfucker! Burn!" Cierra felt great experiencing carefree moments with Terrance. They danced hard, giving their bodies a rhythmic worked out. Sweat ran down their backs, chests, and faces. Terrance started slowing the pace and suggested getting something to drink. Cierra danced over to Kelly and asked where did they find a table. Kelly pointed near the bar. Terrance and Cierra left the dance floor and stopped by the bar on their way to the table. He ordered her a Fuzzy Navel and him a

Jack and Coke. They carried their drinks to the table, sat and tried to talk but the music volume over-powered their voices.

"I can barely hear you," said Cierra.

Terrance slid her chair close beside him. "Now that's better," he responded, happy that she didn't resist. "So, tell me about the new job." Delighted that he expressed an interest, Cierra told him the details of her interview. Terrance told her how proud she should be for such an accomplishment because good jobs don't come easy. He raised the back of her hand to his lips and kissed her soft skin. "Congratulations." At the very moment he intended to plant a flirtatious peck on Cierra's cheek, her friends returned to the table. *Damn* circled in his mind as he thought about his next move.

"So, what are you girls drinking tonight?" Terrance asked wishing they arrived a few moments later.

"I got this one," the guy with Kelly informed.

"Josi, would you like something?" Terrance asked.

"That's OK, I'll get it," Josi responded fumbling with her purse irritated that her dance partner went to the restroom at an inopportune time.

"Put your money away," Terrance told Josi. Naturally generous and kind hearted, he treated her to a drink even though he sensed that she didn't particularly care for him. Terrance and Kelly's friend went to the bar to get the drinks while Kelly and Josi zeroed in on Cierra about Terrance's attempted kiss.

"Girl, what's up? Why are you letting this guy flirt with you and get his hopes up? What about Chris?" Josi commented.

"Terrance is harmless. I'm just having fun," Cierra explained.

"I say go for it," Kelly interjected while watching a hunk of a man walk by.

As Terrance and Kelly's friend returned to the table, Josi's friend joined them. The small group enjoyed themselves as they cracked jokes, listened to the music, and consumed a couple rounds of drinks. "Piece of My Love" by Guy came on and Terrance asked Cierra to dance. They excused themselves and proceeded to the dance floor. As their bodies swayed back and forth, Terrance whispered sweet nothings in her ear.

"You smell so good, I could take you home, put you in a vase of water, and watch you bloom."

"What?" Cierra asked with amusement.

"You feel so good to me I could stay attached to you forever."

"Terrance, you're a nut." Terrance smiled as he noticed Cierra liked his corny jokes. He continued. "You make me so horny I could-"

"Heyyyy," Cierra quickly cutting him off. They laughed and continued to dance. After the slow song finished, they rejoined their friends at the table. They all had another round of drinks then everyone returned to the dance floor as the sound of De La Soul's "Me, Myself, and I" filled the room. Josi tapped Cierra on the shoulder as Cierra shook her groove thang and asked, "Ci, I hope I'm mistaken, but is that Chris over there?" Cierra turned and saw Chris standing at the outer edge of the dance floor watching her.

"Oh shit, Josi. That's him."

Still bobbing to the beat, Josi asked, "What's he doing here? I thought he was at camp."

"He was but he left camp today to try to work things out between us."

"Are you serious? Ci, that's so romantic. Didn't I tell you that you should give him a chance? Look how much he loves you." Josi was almost spellbound. Kelly danced over and interjected, "Ci, don't listen to her. You need to be worried about how long he's been here watching you."

"What are you ladies talking about," Terrance asked curiously.

"Oh nothing," Cierra responded as she looked at Chris out of the corner of her eye. Just then Chris approached her on the dance floor.

"Excuse me partner, you don't mind if I cut in do you?" Chris asked Terrance while looking at Cierra.

"Hell yeah, I mind. Who are you?" Terrance asked agitated by the interruption. Cierra's heart raced as she read Chris' expression. She quickly introduced Chris in hopes that the situation would not amount to anything. But he squared his shoulders at Terrance and warned, "Partner, you need to step off."

"Forget you, man."

Chris ignored Terrance's second remark, looked at Cierra and requested, "I need to talk to you for a moment." Cierra asked Terrance to give her a minute. She knew she had to split the two apart as quickly as possible. Terrance walked away after emphasizing, "I'll be at *our* table."

Cierra and Chris retreated to a corner where he again pleaded with her to get back together. Buzzed from the Fuzzy Navel drinks, she boldly told him, "Chris, you know what? You have some nerve thinking that you can just have me anytime you want. How dare you come on the dance floor and embarrass me like that?" He smelled the alcohol on her breath and persisted that she had been drinking too much and needed to leave with him.

"Chris, I'm not going anywhere. I came here with my friends to celebrate my new job that you don't know about and to have fun for the July fourth holiday, but you're spoiling that right now." She began to walk away.

"Ci, come on let's go. You've had enough." He tugged at her hand but she snatched it back.

"Chris, I'm not going."

"I said let's go!"

"Stop it! You're drunk and you're hurting my wrist."

"I gave up everything for you!" Chris yelled not caring who heard.

"I told you not to. You made that decision so don't blame me!"

Terrance watched the two from the bar as he downed another Jack and Coke. Josi and Kelly watched from the dance floor. Chris became further upset and insisted that she leave with him so they could talk.

"Ci, hear me out. There's so much I need to say to you. You have no idea what's going on with me." *Why the hell did I stop in Reston? Things would be better off if I hadn't*. He wanted to stop the lies that began to take a life of their own and the course of events that followed.

"Chris, I don't want to talk about this."

"But I gotta tell you something important," he begged. He was about to tell her what happened at rookie camp and Reston but at that moment Terrance walked up and asked, "Is everything OK over here?"

"Partner, you need to back off," Chris responded as he glared at Terrance.

Ignoring Chris' warning, Terrance continued, "Ci, are you OK? Do you want to leave?" Cierra nodded yes and tried to move around Chris who stood his ground.

"Man, let the lady go. She said she wants to leave," said Terrance who by this time was extremely serious. Cierra had never seen this protective side of him and subconsciously she liked it. Irritated by Cierra's decision to walk away with Terrance, Chris yelled, "Oh, you don't want to leave with me, but you want to leave with this bamma here!"

Cierra pleaded with Chris to let her go but he didn't move. Terrance stepped forward to take Cierra by the hand.

"Don't touch her," said Chris as he slapped Terrance's hand away.

"Man, you bet not ever touch me again," Terrance said sternly as he gestured for Cierra's hand once more. When Cierra reached for Terrance's hand, Chris sucker punched Terrance in the face and bellowed, "I told you not to touch her!" Then fireworks flew and all hell broke loose.

Chris and Terrance rumbled while Cierra pleaded for them to stop. Josi and Kelly came to her rescue and removed her from the action before she got hurt. Everyone screamed as Chris and Terrance fell over tables shattering patrons' beer bottles and cocktail glasses. One dude tried to step in but after almost catching one of Terrance's right hooks, he backed off. Muhammad Ali and Joe Frazier's Rumble in the Jungle had come to the Underground. Cierra heard someone yell, "Get security!" as she continued to scream for them to stop but the two were at each other in a serious fight. Suddenly, three club bouncers descended upon Chris and Terrance.

"What the hell is wrong with you? Take that shit some place

else," shouted the lead bouncer as he escorted them up the stairs and out the front entrance. People in the upper lobby looked stunned at the sight of their torn shirts and bloody cuts. Cierra, Josi, and Kelly followed.

Outside Cierra ran to Terrance to console him. She felt sorry and embarrassed for Chris' behavior. Terrance's nose bled profusely. He leaned against a nearby car with his head tilted back and placed his handkerchief on his nose. As Cierra stood by his side, Chris yelled at her.

"Oh, so it's like that now, Ci? Just throw everything we had away. Just like that! Ain't this some shit!" He wiped his busted lip as he gazed at her. Cierra looked at him with disbelief and didn't respond. Chris' cousin coached him to his car.

"Come on man, let's go. It ain't worth it."

"Zack, all this shit is getting way out of hand. You have no idea," said Chris squatting to enter the car.

Meanwhile, Cierra turned to Terrance and said, "We better get you home." Terrance gave her the keys to his Benz as he climbed into the passenger side. Josi and Kelly asked if they could help with anything. Cierra appreciated their offer but told them she would catch up with them tomorrow. They left in Kelly's Maxima.

By the time Cierra and Terrance arrived at his house, blood covered his shirt. He sat at the kitchen table pinching his nose while Cierra prepared ice to help stop the bleeding. Terrance kept muttering, "Look at this shit. Ain't this a bitch?" Cierra apologized repeatedly but he reassured her his anger was directed at Chris not her and that she had nothing to be sorry for. Eventually, the bleeding stopped and he removed his shirt. He excused himself to take a shower. After Terrance disappeared from the room, Cierra sat at the kitchen table, put her head down and sobbed.

Approximately twenty minutes elapsed when Cierra heard the shower water stop. She stepped to the kitchen sink and splashed a little cool water on her face trying to refresh her slightly swollen red eyes. She wiped her face with a paper towel and returned to sitting at the wood kitchen table. Terrance walked into the room and filled the air with the fragrance of his Polo cologne. Cierra admired his tall physique as he walked to the refrigerator and placed the ice pack back into the freezer. She stared at him and softly said, "Terrance, I'm truly sorry about tonight." He smiled slightly and then planted a peck on her cheek. His jaw ached but he kissed her anyway.

"It's not your fault." He stepped around her, grabbed his keys off the kitchen table and said, "It's kinda late. Let's get you home."

The two didn't talk much during the thirty-minute drive to Cierra's house. She felt awful and repeatedly replayed the fight scene in her head. She couldn't wait to confront Chris about it. As she daydreamed out of the window about what she wanted to say, Terrance kept glancing at her when he thought she didn't noticed. He questioned himself about whether he wanted to pursue her. After they arrived at Cierra's home, he opened her car door and escorted her to the front porch. She looked concerned as Terrance kissed her on the forehead and told her he would talk with her later.

"Wait Terrance. Here's my phone number. Let me know how you're doing when you feel up to it. Okay?"

"Yeah," he replied as the night's event hovered in his mind. Cierra entered the house and watched Terrance backed out of the driveway.

Early the next morning, she phoned Zack who in turned gave the phone to Chris. Cierra and Chris argued about last night. He did not apologize for the fight and made it quite clear that he did not appreciate her leaving with Terrance. He insisted that they work out their issues and see each other before he returned home to Baltimore.

"Chris, you've gotta be kidding. After what you did last night? You practically beat my friend. I barely recognize who you are anymore. You had no right to go off on Terrance like that. Haven't you realized that the more you do to force us together, the more you only push me further away?" She tried to talk rationally with him but he had his own agenda.

"Ci, I'm sorry about last night, but you have to understand what I'm going through."

"What are you going through Chris? You seem to be the cause of everything. So what can you possibly be going through?"

He wanted to tell her the whole truth but how could he at this point? *Things are getting way too complicated. How can I explain this to her?* They continued to go round for round until the conversation escalated to cursing each other. Cierra grew tired of the battle and hung up the phone in his face. He called back and tried to talk more calmly but that didn't work either. Cierra made it clear that she did not want to talk or see him. She suggested that they both take time to cool off and perhaps talk at a later date. Chris reluctantly agreed.

At mid-day, Josi and Kelly made an impromptu stop by Cierra's house dying to get all the sordid details of last night. They crept into the house like two church mice unsure if Mr. Sykes was around or not.

"Ci, where's your dad?" asked Josi. She was always the first to ask of his whereabouts because she feared him the most.

"Around at Nippy's I guess. He's been gone for a while. He won't be back until later," Cierra explained. The three friends camped out in the kitchen snacking on microwave popcorn and fruit punch while Cierra filled her friends in on every detail.

"Ooh girl, seems like Terrance is pretty pissed," Josi commented.

"Wouldn't you be if someone punched you in your face?" Kelly quickly responded.

"Ci, is Terrance mad at you?" asked Josi.

"Well, he said he's not, but I'm not really sure."

"Josi, what kind of question is that? Ci, didn't fight him, her crazy ass ex did." Kelly shook her head at Josi.

"Maybe he just needs time to cool off," stated the optimistic Josi.

"Girl, I thought Chris was going to kill him. He just went ballistic," Kelly said as she put another bag of popcorn in the microwave.

"I know. I'm definitely seeing a different side to him these days. He's changed so much in the last year, first his affair with

Amy, then him leaving the Jets, and now fighting Terrance. It's like I don't even know who he really is anymore," Cierra said as she scooted her chair away from the table to put her glass in the sink.

"Ci, all I can say is Chris is crazy in love with you. You better be careful how you handle him 'cause no telling what he might do," Kelly cautioned as she joined Cierra at the sink.

"Yeah really. Suppose he tries to hurt you or be like some people and think that if he can't be with you then nobody will and do some crazy mess like kill you and commit suicide."

"Josi, shut up that's just sick," snapped Cierra, "Chris wouldn't hurt anybody!"

"Well, he sure did a number on Terrance," Kelly sarcastically stated.

"OK look. If y'all don't have anything nice to say then don't say anything at all. I have enough on my mind without you two making matters worse."

"Fine," Kelly and Josi said harmoniously.

"So, what's up for the rest of the weekend?" Kelly asked acknowledging the fact they needed to change the subject.

"Nothing really, my holiday mood is shot. So, I'm just going to get ready for my first day of work at HFIC," Cierra responded.

"Oh, that's right. With all the excitement, I almost forgot you start your new job on Monday. Girl, you're gonna love corporate America. There are golden opportunities around almost every corner. Josi, when are you going to get your act together and start working, or is ta mère and ta père going to take care of la petite femme forever?" Kelly commented and teased.

"Fremmez la bouche, Kelly."

"You shut your mouth. All I'm saying is, you need to figure out what you're going to do. Have a plan for goodness sake, Josi. Stop waiting on prince charming to come save you."

"I'm not waiting on anyone."

"Yeah right," Cierra and Kelly chimed together.

The friends chatted for another hour or so then Kelly and Josi left. Cierra returned to her room and selected her clothes for her first day on the job as Assistant Product Manager.

Lord, I pray things go smoothly at the new job. I look forward to this new opportunity. I sincerely thank You for blessing me with the very job I prayed for. Lord, I pray that Terrance doesn't hold the fight between Chris and him against me. I know Chris is upset and hurting. But I don't want to rush back into a relationship with him until I'm clear that's what I want. I pray he understands my feelings and finds peace for himself so that his hurt and anger can subside. I also pray that some day down the road we are able to reconcile and be friends again so that our four years together was not in vain. Amen.

The early morning dew evaporated and the sun rose for another hot Virginia day. Cierra drove down West Broad Street to Staples Mills Road and into the parking lot of HFIC at seven forty-five, Tuesday morning on July fifth. She found her parking space number far behind the five-story tinted glass building. After crossing what seemed to be a mile in heels to the "Employees Only" entrance, she made her way down a small corridor to the front lobby where a security guard signed her in.

"Morning. Haven't seen you before. You must be new here," the Security Guard commented as he looked at Cierra. She glanced at his nametag and replied, "Yes sir, Mr. Hughes. Today is my first day on the job."

"Okay. Well, you'll need a visitor's pass for today. You'll get your employee badge at orientation."

"Yes sir. That's what the HR representative told me too."

"What department will you be in?" he inquired as he handed her the visitor's pass.

"Marketing."

"Oh, you'll like it up there. They have a lot of nice folks in that department. You have a good day now," he said as he allowed her to pass through.

"Thank you."

Cierra walked across the beige marble floor to the other side of the lobby and waited for the elevators with several other people. The elevator doors opened and the people scrambled in. The metal doors closed and folks sounded out, "Press three please, four please, five please." One brave soul said, "Two please." Everyone turned and looked at a rather short narrow framed gentleman standing in the middle.

"Harry, you know you should have taken the stairs," a man in the back commented. Everyone laughed. The doors open and the little man pushed his coke-bottle, eyeglasses up onto his nose, pressed his raggedy, brown briefcase close to his chest and said, "'xcuse me, 'xcuse me," as he exited the elevator. The man in the back further commented, "Harry has been working here for twenty-five years and still won't take the stairs to the second floor, don't make no damn sense." Everyone laughed again. Cierra enjoyed the lighthearted humor that started her morning at the office.

She exited onto the fourth floor with a couple of other young ladies. They walked through the glass and brass doors labeled HFIC Marketing Division. The receptionist sitting behind the desk greeted them. Cierra approached her and asked where she could find her office.

"Right this way Ms. Sykes," said the receptionist as she proudly guided Cierra down the hall and around the left corner. "Your office is the second one on the right hand side."

"Office? I thought that I was getting a cube," said a shocked Cierra.

"There have been a few changes around here and you were assigned this office. Let me warn you, some folks are ticked off about it, but you didn't hear it from me. Enjoy it."

"Thank you," Cierra replied.

Once in her office, Cierra looked around, checked out what was left behind in the cabinets and desk drawers then sat in her black leather chair to get a feel for her new space. Suddenly, her manager, Mr. Bill Wilburn knocked on her door.

"Good-morning, Cierra. How are you this fine morning?"

"Very well, thank you," she replied standing to reciprocate the

Director of Marketing's handshake.

"I see you're getting settled in. We cleared out everything. So feel free to get what you need and fix the office how you like. You can make a list of items and give it to the receptionist. She'll make sure that you have your supplies within a day or so."

"Yes sir. And thank you, sir for the office. I'm more than surprised."

"Yes, well we've had some changes and I thought this space suited you best. I have a hunch about you and I always play my hunches. This is a good fit for where you're headed."

"Thank you, again," replied Cierra giving him a warm professional smile.

"After you get settled in, stop by my office. I'll take you around and introduce you to everyone. Let's say around nine this morning. Everybody is usually here by then."

"OK. I look forward to it," Cierra replied as she returned to sitting in her chair. She liked her new office. The maple and chrome modern style office furniture suited her taste fine.

Noon approached and two employees that Cierra met on Mr. Wilburn's nine a.m. tour asked her to join them for lunch. Terri Moore and Lisa Dexter worked for the Director of Marketing, Terri as his Secretary and Lisa as his personal Computer Systems Administrator. At lunch, Lisa drove them to a nearby soul food restaurant. They talked about everything from the nasty cafeteria food to the office gossip and finally to asking Cierra about her background like what school she graduated from. Because she was new to the office and cautious of loose lips, Cierra only told them things on a need to know basis.

By the end of the workday, Cierra felt exhausted. She went home, changed clothes and relaxed. Just as she was about to close her eyes for a power nap, Kelly phoned to hear all about her first day on the job. The two talked for an hour about life in corporate America and all that they wanted to accomplish. Later that night, Rachel called Cierra in tears.

"Rachel, what's going on? Why are you crying?" Cierra asked with concern.

In between sobs, Rachel began to explain her predicament. She continued to have problems getting a church and a reception hall on the same day, as well as a caterer that could accommodate Damien's football schedule. In addition, her mother and Damien's mother tried taking over planning the wedding. Overall, the entire planning process began to take its toll on her. Cierra tried to reassure her that planning weddings wasn't easy for most couples but that everything would work out. The more Cierra talked about how wonderful Rachel's wedding would be and how beautiful she would look in her wedding gown, the harder Rachel bawled.

"Rachel, what's gotten into you?" Cierra asked confused by Rachel's reaction to her comments.

"You don't understand," Rachel wailed.

"Understand what?"

"I'm not going to look good in my dress."

"Rachel, you've already picked out your dress. It's gorgeous and it fits you perfectly."

"Cierra, I won't be able to wear it," Rachel wept louder.

"Why not?" Cierra asked wondering what could be so devastating.

"Because instead of hemming the dress one inch, some idiot hemmed it one foot. They cut off twelve inches, now it comes to my calves. Now what am I supposed to do?" Rachel cried harder.

"Damn. That is jacked up. But can't they replace it?" Cierra asked feeling sorry for her friend.

"The style is being discontinued. They can't order it again. Now I have to start all over. The best they said they could do is give me a store credit."

"Well, maybe you'll find something you like even better," said Cierra trying to look at the bright side.

"They did say that they received a couple new bridal books," Rachel informed as she began to calm down.

"Trust me, it's going to work out," Cierra assured.

"Ci, I was wondering, would you come and help me look for a new wedding gown?" Rachel asked desperately needing the support of her friend.

"Sure Rachel, but you know Damien would marry you in jeans and a T-shirt if he had to," Cierra joked making Rachel laugh a little.

"Thanks, Ci. You're a life saver."

"No problem. This will be great. I can see you and call Terrance while I'm there. I still feel badly for him," said Cierra.

"Who's Terrance?" Rachel inquired.

"Oh, I didn't tell you about the fight."

"What fight?" Rachel's toned changed from a damsel in distress to Curious George.

"Terrance is this guy I met at the Underground who is interested in going out, but I only view him as a friend. He's very nice, personable, career minded, and goal oriented. I probably would date him if I hadn't just got out of this relationship with Chris. Right now, it's just too soon. Well anyway, he and Chris got into a fight at the Underground."

"Girl, you're lying. What happened?" Rachel inquired.

Cierra recounted the event and Rachel couldn't believe her ears. Rachel insisted that Cierra needed a reprieve just as much as she did. They ended the conversation with well wishes and plans for Cierra to travel to Reston, VA.

The remainder of the week seemed to fly by as Cierra anxiously waited for Friday. Work became challenging as Mr. Wilburn assigned her the Medicare Supplement product account for senior citizens. She started putting together her project plan, selecting team members, and scheduling meetings for the following week.

Chris called a couple of times during the week. They engaged in small talk about her job but the conversations didn't last long at all. He maintained his composure and managed not to talk about their relationship even though he wanted to. He believed if they could be friends again, the rest would follow and he would have her trust once more.

During their second conversation on Thursday, Chris asked Cierra about her plans for the weekend. Cierra hesitated at first but decided to tell him that she planned to go to Northern Virginia to visit Rachel and some other friends. She had no idea how her trip to visit Rachel concerned him. *Damn. I wonder if Damien or Rachel will tell her that I stopped through Reston on my way to Richmond when I left camp on July third. I need to call them and make sure they don't let the cat out of the bag. I'll tell Cierra what really happened when the time is right.* Chris played cool and told Cierra to tell Rachel and Damien "Hello," and that he'll talk to them soon. She sighed with relief and ended the conversation before he asked more detailed questions.

She spent the remainder of the evening packing so that she could leave directly after work the next day. As she packed, she heard her intoxicated father in the family room blasting his stereo to the tunes of a classic Mahilia Jackson album. His boisterous noise gave Cierra a huge headache. *Hypocrite. In there, trying to sing with one of the best, gospel singers there ever was with his drunk, crazy ass. Listen to him. He can't even say the words for slurring.*

Her father called after Mrs. Sykes to join him. When she heard her mother reply, "Gregory, I don't want to be bothered with you and all your loud music," Cierra rolled her eyes upward in her head. *Here we go again. I can't wait to move out of this hellhole. As soon as I earn my first paycheck, I'm as good as gone.* She left her suitcase opened and met her father stumbling down the hallway, headed in the direction of her mother who was mending a pair of his trousers in the guest room. Cierra intercepted him in the hallway where she successfully convinced him to return to the family room. That night her soul felt wearied.

> *Lord, how much longer do I have to endure my dad? Managing him is so draining. I'm truly tired of his drinking and abuse. Please intervene. I've been praying for years. What else can I do? My mother is aging with each passing year and I'm afraid the continued stress of all this will send her to an early grave. She tries to hide the strain but I see it in her face. Lord, please hear my prayers. Protect my mother and me from my father. In the mean time, I pray for continued strength. Amen.*

After work on Friday, July eighth, Cierra traveled to Reston,

VA as Rachel and she planned. She rang the doorbell of her luxury townhouse that was nestled in a community where several of the Washington Redskins players lived. Damien and Rachel greeted her at the door with long awaited hugs. Damien then carried her suitcase to the guest room.

"It's so good to see you, Ci," said Rachel giving Cierra another sisterly hug.

"You too. This is a very nice neighborhood and your townhouse is beautiful," Cierra complimented as she looked around the French styled décor.

"I know. Girl, I can't complain," said Rachel giving Cierra a high-five. The two snickered as Damien reentered the room.

"What's so funny?" he asked.

"Oh, nothing. Just girl talk," Rachel responded.

"You two have started already," said Damien humorously.

"You know how it is," Cierra replied.

"Yeah, I do. So, when was the last time you talk to my man?" Damien asked as they all walked to the family room to chat a minute.

"I spoke to Chris last week before I left to come here."

"Yeah? Well, you know he was very upset with you," informed Damien.

"What are you talking about?"

"The fight with that dude."

"How do you know about that?" She looked at Rachel.

"Ci, I didn't say anything. Chris told him. C'est ça," Rachel quickly explained.

"Ci, you know how the fellas stick together. We're tight as thieves."

"What do you want me to say, Damien?"

"Nothing. All I'll say is, Chris wasn't too pleased to see you out on a date."

"I wasn't on a date. We were just dancing, damn. Damien, I tell you what, whatever you want to say go ahead and tell me now. Get it off your chest 'cause I don't want to hear all this talk about Chris while I'm here visiting," said Cierra a little annoyed at the conversation. Rachel sat quietly across the room anticipating Damien's reply.

"Look, what happened is between you and Chris. I know you guys will work it out eventually," said Damien.

"So, do you think I'm wrong to move on?" Cierra asked.

"Have you really moved on or are you just trying to get back at him?"

Damien's suggestion that she was being spiteful irritated Cierra. She replied, "Damien, he screwed up. So, why should I just go back to him because he says 'I'm sorry' after deceiving me for almost the whole damn school year?"

"Look Ci, I just want what's in the best interest for you both. He's my boy and you're my girl's best friend. I don't want to see either of you do something you may regret," Damien said sincerely.

"I understand where you're coming from but quite frankly Damien, I don't trust him."

"Ci, the man messed up. There's no question about that but he's truly sorry."

"So, he's talked to you about it, huh?"

"Yeah. The brother gave up his dream to come back and be with you. Doesn't that mean anything to you?"

"Yes, Damien, it does. But I shouldn't be held accountable for his actions. I didn't ask him to leave the Jets."

"I know and that's what I'm saying. Do you know how hard it is to get into the NFL? Do you realize how hard he worked all these years to get there? Ci, the brother loves you so much he gave that up. Now he sees you out with some other guy. He's pissed. But you didn't hear it from me."

As a pro-football player himself, Damien's heart went out to Chris for the sacrifice he made. But unknowingly, he spread Chris' distorted version of the true reason why he left the Jets' preseason training camp. Throughout his conversation with Cierra, Damien kept his promise to Chris not to tell her that he stopped through to visit them on his way from camp. For a moment, Cierra felt at fault for Chris leaving the Jets. Perhaps she was too hard on him and should have taken him back.

"Okay you two, that's enough talk about Chris. Come on Ci, let me show you around," Rachel interjected.

She took Cierra on a tour of the large townhouse and made plans for the weekend. Damien approached them in the game room and announced he was headed to a sports bar with a couple of teammates. He gave Cierra a friendly hug and told her to think about what he said. He then gave Rachel a juicy peck on the lips, said, "Love you girl," then exited the home.

On Saturday, Cierra and Rachel spent the afternoon at the bridal shop in Tysons Corner searching for a replacement, wedding gown for Rachel. Although they didn't find the perfect gown, they enjoyed a minor shopping spree and lunch at Armand's. When they returned to the townhouse, Cierra phoned Terrance to check on him and say hello. Surprised to hear from her, he talked for a while about general things such as work and his master's degree. When the conversation reverted to the incident at the Underground with Chris, he assured her that he wasn't mad at her about the fight and that everything was cool. Cierra felt relieved because she truly liked him as a friend and was regretful about the fight.

Later that night Damien treated Rachel and Cierra out to dinner at Clyde's. The three ate dinner with laughter and good conversation. Damien invited Cierra to a Redskins pre-season game. She gladly accepted the kind gesture but forewarned that she didn't want him playing cupid and have Chris there at the same time. Damien wiped his mouth, placed his napkin on the table, and said, "Now see, there you go. Nobody mentioned anything about Chris. I know you like the sport and thought you may want to come and hang out with your girl and see the game. That's all."

"OK. In that case, I'll come."

"Cool. Now, do you two ladies want dessert?"

"No thanks, sweetie. I'm stuffed and tired," replied Rachel.

"Me too. Plus, I need to leave early tomorrow morning," expressed Cierra.

"A'right, but don't ask for any of my ice cream," he joked as he ordered his dessert to go. After they arrived at the townhouse, they all relaxed in the basement recreation room and watched Sylvester Stallone in Rocky IV for their evening entertainment.

Early on Sunday, Cierra left Reston, VA and returned home. She entered her neighborhood and turned the corner to her street. To her surprise, Chris' black Pathfinder was parked in her driveway. *I don't believe this shit.* Upon, entering the kitchen door her mother greeted her, "Cierra, look who came to town to see you."

"Hi Chris," Cierra said with a look of shock and disapproval. Chris stood to hug her. Mrs. Sykes interrupted, "Well, I'll leave you two alone. Chris, it's nice seeing you. Hope to see you again soon." Mrs. Sykes placed her apron on the back of a chair and exited the room.

"Chris, what are you doing here?"

"Obviously, I came to see you."

"You just can't pop up like this. You should've called first." Cierra walked around him avoiding his gesture for a hug.

"Damn, Ci. So, it's like that? I don't even get a hug?"

Cierra opened the fridge to take out the ice tea her mother just made and said, "Chris, I know how you feel. But you have to give me some space." She poured the tea into a glass and took a sip. Chris pushed her glass aside so he could have her complete attention.

"Ci, are you telling me that you don't want to see me anymore?"

"I just need my space that's all."

"Why, so you can go out with that dude from the club, like you don't have a man in your life?"

"Chris, you stopped being my man when you decided to put your dick in that skank bitch Amy."

"This is ridiculous."

"Ridiculous? Chris, not only did you cheat on me, but you picked one of the trashiest girls on campus to do it with. How do you think that makes me feel?" Cierra angrily asked him.

"Look Cierra, I didn't come here to fight with you. I was hoping we could work through some of this. Can we do so without all the anger and name calling?"

"I don't know, Chris."

"Well, what is it that you want? What do you want from me?" Chris asked desperately.

"I told you. Give me space," said Cierra.

"Why?" Chris asked. Cierra remained silent. "Why?" he demanded again.

"Because- because- I might want to date other people," Cierra replied, wanting him to feel uneasy.

"What? Are you serious? You can't be serious. Ci, are you sleeping with this guy?"

"I'm not discussing this."

"Ci, I asked you, are you sleeping with this guy?"

Cierra looked him in his eyes and said nothing. Chris grew agitated and raised his voice, "Are you sleeping with this guy?"

"Chris, lower your voice. You're in my parents' house and my mom is here."

"You know what? Forget about it."

"Chris, you're going off on a tangent."

"Am I? This is bullshit you know that, right? I mean, Ci, how long have you known this guy, huh? What could he possibly mean to you?"

As much as she wanted to tell Chris her friendship with Terrance was platonic, she again stood in silence. Chris walked toward her, looked into her eyes and asked, "Do you still love me?" Cierra's heart pulsated heavily because she knew deep inside her soul she did but pride prevailed.

"Chris, I just need some space from you that's all."

Chris' brown eyes watered, as he consented. "Fine. I see that this is what you really want and I don't want to cause you any more grief. Ci, have it your way but know this, no man will ever love you like I do and you will never have the love that we had because we were friends and lovers. What we had no other man can ever replace. If you find that genuine thing that we shared, then more power to you." He turned to leave out of the door.

"Chris, wait."

He turned around to see what she wanted. Cierra walked to him and gave him one of their special bear hugs.

"I still care about you, Chris."

"Yeah. I hear you."

"I do. Are you staying with Zack?"

"I was, but I think I'll head back to Baltimore. You've made it painfully clear that there's nothing for me here."

As he descended the back porch, Cierra watched him wipe the tears from his eyes and climb into his SUV. Regretful thoughts twirled in his mind. *Everything is wrong. I've messed up so badly.* Losing Cierra and getting cut from the Jets was more than he could handle. The idea of her dating another man made him angry, jealous, and sick on the stomach. He then thought about how he lied to Damien. The deceit ate at him like a slow, deadly cancer. He felt bad about his actions, but he just couldn't summon the courage to tell Cierra or Damien the truth, particularly now that his lies festered. *Damn, what am I becoming?* He replayed his July fourth visit to Reston, VA over and over in his head. He was more than sorry that he stopped to talk to Damien about joining the Redskins. Cierra watched him drive away.

> *Lord, what have I done? I pray I made the right decision. God, if it's meant to be, I pray you will bring us back together and if not, then may we both find happiness elsewhere. Amen.*

September

The week of Labor Day marked eight weeks into Cierra's financial plan. A plan she derived to save three months worth of salary before moving out of her parents' home. Two months into her plan wore at her spirit like burlap against bare skin. Weary and with $4,500 saved, Cierra wanted to jump ship and leave 1810 Berman Street once and for all. But each time she told Kelly she wanted to quit, Kelly encouraged her to stick with her three-month plan.

The phone rang interrupting her light sleep. She looked at the digital clock, eleven-thirty p.m. *I know this has to be Kelly. Who else would call at this hour?* But to her astonishment, another familiar voice occupied the phone, one she hadn't heard since July tenth. She immediately recognized the charismatic voice.

"Hey, Ci. How are you?"

"Hi, Chris." She was surprised and excited to hear from him and desperately needed to talk to the only man she every shared her family's problems with.

"What's up?" he asked relieved and delighted to hear the warm welcome in her voice. Since he last saw her in July, he conquered most of his depression and wanted to try to reconnect with her in some small way, if possible. Their pleasurable tones indicated they missed each other.

"It's so good to hear from you," Cierra said with enthusiasm.

"Yeah? It's good to hear your voice too. I was thinking about you and just thought I'd give you a call. So what's been up? How's the new job?" Chris asked wanting to know the latest events in her life.

"Chris, the job is great, but I'm so miserable at home."

"Baby, what's wrong?" he asked. She liked that he still called her baby. She explained her financial plan and how she wanted to throw in the towel at this point, and move away. Much to her surprise, he agreed with the financial plan and encouraged her to hang in there.

"Ci, I know it's hard for you, but you will come out better in the long run," he commented.

"But Chris, dad is drunk almost every night. His yelling and cursing is none stop and he keeps trying to pick fights with mom and me. I'm so stressed all the time. I just want out. I want some peace in my life!"

"Baby, I know how you feel. Believe me. I don't want you in that situation no longer than you need to be. But if you have an opportunity to save nine grand, you should. Plus, you're already half way there."

"I know but it's so hard," Cierra admitted.

"Are Kelly and Josi supporting you?" Chris asked hoping that they were.

"Yeah, mostly Kelly," Cierra replied.

"I don't mean to pry, but do they know what goes on in your home?" Chris asked.

"Not really. I mean they know my dad drinks and curses but that's it. I never disclosed everything about the abuse to them. It's too embarrassing."

"All these years, I thought they knew," Chris commented rather stunned. Instantly he knew this was his connection to her that would keep a door open if handled properly.

"Okay, well look, you know you can talk to me anytime. I know we've had our ups and downs but I still care about you and don't want to see you hurt." Cierra didn't speak but felt some relief in his words. He continued, "Listen, tell you what, if you don't mind, I'll call you once a week to check on you and see how things are going. OK?"

"OK," Cierra agreed. She needed the outlet and was thankful he was still there for her in that capacity. The two continued their conversation into the early morning, catching up on all the latest happenings in each other's lives. Chris told her how he got a job with the prestigious Johnson and Patterson Architect Group known as JPAG in downtown Baltimore.

"Chris, that's wonderful. You're so talented at drawing and building. You will do great. I'm glad to see you're putting your college degree to work."

Cierra's encouraging words reassured him that he accepted the right offer. He explained how he interviewed with a number of different companies but either the pay or the position didn't fit his requirements. Then JPAG contacted him to schedule an interview.

"Ci, that was the toughest panel interview I've ever been on. They have a rigorous process."

"But it paid off you got the position, salary, benefits, and perks that you wanted."

Proud of his accomplishment, Chris smiled and said, "Yes, I did. I'm just glad that I got my degree and that there's life after football."

"Chris, I'm so proud of you. You'll always be a winner no matter what you do because you're smart and have the drive."

"Thanks, Ci. That means a lot to me. Well, I better let you get some sleep."

Cierra wanted to chat just a little longer so she continued, "Before you go, when do you start your new job and what's your title?"

"I start this upcoming Monday and my title is Senior Architect Consultant. My first assignment is to help Price Walters & Associates design a new office building in Towson, MD."

"Wow, Chris that's exciting. I wish you well and it was great talking with you."

"You too, Ci. Say uh, you know I'm going to be in Richmond for Labor Day to see Zack. It would be great to see you while I'm there. I'm thinking maybe we can do lunch or something small like that."

Cierra's heart took a weird turn and she felt excited about the idea.

"Uh, yeah, that would be nice," she agreed.

"OK. I'll call you when I get in town."

"Okay, Chris, I'll talk to you later."

Cierra hung up the phone feeling all warm and bubbly inside. She looked at the digital clock on her nightstand. *How in the world am I going to wake up in six hours for work?* She tried to sleep but Chris' smooth sexy voice played over and over in her head. His invitation to lunch floated through her mind like a falling feather. Finally, at three thirty a.m., she dozed off to sleep.

The Labor Day weekend quickly arrived, marking the last 1988, summer holiday. As promised, Chris called Cierra to meet for lunch. When she drove into Bennigan's parking lot, Chris' SUV was already parked. Butterflies circled about her stomach as she entered the restaurant. He greeted her with a hug and she hugged him back just as affectionate. Chris shook his head while he smiled and absorbed her presence.

"Why are you shaking your head?" Cierra asked out of curiosity.

"You're so beautiful. I just can't believe I-, never mind."

"No go ahead, tell me."

"Let's just say you never know what you have until it's gone. It's really nice seeing you, that's all."

"You're not looking so bad yourself, Christopher Jackson. I see you're still in shape," Cierra commented admiring his athletic build. She still found him very sexy and pleasing to the eyes. There was a moment of silence as they stared reminiscing about each other. Then the hostess interrupted and sat them at the booth he requested. They started their evening conversation with a discussion about Cierra's financial plan. Chris encouraged her again to stay the course and don't quit. He then offered that if she liked, he would come see her again after she settled into her new apartment at the end of October. The mere thought of them alone made her body tingle. *How would I handle that? I would be cool. We're just friends, nothing more and nothing less. After all, we have a history together. He could see my life's progress.*

"Yeah Chris, that would be cool. I move into the apartment the weekend of Halloween. So, you could come and help me hand out candy."

"Word. That's settled," he agreed.

The conversation was going so well that Cierra decided to ask, in a joking but serious way, "Chris, are you dating now? Surely, a young, fine brother such as yourself is not without someone," her inquiring mind wanted to know.

"Actually, I'm not dating anyone seriously."

"You're not dating anyone? Come on, no way," she said in disbelief.

"Seriously. I mean I go out but that's about it," he replied.

Cierra looked at him sideways as if that would help her determine his sincerity. Chris thought about telling her how he had met a young lady who he had been out with a few times to the movies and dinner and had one or two intimate encounters, but he believed she had enough on her mind to deal with and he was afraid it may hurt her feelings regardless if they were just friends or not. So, he kept his love life to himself and asked her about her social dating.

"What about you? Are you dating someone?" He expected her to say something about Terrance, but she didn't.

"No," she replied.

"What about that dude at the club?"

"Who, Terrance? He's just a friend. We talk every blue moon."

"I see," Chris remarked. He changed the topic of their discussion back to their careers and goals, something he believed that was less stressful than conversations about dating activities. Cierra enjoyed the exchange of dialogue.

Their luncheon ended with a bear hug and kiss on the cheek at Cierra's car. As Chris released her, his arms moved slowly down around her, stopping at the right spot on her lower back that made her tingle inside. Being that close, only heightened the chemistry that sparked all afternoon while they ate. Their bodies meshed as if each part knew where to go without consciously wondering if this was right or wrong. She wrapped her arms around him landing her hands softly on his strong, back muscles, the very ones she used to watch flex in her dresser mirror as he made love to her just the way she liked it. They held each other a moment longer. Chris leaned toward her neck, took a whiff of her Tiffany cologne, and softly said, "You smell so pretty."

For a split second, Cierra wished he would kiss her right in the spot he sniffed because no matter how minuscule, she recognized that something about their love still existed. After one last hug and peck on the cheek, they each drove their separate ways.

Cierra drove home, rushed into the house and ran upstairs. She grabbed the phone and quickly dialed Rachel. She told Rachel all about her outing with Chris. Rachel was glad to hear they had a good time and hoped they worked things out. She also apologized to Cierra for not calling more frequently.

"Ci, I've been meaning to call you. But I've just been so busy with the wedding plans and traveling to New York for modeling gigs. And, to top everything, I can't seem to shake this virus thing that is making me feel sick, emotional, and has made my menstrual crazy. I didn't come on again this month."

"Rachel, you sound like you're pregnant not sick," Cierra informed remembering the pregnancy symptoms she experienced earlier this year with Chris' baby.

"I sound what?"

"When was your last period?"

"I think my last one was in June," Rachel said nervously as she calculated the days.

"Girl, you need to go to the drug store and buy an EPT and see what's up," Cierra instructed.

"I think you're right. I'll pick one up today and do the test in the morning. I'll call you with the results."

"Okay girl, I'll chat with you then."

At six a.m. the next morning, Rachel started Cierra's day with a squeal into the phone.

"Ci, you were right! I'm pregnant!"

"I knew it. Rachel, that's wonderful. How far along are you?"

"Six weeks."

"Did you tell Damien?"

"No, not yet."

"Why not? He should know," Cierra said puzzled. She remembered how excited Chris was about their baby and thought Damien should have the same experience.

"I don't want to tell him because he's traveling. The team has a series of away games and I don't want him to worry and mess up his game, especially since he's doing so well. I'll tell him when he comes back home for their next home game."

"Okay, if you say so. Have you told your mom?" Cierra asked still excited.

"I haven't told anyone except you. I want to tell Damien first then I'll tell my mom," Rachel said.

"Okay," Cierra said looking at the clock, needing to get ready for work.

"Ci, you have to promise me that you won't say a word to

Damien, Chris, or anybody. When I'm ready, I'll let him know," Rachel insisted.

"OK already. I promise." Even though Cierra disagreed with Rachel's decision not to tell Damien until he returned home, she respected Rachel's wishes.

"Thanks, Ci. C'est ça. I'll talk to you soon. Smooches."

They ended their conversation both being excited about Rachel's pregnancy and Cierra's rekindled friendship with Chris. It was a good Labor Day weekend.

> *Lord, so much has happened, as You know. I'm ecstatic that Rachel is gonna be a mom. I pray she has a healthy pregnancy and baby. I pray for her and Damien as new parents. I'm also thankful for the friendship You have allowed Chris and I to restore. I pray You make clear his purpose in my life. Amen.*

Fall 1988

Between Labor Day and the end of October 1988, Chris called Cierra once a week like he promised. She looked forward to his Tuesday night calls because they helped her face the remaining days of the week at her parents' home.

When Terrance traveled to Richmond, he generally called Cierra on Thursday to confirm any friendly outings for the weekend. He could always tell when he called the Sykes household on a bad night; Cierra seemed a very different person, distant, moody, short patient, and sometimes just mean. He took the brunt of all of her mood swings and begged her to tell him what was happening, but she refused to share that part of her life with him.

The weekend of Halloween arrived, marking the end of Cierra's financial plan. Mr. Wilburn gave her Friday off from work so she could move into her new apartment. She and Josi made most of the trips back and forth from Berman Street to her spacious, swank, one bedroom apartment in the West End. Kelly participated after the end of her workday at Merrill-Lynch.

Mr. Sykes watched from the kitchen table as Cierra and her friends walked in and out like army ants carrying Cierra's belongings. Kelly and Josi didn't mind him as long as he didn't say anything to them. Even when sober, his presence made them uneasy. The girls loaded Cierra's last boxes while Cierra did a final walk through. They tried to contain their excitement, but they each knew how important this day was to Cierra physically, mentally, emotionally, and spiritually. Cierra gave her mother a huge hug and thanked her for everything. Her mother's eyes watered as she said, "Cierra, you act like you're never coming back."

"Mom, you know that I had no intentions of staying here."

"I know. It just seems so soon."

"Soon? It seemed like a lifetime to me. Mom, I'll be around. I'm still in the area."

"I know. I just wish you would stay. I worry about you when you're not home." Cierra suspected that her mother's worries really weren't about her but more about her mother's dealings with Mr. Sykes.

"Well, don't worry, mom. As always, I'll be fine."

Her mother wiped away her tears with her apron. Cierra looked at her father and said, "Later dad." He grunted. She opened the back door, stepped onto the porch, spread her arms as wide as she could and yelled, "Free at last! Free at last! Thank God Almighty, I'm free at last!"

"Alright Martin, get down off your podium and let's go," joked Kelly and Josi.

Cierra jumped from the top step and jogged to the Beamer. With water filled eyes, Mrs. Sykes watched from the front living room window as Cierra drove out of the driveway. Cierra, Kelly and Josi worked diligently through the evening to clean and start setting up the new apartment. To close out the night, they ordered pizza and soda and had a picnic on the empty living room floor as they gossiped about Cierra's new neighbors and joked each other as usual. They left around midnight.

At eight a.m. the next morning, the phone line was turned on. Cierra called Terrance and told him that she finally moved in. Excited for her, he expressed how badly he wanted to come check out her place but was tied up at work and wouldn't be back in town for two weeks. He apologized then made plans to see her the second weekend in November. She agreed then phoned Chris.

"Hey Chris, guess what?" Cierra questioned excitedly. By the enthusiasm in her voice, he suspected she wanted to share good news of some sort.

"What? You sound very cheerful."

"I did it! I have my own place and money in the bank. I feel as free as a soaring eagle."

"Ci, that's great! I knew time was getting close for you to make that move. I'm happy for you. You, more than anyone I know, deserve this. Have your friends checked it out?"

"Yeah, Kelly and Josi helped me move," she answered appreciative of their help.

"Cool. So, when do I get a chance?" Chris asked, letting her determine when or if she still wanted to see him.

"Are you serious?" Cierra asked surprised by his question.

"Yeah, remember I told you a while ago I'd come see you."

Cierra thought about his request and believed she was ready to be around him again.

"OK, um, when were you thinking about coming?" she asked believing he would say next week.

"How about today?" He waited for her response with his fingers crossed.

"Today? Well um, I don't have any furniture right now. It won't arrive until five today. If you come any sooner, it won't be very comfortable. I only have my air mattress to sit on," she explained while stumbling over her words.

Chris didn't mind and persisted he come. He desperately wanted to see her again. With some persuasion, Cierra agreed to his visit. She hung up the phone, looked at the clock and thought, *OK it's nine a.m. He'll be here by eleven thirty. What to do first?* She scanned the apartment and quickly realized that she didn't have any food. She made a mad dash to the store to buy a few things they could snack on plus a bottle of wine and a small case of beer. She returned home at eleven to finish arranging the apartment as fast as she could in the allotted time. She hung the remaining clothes in the closets and unpacked her shoes. She ran empty boxes to the dumpster and placed unopened boxes along the back wall of the dining room. Then she took a quick shower and changed into a pair of stone washed jeans and a white, v-neck cashmere sweater. At eleven forty, she heard the highly anticipated knock at her door.

I hope she likes this. Chris held his housewarming gift behind his back. His heart pounded heavy in his muscular chest as he heard Cierra approach the door. She inhaled deeply to control her breathing then opened the door as she exhaled. There stood Chris with a small bouquet of flowers in one hand and a 'Welcome' mat for outside her door stoop in his other hand.

"Chris, this is so sweet. You really didn't need to get me anything." She hugged him and her touch sent surges through his yearning body.

"It wouldn't have been right to come empty handed. Besides this way, I'll always be here to welcome you home every day. All you have to do is look down at the mat."

"How cute. Well, don't just stand there. Put the mat down and come in."

She gave him a tour of the empty apartment and again explained the furniture was on its way. Chris barely heard her explanation, as he was thrilled just being alone with her. While she waited for the furniture delivery truck, Chris helped her unpack the last of her kitchenware. They engaged in light hearted, friendly conversation that came effortlessly. Cierra enjoyed the feeling of him in her apartment. It reminded her of old times at Virginia Tech.

At one o'clock that afternoon, Ashley's Furniture movers knocked at her door. Cierra looked through the peephole and was delighted to see that the furniture delivery was four hours early. The furniture was "starter furniture", nothing high-end, just good sturdy transitional furniture to get her established and comfortable. The poplar wood and glass living room tables accented the sage chenille sofa. Four wrought iron dining room chairs accompanied a round glass table, and the bedroom furniture made of light maple wood with pewter hardware completed her new furnishings. Chris liked the new pieces and helped her arrange them where she wanted. Desiring to make her living space feel like home, Cierra convinced Chris to go shopping with her at Marshall's for some accessories.

By evening, they were tired of fixing up the apartment and decided to take a break. They drove around town to some of their favorite spots like Bryan Park and the Fan District. They then ate dinner at Red Lobster finishing in time to catch a seven o'clock movie at the Regency Square Mall. Cierra was dying to see

"Halloween 4: The Return of Michael Myers". As dusk settled, the day came to an end, and they returned to the apartment around eleven p.m. Cierra decided to ask Chris to spend the night so he wouldn't have to travel back to Baltimore so late.

"Sure, that'll work. Where do you want me to sleep on the sofa?" Chris asked looking at the large sofa. As comfortable as it appeared, he would only sleep there if necessary.

"You can bunk with me," said Cierra expressing a familiar smile to him.

"Bet," Chris replied glad of her offer.

Cierra lit candles in her bedroom and turned on the stereo to the Quiet Storm as Chris started the shower.

"Are you coming in?" he questioned as he held out his hand gesturing her to join him. She hesitated for a second as a brief thought raced through her mind. *Am I really ready for this?* She wanted this moment to belong to her man of four years. She wanted to pleasure him and be pleased by him. She needed to feel the closeness she secretly longed for. She undressed and stepped into the shower. Within seconds, Chris made her forget about her doubts. He savored every moment as the shower became their seductive rain forest. As the water ran down their bodies, Chris gave Cierra the most sensuous soft kisses all around her neck. His large strong hands touched all her erogenous zones that only he knew. He suckled her breast giving extra attention to her hard nipples. He kneeled and became eye level with her stomach then swirled his tongue in her navel then into her neatly trimmed patch. He spread her legs and continued to swirl his tongue around her labia. Cierra's head filled with thoughts of how badly she wanted him to penetrate her. She missed their perfect fit. She ran her fingers through his freshly cut hair, holding tighter as he teased her clit. She climaxed with so much pleasure that she forgot they were in an apartment and hoped that her neighbors did not hear her loud moans of satisfaction. Chris stood and faced her. The water fell romantically from his eyelashes.

"Chris-" she began.

"Shhhh. Don't say anything. Just enjoy tonight," he replied as he placed one finger on her lips. Cierra listened and placed his finger in her mouth. She then returned the body exploration and Chris found himself as delighted as Cierra, except he didn't care who heard him.

Their lovemaking continued outside of the shower and for the remainder of the night. Chris carried Cierra's wet, naked body from one end of the apartment to the other as they christened each room with their passionate affections. He wanted her to remember him making love to her in every room of her new home. He wanted her to think about him the next time she sat a glass on the kitchen counter, the next time she rested her hands on the bathroom basin, the next time she sat in her kitchen chair, the next time she relaxed on the sofa, the next time she hung her clothes in the closet, the next time she crawled on her knees on the carpet, and definitely every night as she rested in her bed. *She has to know this is my heart I'm giving her. She has to know nobody had me like this. God, I've missed her. Please let her be mine again. I love her so much*, he thought as they went from room to room.

Cierra felt like she was suspended in time and tossed to another world where nothing bad had ever happened between them. She loved Chris back as intensely as he made love to her, touching, kissing, and caressing him on every spot that she knew would excite him. She wanted all of him, every internal and external part of him.

"Chris baby-," she began.

He quieted her again, "Shhhh," and continued with his mission to satisfy her until they fell asleep, arm in arm, completely exhausted.

Cierra and Chris awoke Sunday morning still in each other's arms, one not knowing quite what to utter to the other. Their hearts had done all the talking last night so what was left to say? They dressed in almost complete silence with just a few small jokes here and there. They tried to make the morning less awkward.

"Ci, you were a trip yesterday, screaming at the movie. I don't know why you like watching scary flicks at Halloween. You're always frightened. You stayed up under me the entire night."

"Don't flatter yourself," she teased knowing that he was partially right. Her other reasons for being so close to him had nothing to do with the movie. They both understood that.

After brunch, Chris prepared for his trip back to Baltimore when the phone rang.

"Are you gonna answer your phone?" Chris asked.

"Huh? Oh yeah," Cierra replied as she walked to the furthest phone away from him. As she suspected, Terrance called to say hi and check on her. Chris sat patiently on the sofa and waited. When she returned to the living room, he asked, "So, um are you still friends with Terrance?"

"Yes, I am." She felt a large lump in her throat. *How is he going to respond after last night?* Chris stared at her eye to eye then replied, "A'right. You know what you want and what you need." He felt confident that her friendship with Terrance wasn't a threat anymore, especially after their night of passion. *What? Is this the same Chris? No argument this time?*

"Chris, you're fine with that?" Cierra asked bewildered at his new disposition.

"It's your life and your decision. I just want whatever makes you happy. If he's a good friend for you, well I have to accept that."

Cierra, caught off guard with Chris' acceptance, didn't know quite how to take it. *Does he mean it or is this reverse psychology?* Whatever it meant, she welcomed the refreshing attitude.

He did not try to change her mind. He remained cool and collected, like his old charming and charismatic self. There was something nouveau about him that Cierra found attractive. He seemed more certain about himself. *Perhaps landing the job was just what he needed.*

Chris left Sunday afternoon glad he had a great visit with Cierra. They promised each other to talk more frequently then hugged and shared one last French kiss. He ran the back of his hand along her cheek and whispered, "I've missed you, Ci." Instead of telling him what she felt in her heart that she missed him too, she stood there not sure what to say. Cautiously, she replied, "I know. I'm glad you came and I enjoyed our time together." Chris smiled, gave her a peck and said, "I'll call you soon." She watched him descend the building steps, and then she closed her apartment door. She waved to him from the balcony and watched the Pathfinder leave the parking lot. Back inside the apartment, she danced a jig in the middle of the living room then dashed to the kitchen and dialed Rachel. She shared her weekend adventures, everything from move-in day, to the furniture, and of course she saved the best for last, Chris' visit.

"Oh Ci, I'm so happy for you guys. It's been so long since you two connected like that. I hope this is a new beginning for you," Rachel said kindly.

"Yeah. I must admit. It was the best breakup makeup session we've ever had."

"How long has it been since you two were together?"

"Since July when I went to see him in New York. So about four months."

"Wow, that's a long time."

"Hey, switch topics. Did you tell Damien about the baby yet?"

"No. I wanted to tell him last month like we talked about, but the team was going through a lot of adjustments being that it's the beginning of the season. I didn't want to put any extra pressures on him," Rachel answered as she braced for Cierra's response.

"Rachel, that's crazy. Damien would be thrilled. He probably needed some good news. Why won't you tell him? I don't understand."

"Well, we're in Houston, Texas today. He has a game against the Oilers. My flight returns home before his so when he gets back I plan to tell him regardless if they win or lose."

"If you're in Houston, how did you get my call? I phoned your home."

"Girl, you need to keep up with the times. I got call forwarding to my mobile. Damien loves all this new technology and gadget stuff."

"Must be nice."

"Yeah, it is."

"Anyway, you'll be through your first trimester and just telling your fiancée about his baby. You better hope he doesn't get mad with you for not telling him."

"He'll be fine. Besides, that's the least of my worries," Rachel stated.

"What do you mean by that?" asked Cierra with raised curiosity.

"Nothing. You know it's just that so much is going on, that's all."

"Well look, I gotta go. I need to finish organizing my apartment. I have to report back to work tomorrow."

"Okay, Ci."

"Let me know how Damien reacts to the news. I know he's going to be overjoyed."

"OK, c'est ça," Rachel replied rubbing her belly.

They ended their conversation and Cierra remained busy the rest of the day putting the final touches on her new eclectic home.

Rachel sat in the stands that Sunday afternoon watching the Redskins trying to out maneuver the Oilers. The Defensive Coordinator decided to play a few rookies in the first quarter. He called Damien to the front line. The coach wanted to see his competitive edge against a worthy opponent. As a rookie, Damien knew every minute on the playing field was a moment to earn or keep a spot on the team. He ran out to the huddle with his heart pounding like a herd of elephants. He bent over, listened to the Linebacker call the play then went to the line of scrimmage with his teammates.

At 2nd and 10, Coleman suspected the Oilers' offense would throw for a touchdown. Lined up at the thirty-yard line, the Quarterback yelled out the audible. Concentrating on the play at hand, Damien focused on the Wide Receiver, his opponent to stop. The Center snapped the ball to the QB, Damien ran like lightning to cover the receiver. As the ball descended toward them, Damien leaped, intercepted the ball then ran for fifteen yards before someone tackled him. His defensive coverage was spectacular. The crowd roared and cheered for him as the teams switched their offense and defense because now the Redskins had possession of the ball. Damien's teammates saluted him by colliding their chests and helmets with his. His coach didn't say anything. He just wrote something down on his clipboard. Thrilled, Damien returned to the sideline pleased with his performance. The coach didn't play him again until the last three minutes of the game during which he remained focused and perfected his plays.

Although the Redskins lost 41-17, Damien was pleased with his competence. His coach spoke to the team coarsely in the locker room about their overall poor performance because the lost ended their three games, winning streak. However, when he passed Damien on his way out, he said, "Not bad, Hall. Not bad at all. Keep up the good work."

"Thanks coach," Damien replied as he packed his gear. He couldn't wait to tell Rachel. She had already left for the airport to return home with some of the other girlfriends and wives.

When Damien entered the townhouse that night, Rachel greeted him with a warm hug and kiss.

"There's my superstar," she proudly announced causing Damien to blush beneath his dimples.

"You liked how I played today, huh? A brother got skills." He placed a kiss upon her soft lips.

"Sweetheart, you were terrific. I knew you had that guy beat for the interception."

"Coach seemed pleased too," he remarked.

"What did he say?" Rachel inquired hanging onto his every word. Damien placed his arm around her shoulders and told her about the coach's "good work" comment. He liked being able to talk to her about the sport. She absorbed all that he taught her. She'd come a long way since her days sitting in the bleachers at Virginia Tech with Cierra trying to understand the game.

"Baby, do you want to watch some TV with me?" he asked as he made room for her to lie beside him on the sofa. Without a word, Rachel picked up the remote, turned off the television, faced him and in a serious voice said, "Damien, we need to talk." He sat up immediately suspecting something major was wrong because she never disturbs him while he cools out after a game.

"Baby, what's up?" He wondered what had her so serious.

"Well, you know how I've been kind of sick lately and always running out of energy?"

"Yeah."

"Well, there's a reason for it." She looked at him hoping he would take the words out her mouth so that she wouldn't have to say them for fear of his reaction but he only looked puzzled and sat in silence.

"Damien, I um, I um," she stammered.

"What Rachel?" he asked becoming more alarmed.

"I'm pregnant," she said softly.

"Come again. You're what?" Damien asked shocked at the words that fell from her lips.

"I'm pregnant," she said unsure of his next reaction.

"Are you serious?"

"Very."

Damien then jumped to his feet and screamed, "Baby, that's terrific!" He held her in his arms and embraced her joyfully. Suddenly, Rachel broke down and cried.

"Rachel, baby, what's wrong? You're not happy about this?"

"Yes, no. I mean yes. I'm worried," she replied.

"Worried about what?" Damien asked still trying to absorb the fact he was going to be a daddy.

"What about my modeling career? I've worked so hard for this. Now, I'm gonna miss out on a lot of shoots and opportunities when my belly starts to get big."

"Well that won't be for a while, right?" Rachel remained silent causing Damien to grow suspicious.

"Rachel, how far along are you?"

"I'm at the end of my first trimester. We conceived in early July."

"Three months?" He paced the floor upset with her decision to withhold such crucial news. "Why didn't you tell me sooner? I have a right to know. Why did you wait so long to say something?" he angrily quizzed.

Thoughts of Cierra telling her that he would be upset raced

through her mind as she search for a logical explanation.

"Well, the doctors said that most anything could happen in the first few months and a lot of woman miscarry. I didn't want to get your hopes up when something could go wrong. I wanted to wait until I was out of the early risk stages before I told you. You have so much on your plate with football."

He walked towards her, touched her stomach and said, "Rachel, understand this. Nothing, and I do mean nothing, is more important to me than family, not even football. You should've told me. I don't want to miss out on any parts of you being pregnant. That's my son or daughter you're carrying. Don't leave me out."

"I'm sorry, Damien. I thought I was doing the right thing."

He gave her a peck and said, "It's water under the bridge. We'll go forward from here. But please include me. I don't care if I'm on the road, I don't care if we've lost a game, just let me know what's happening. OK?"

"OK," Rachel replied.

"When is your next doctor's appointment?" he asked excited.

"At the beginning of December."

"Let's try to coordinate with my schedule so I can go with you. We play the Eagles on December fourth in Philly. But we play the Cowboys on the eleventh here at RFK."

"That'll work," Rachel replied, happy that things would work out.

"Come on," he instructed. His eyes beamed with joy.

"Where to?" Rachel looked confused as he led her upstairs. He stopped at the top of the stairs and said, "Alright, so tell me, which room have you picked out for the nursery?" She pointed to the second largest bedroom. He walked her to the door, stood behind her and placed his arms around her middle.

"Now tell me, what do you envision for the room?"

After discussing everything from baby furniture to window treatments, Damien then led her to their bedroom.

"Damien, what are you doing?" Rachel asked half laughing.

"I want to get a taste of my little sexy momma," he replied as he nibbled on her ear.

"See that's how we got this one," she replied giggling.

"Exactly," he replied. Something sparked in him and for a reason he didn't quite understand, her being pregnant turned him on and Rachel liked it. She regretted not telling him sooner. *Cierra was right. I should've told him when I first found out.*

Rachel cuddled closer to Damien as he caught a nap after their evening rendez-vous. She savored the moment of the three of them laying there, him, her, and their unborn child. She wished Damien didn't have to travel so much but that was the nature of their world. He was always in and out of town. She calculated her weeks and realized that she would be due the first of May and contemplated about the best time to get married. *The regular football season isn't over until they play Cincinnati on December seventeenth, then there are the playoffs for the Super Bowl in January, then there's the Pro Ball in Hawaii in February, then mini camp starts in April. Good grief March is the only open month. I'll be eight months pregnant in March. Well, it is what it is and if folks don't like it, too bad. C'est ça.*

Early the next day Cierra received Rachel's exciting phone call about how she told Damien about the baby.

"Finally! Now, I can congratulate him."

"Ci, I have to admit, you were right. I should've told him long ago."

"Was he excited?"

"Very. This is going to be an exciting time for both you and me. We're both getting what we want. I can't wait to see what the future holds."

"Yeah, me too. Things are going well with Chris."

"Will you see him this weekend?"

"No, but we'll probably see each other at Thanksgiving. Plus, Terrance is stopping through this weekend to check out my new spot."

"Terrance? Girl, you bet not let him interfere with you and Chris."

"I'm not. He's just a very sweet guy."

"Mmm Mmm. Yeah ok, I hear you."

"Seriously. Anyway, I gotta run. I'm glad everything worked

out with Damien. I'm happy for you two. Take care."

"Thanks, Ci."

> *Lord, I hope she's right about Chris and me. We are working through our heartache. I pray we continue to grow together. I love him so much. Thank you for reuniting us. I also pray for the health and wellbeing of Rachel and Damien's baby. I wish my baby was here. The kids would've been best buddies. Nonetheless, I pray Rachel brings new life into the world and may they always be a happy family. Amen.*

November

When Terrance arrived in town on Veteran's Day to see Cierra's new apartment, he noticed something different about her. She seemed happier and more at ease.

"Ci, what's up? You seem a little different today," Terrance asked wondering if she was happy to see him.

"What do you mean? I'm just glad to be in my own place that's all," Cierra explained although her delightful mood had a lot to do with Chris' visit.

"Word. Well, close your eyes. I brought you something," Terrance instructed. He reached in his coat pocket and pulled out a beautiful, lead crystal swan figurine and placed it in Cierra's hands.

"Alright. Now open your eyes."

"Terrance, this is beautiful. Look how the light spectrum reflects off of its wings."

"I thought you might want to start a collection of some sort for your place. So, I thought crystal would be nice. Then I thought how graceful and sweet you are, so I picked out the swan."

"Thank you. This is so nice of you. You're always so generous." Cierra hugged and kissed him on the cheek. She placed the swan in the middle of her coffee table next to Chris' flowers and continued their usual hour-long casual visit. Before leaving, Terrance built up the nerve to ask Cierra about her Thanksgiving plans.

"So, pretty lady, what are you doing for the holiday?"

"I may visit Chris. Over the years, I've always gone to his parents' home in Baltimore for the holiday. It's no fun hanging around Richmond, especially dealing with my dad who is always drunk on the holidays."

"I see." Terrance paused and contemplated inviting her to his mom's for Thanksgiving dinner but decided not to because he sensed something else was going on with Cierra, something more than her being happy about moving into the apartment. He suspected Chris was the source of her joy and felt best to just let things be.

"Well, Cierra, it was great seeing you again as always. You have a really nice place. I'm sure you'll enjoy it."

"Thank you, Terrance."

"Well, I better get going. Have a wonderful time in Baltimore. Perhaps we'll catch up with each other some other time." He reached for his coat.

"Sounds good. Terrance, thanks again for the beautiful swan. It was very sweet of you."

"You're welcome." He departed her apartment with mixed emotions. He wished he knew how to better approach her to get her attention but she seemed too uninterested.

As Cierra gave in more to her feelings for Chris, she asked him if she could visit him in Baltimore for Thanksgiving. He agreed, thinking it would be nice for her to join his family for dinner. Besides, the girl he had started to date was out of town visiting family and Cierra wouldn't be missing anything at her parents' house except a guaranteed intoxicated father. They made plans and the trip was set, she would leave Wednesday, November twenty-third after work and return Friday.

Lord, I have always hoped that if You brought Chris back into my life then our relationship was meant to be and I would give him a second chance. So far, he has started to do the right things to win my heart back. I pray that I have the courage to trust him again and that he and I continue to regain our relationship. I also pray Terrance will always be a dear friend. He looked sort of disappointed when I told him I wanted to spend Thanksgiving with Chris. I hope he understands my feelings. Amen.

Winter 1988

On the morning of December fifth, Rachel prepared for her doctor's appointment. Damien drove into the driveway from practice and stopped her at the car.

"Baby, did you think I was gonna let you go by yourself?" he asked escorting her to his car.

"Well, yeah," Rachel replied surprised he made it home in time.

"Do you want me to go?" he questioned.

"Of course," said Rachel as she climbed into the car.

The new parents-to-be appeared anxious as they arrived at the doctor's office. After signing in and waiting fifteen additional minutes, the nurse asked them to follow her. She took them to the lab and took Rachel's vitals and weight. The nurse then instructed Rachel to roll up her sleeve so she could draw some blood. The nurse marked five vials. Rachel asked, "Do you have to fill up each one of those?"

"Yes, sweetie, I do."

Damien made a squeamish face and watched Rachel endure the extractions. Afterwards, the nurse led them to the examination room and instructed Rachel to get undress and put on the pink paper gown.

The doctor and nurse entered shortly afterwards. The doctor examined her uterus, listened to the fetal heartbeat, and performed a sonogram. Rachel and Damien marveled at everything. Damien held her hand as the doctor pointed out the different parts of the baby's body.

"Wow. That's so amazing," Rachel commented, astonished at

the life growing inside of her.

"Can you tell if it's a boy or girl?" Damien asked curious to find out the baby's gender.

"No, it's too early for that. We'll do another sono at the end of your second trimester. If you want to know at that time and if the baby cooperates with its position, we may be able to tell. Let's see, it looks like your baby's due date is May 4, 1989 give or take two weeks."

"What do you mean 'give or take two weeks'?" asked Rachel.

"Well, the baby was definitely conceived around the first of July. However, any baby may be born two weeks before the due date or up to two weeks afterwards. The date is just a good estimate."

Rachel and Damien intently watched their baby on the monitor. Then the doctor printed some snapshots for them, turned off the monitor, and told Rachel when she wanted to see her again. Damien looked at the sonogram pictures while Rachel dressed. He was extremely moved by the experience. When Rachel reached for her purse to leave, he stopped her. He kissed her on the lips and said, "I love you. I can't wait to see our son or daughter. I want to be right there when you give birth." He rubbed her belly and his dimples deepened as he smiled and beamed at Rachel. They left the doctor's office hand-in-hand.

December first marked a different beginning for Cierra. She felt ready to build a closer relationship with Chris, especially since her Thanksgiving trip went so well. Excited, she called him.

"Hey, Ci. I was just about to call you and wish you happy birthday. I figured that would be alright with you," replied Chris.

"Thanks, Chris. That's more than fine," she replied glad that he was thinking about her.

"So how does it feel to be twenty-three?" he asked jokingly.

"The same. You should know. Your birthday was before mine," she answered playfully then continued, "Chris, I need to see you. There's something I want to tell you."

He tried to get her to tell him over the phone. He suspected her news had something to do with her birthday or Thanksgiving but wasn't a hundred percent sure. He attempted again to get her to tell him, but she insisted telling him in person. They planned for her to travel to Baltimore on the upcoming Friday.

When that Friday arrived, Cierra changed in the ladies' room at the end of her workday from her business suit into one of Chris' favorite outfits. Her ensemble included a soft, rayon burgundy V-neck sweater, black mini leather skirt, black sheer hose, and black leather three-inch pumps. She smiled at her reflection in the mirror, pleased with how gorgeous she looked. *He's not going to be able to keep his hands off of me. This is going to be the best birthday I've ever had.* She exited the building, walked to her car, and then raced North on I-95.

When Chris answered the door, Cierra wrapped her arms around his neck giving him a big kiss. Caught off guard by her zealous greeting, he became very curious to hear her news.

"Wow. What's gotten into you?" Chris asked.

"Sweetie, I haven't felt this good in a long time," Cierra responded.

"So I see. What's up?" He intentionally gave her a platform to announce her news. They walked to the family room and sat on the sofa. Cierra held his hand. Her face and eyes beamed with joy. He liked the sparkle in her feline shaped brown eyes. She took a deep breath then poured her heart out.

Chris sat quietly as he listened to her describe how she realized that she needed and wanted him in her life, and how she discovered there was no other man for her but him. She confessed that although she was attracted to Terrance's gentlemanly ways, she never wanted a relationship with him.

"Chris, I believe we can work out our situation. We have already established the basis by rebuilding our friendship. I think we're off to a great start and trust and more love will blossom from here." She looked at his piercing brown eyes and continued, "Chris, I love you so much. I miss you and I want to get back together."

Shocked by her words, he continued to sit in silence. Cierra broke the dead calm, "Well, aren't you gonna say anything?"

"I don't know what to say. Where did all this come from? For months you have told me that you didn't want us together, that you needed your space. Even when I came to see you when you moved into your apartment, I poured my heart out and made love to you everywhere. I thought showing you how I felt instead of just telling you would've made a difference. But you said nothing of the sort. I told you that I missed you after loving you until I was breathless and all you said was 'I know'. I showed you how much I love you and care for you, how sorry I've been for my mistake, and you didn't acknowledge any of it. That hurt, Cierra. That hurt like hell."

An uneasy moment of stillness occupied the space between them as Cierra reflected on his words, knowing that he spoke the truth. Then Chris asked, "So, what happened? Why the change of heart?"

"I felt the same things you did when you visited me, Chris. I was just afraid to verbally express my feelings, but I made love to you just as passionately as you did to me. Couldn't you see and feel my heart? I revealed mine to you too. I didn't mean to hurt you and I'm sorry if I did. As for what happened, I told you. I know it's you that I want. You touch a part of my soul I just can't deny. We belong together. Chris, I thought you would be happy to know this. After all, isn't this what you've been wanting?"

"Yeah, I did, Ci but that was a while ago. You did a really good job of pushing me away."

"Chris, I did need space and having that space helped me come to this decision." Cierra's heart started skipping beats as the conversation took an unpleasant turn.

"Ci, what really happened? Did you break up with Terrance or did he break up with you?"

"Chris, we never dated."

"Yeah right. I see where this is coming from now. Terrance broke up with you, didn't he?" Chris stood.

"Chris, I told you, we were not in a relationship and I was never intimate with him. My heart is with you and has always been with you."

"Cierra, I don't believe you." He shook his head in disbelief.

"What?" How can you say that?" she exclaimed standing to face him.

"I say that because look how many times you've gone to visit him and he has visited you. I doubt they weren't platonic visits because men don't think that way. And he's always calling you. Every time we're on the phone, he beeps in. That dude wants you. I know what time it is."

"Chris, what are you talking about?"

"Cierra, up until I came to see you at Halloween, we hadn't been intimate since you visited me in New York back in July. That's four months, Cierra. And then you went to D.C. too? I ain't stupid. I know you have needs."

"Chris, I went to visit Rachel and called Terrance while I was in town. I didn't see him. And he's only been to my place once. Other than that, we've been out to dinner a couple of times when he came to town. Why are you trippin'?"

"Ci, tell the truth, you were intimate with him, weren't you?"

"No, Chris, I wasn't," Cierra retorted abruptly.

"I asked you at your mom's house back in July were you intimate with him and you kept quiet. What was that about, huh? What did that mean?"

"Chris, it meant nothing." She thought about the moment he came to visit her in Richmond and regretted her silent treatment. Cierra's head throbbed as much as her heart and an intense headache instantly set in. *This can't be happening.* She found herself in the midst of explaining her actions and decisions, pleading with Chris to believe them.

"Chris, what about Thanksgiving when I visited you?"

"Ci, that was a nice weekend, but we didn't talk about a relationship. We talked about being friends. You made it clear that's what you wanted. Not even just holding you was good enough. I expressed my affections for you platonically over the course of those three days to show you that I can give you whatever you need from me. But every time I tried to have you close to me, you pushed me away. Whenever I tried to kiss you, you turned your cheek, leaving me with only landing a peck. I wasn't trying to have sex with you. Baby, I just needed to feel close to you."

"I just wanted us to start over as friends and take things slow. That's why I talked about us being friends and I enjoyed your hugs and peck kisses. Maybe I just didn't trust myself because I wanted to go slow and I knew that if I allowed myself to be that close to you, I would've done more with you and I wasn't emotionally prepared for that then."

"And you are now? Ci, I don't know what else to say. You always spoke of us as being friends, nothing more. So, after the Thanksgiving weekend when my friend came back in town, I told her that I wanted to date more seriously and that it was just about her and me now. At the time, all you wanted was to be friends. I wanted more but you didn't. Not once did you say anything about getting back together."

"But Chris-"

"But Chris, what? I showed you how much you mean to me time and time again. Don't actions speak louder than words?"

"Yes sweetie, they do and I'm here now. We can have the life we've always wanted together. We can have the family we always wanted. We can make our dreams come true. You don't have to stay with this person. I love you. You're in my soul and I know I'm in yours. Let's just start over," she cried.

Chris' heart felt the common threads that bonded them. He thought about the loss of their baby, their four-year relationship and their deep kindred spirits. He badly wanted to reach out and hold her, but things were different now.

"Ci, it just wouldn't be right for me to walk out on this person. Surely, you can relate to that."

"Chris, please."

"Ci, I can't."

"Why not?"

"I just can't. It wouldn't be fair."

"What about what's fair to me, what about us?"

"Ci, I can't. Please try to understand."

Defeated by his determination, Cierra pulled herself together.

She wiped the salty tears from her cheeks, gathered her keys and walked towards the front door. As she turned the brass knob to exit, she faced Chris and said, "You're right, Chris. You're absolutely correct. It wouldn't be right or fair since you've made a commitment to her. I understand where you stand."

"Ci, baby, I'm sorry," he replied feeling frustrated by their conversation.

"No need. Take care and remember that I love you most."

"Love you too, Ci."

Cierra returned to her car. Chris closed the door and returned to the living room. He sat on the sofa with his head in his hands and yelled, "Shit, shit, shit!" He wished the strange turn of events didn't happen, especially on Cierra's birthday. He felt bad for her but believed he was doing the right thing by staying with his new girlfriend, if for no other reason than to prove to Cierra that he could be faithful to the one he was involved with, even if it meant turning her down.

Cierra drove home crying and broken hearted all over again. What she believed was going to be great news and a wonderful gift turned into the worst news flash ever. Weary and down, she needed to talk to a friend. Kelly and Josi would only make her feel worse with their opposing views, Rachel was with child, and Bridget was visiting one of her boy toys. Terrance was out of the question. She talked to the only friend who was always available.

Lord, where did I go wrong? I followed my heart in all of this only to end up back where I started. If there is any sense to be made out of it all, I pray You show me the way. I feel like Chris and I are two ships that keep passing in the night. I remember my prayer of long ago when I asked that You show me Your will if Chris and I are meant to be together. But I'm confused with the answers around me. He showed me his inner most feelings, love that feels so true, but now the timing is wrong. I know I love him and want to be with him. He still loves me too, it's written all in his eyes. I pray that our feelings for each other live on and that the timing for us to reunite is set to one accord so we can be together again. Amen.

For Cierra, the rest of December was cold and bitter, not just from inclement weather, but also from the lack of phone calls from Terrance and Chris. What happened to the joy she longed for? How did she end up losing both men? She often thought *where did I go wrong?* In order to preoccupy her mind with something other than her social life, she concentrated even more on her job. She successfully managed several projects simultaneously, making her manager Mr. Wilburn glad that he hired such a competent person. He often told her, "Cierra, the Marketing Department is fortunate to have you as a team player. I don't know where we would be without you." Cierra's co-workers Lisa and Terri, as friendly as they tried to be, envied her good standing with Mr. Wilburn. They often overheard him commenting to the Marketing Vice President about how the new girl was doing an outstanding job.

Cierra continued to hone her skills and perfected her craft. She welcomed the challenges Mr. Wilburn gave her and was grateful for the opportunities to showcase her business talents. She received raved reviews and acknowledgements for her efforts.

Then, one cold and windy December afternoon, Mr. Wilburn seemed as brash as the weather. He, like many other managers, was concerned with the news about additional company layoffs. While making hot chocolate in the break room, Cierra watched three senior level employees and two newly hired, entry-level employees leave with severance packages in hand. She was shocked to see the senior level employees released from their jobs because they only had a couple years left at Health First to receive full retirement benefits.

That Wednesday, Mr. Wilburn was in a very bad mood. He summoned Cierra to his office. She nervously wondered if she too was being relieved of her job. Her heart raced with anticipation.

"Cierra, come in. Please close the door." She did as he asked. Mr. Wilburn explained the layoffs and addressed the latest rumor that Health First was moving its operations overseas.

"Cierra, I'm sure you've heard about the layoffs."

"Yes sir."

"Well, before we go any further, let me assure you that your position is not being eliminated."

"Thank you, sir." She breathed with relief.

"The reason I've call you here is because I could use someone of your caliber to help bring restored order and productivity to our unit. As such, I would like to promote you to Senior Product Manager. Would you be interested in the position?"

"By all means, yes, sir."

"Very well. I will have my secretary work out the details for your position and pay adjustments with Human Resources."

"Thank you, Mr. Wilburn. Thank you so much."

Cierra contained herself until she stepped outside his office then she let out a loud but controlled, "Yes!" Mr. Wilburn heard her and smiled as he swiveled around in his chair to look out his window at the falling snow.

The Christmas holidays arrived and Cierra took a week's vacation from work. On the morning of Christmas Eve, she delivered her gifts to her parents. At ten in the morning, Mr. Sykes greeted her at the back door with the distinct order of bourbon on his breath. She brushed by him and ignored his attempt to converse, placed her gifts under the tree and chatted awhile with her mom in the kitchen then soon left. She didn't want to stay any longer than what was necessary.

Later that evening Josi and Kelly picked up Cierra from her apartment. The trio then ventured to Bixby's in Shockoe Slip downtown. The city of Richmond sparkled with white Christmas lights everywhere. The Sixth Street Market Place looked like one big Christmas tree. They drove to the slip where Kelly parked the car a block away from Bixby's. The fabulous trio entered the club like they just stepped off an Yves Saint Lauren fashion runway.

Sporting varying lengths of wool mini skirts with high heel boots, they left just enough of their toned legs to taunt a man's imagination. Wearing the appropriate color and textured top to match each of their individual caramel, butterscotch, and cocoa complexions, the three friends looked sexy with their flawless hair, makeup, nails, and outfits.

As they strolled through the establishment, they ignored the guys licking their lips at them saying, "Yo baby, what's your name? Can I holla at you?" even though they enjoyed the attention. The brothers that offered to buy them a drink, was capable of having a decent conversation, or politely asked if they would like to dance, the girls gave them the time of day. The trio's mission was quite simple, look great, have fun, and get as many free drinks as possible. Cierra loved hanging out with her friends. Around three a.m., they ended their Christmas Eve outing and returned home.

On Christmas morning, Cierra cuddled beneath her favorite cotton sheets in her silky chemise feeling delighted that she did not have to deal with the loud cursing and fussing of her father for a change. *Finally, I have a peaceful Christmas morning.* As she rested giving thanks to the Lord for her new home, Rachel called to wish her Merry Christmas and apologized for not calling sooner. Cierra told Rachel that she didn't need to explain herself while Rachel rambled on about trying to establish a normal household between Damien's trips and practices, and her modeling trips to NYC for a cosmetics line.

"Rachel, I truly understand. Don't sweat it."

"Thanks for understanding, Ci."

"How's the baby?"

"Growing like crazy. My pregnancy is the reason why I started doing cosmetics commercials and print ads. This way I can hide my belly and stay in the business longer. I'll do runway shows again later."

"Sounds like a plan."

"What's up with you and Chris? Did you get back together?"

"Nope. I wanted to but he's in a committed relationship with that girl he's been going out with."

"Did you tell him how you feel?"

"Yep. We talked face-to-face. He said that it wouldn't be fair to her for him to break it off because I always told him I just wanted to be friends."

"Are you serious?"

"Yep."

"Well, what else happened?"

Cierra recounted her Thanksgiving and December visits bringing Rachel up to date about Chris and Terrance.

"Damn Ci, all that happened since Halloween?" Rachel asked feeling almost as disappointed as Cierra. She had hoped Cierra and Chris would reunite.

"Yep. I'm bringing in the 1989 New Year by myself. I think Kelly, Josi and I are going to a house party, but enough about me. Have you guys set a date yet?" Cierra asked about the wedding.

"No, not yet. It's a little more complicated than I thought and I don't want to go into it but it should be soon. Most definitely before the baby is born."

"That's fine. I'm sure you'll have everything straight. How's your mom and dad?" Cierra asked to change the subject. They talked a little while longer then ended the conversation with best wishes for a Happy New Year.

Terrance drove to Richmond as he always did for the holidays. He couldn't resist being in town and not seeing Cierra. So, he visited her Christmas afternoon to say "Hi". His short stay at her apartment pretty much went the way she expected, a how are you doing and what are your plans for the holiday? She told him about her Christmas Eve outing with her friends and Rachel's upcoming wedding.

"Well that should be interesting. You get a chance to see your boy," he commented sarcastically.

"Terrance, don't start," said Cierra.

"I know. That wasn't right. My bad," he apologized. His ill feelings about Chris still surfaced every now and then. Cierra didn't like his sly comments but accepted the fact that there may always be bad blood between the two as a result of their fight.

A couple hours later, Diane Sawyer began the evening newscast and Terrance hinted at his departure.

"Well, pretty lady, I need to get back to my mom's."

"Okay, Terrance. Thanks for stopping by. It was nice seeing

you again." She walked to the coat closet and handed him his jacket. He draped the garment over his arm and just stood at the doorway staring at her.

"Terrance, is everything alright?"

"Yeah. Why?"

"You're acting a little strange. I thought you were ready to go."

"I'm-, it's just that-, well um-, never mind. Take care, Ci." He leaned down and gave her a peck on the lips, a first.

"Terrance, what's up? Are you sure everything is ok?" she asked concerned about his mood and unusual behavior.

"Yeah. I better go. You take care," he commented as he looked at her in a peculiar way then walked through the doorway.

"You too," Cierra replied.

She closed the door, watched him get into his Mercedes and drive away. Her heart drifted to her feet because for some strange reason she sensed this was a final farewell.

Lord, please tell me what just happened here. Why do I feel like Terrance just ended our friendship when he obviously cares for me? I wonder if over the months I sacrificed the possibility of a good relationship with him by desiring Chris? Will I ever see Terrance again? Lord, I pray that I do. Amen.

January

Cierra kicked off 1989 at a New Year's Eve house party on the eastside of town with Kelly and Josi. At midnight, everyone except those passed out, participated in the count down. When they all yelled, "HAPPY NEW YEAR," Cierra watched couples embrace and share that special New Year's kiss. She wished Chris stood with her. Kelly nudged her, "Come on girl. No time for reminiscing about Chris. There're far too many fine, single brothas here."

"Yeah, I know but-"

"But nothing. Come on." Kelly grabbed Cierra by the wrist and led her to the other side of the room where a group of guys huddled. Without hesitation, two well-dressed young men in the group approached Cierra and Kelly and naturally asked them to dance. As they did, Kelly winked at Cierra with her "See, I told you so" look. After a couple more hours of fast tunes and refilled glasses of champagne, the girls called it night and returned home.

Tuesday, January third ended Cierra's week long vacation and she reported back to work. With their nosey minds in overdrive, Lisa and Terri sensed Cierra's down trodden mood. When they asked Cierra how was her holiday, Cierra casually mentioned that the holidays were quiet and peaceful but a little lonely at times. Her thoughts drifted to Chris. She never shared her personal business at work and she thought the vague answer would suffice and send them on their way. Instead, it sparked a notion with Lisa and Terri to pay her back for all her good work and rapport with their manager, Mr. Wilburn.

"We're sorry to hear that, Cierra," said Terri.

"Excuse us a moment, will you?" asked Lisa with a fake expression.

"Sure," replied Cierra thinking her answer served its purpose and sent them away. Lisa and Terri met in the ladies' room as they often did to vent or talk about people.

"Girl, we can get her vulnerable ass now," voiced Lisa.

"Yeah, we can set her up with your no good brother, Kyle," suggested Terri.

"Oh, hell yeah. You took the words right out of my mouth 'cause that's exactly what I was thinking too. That would be the perfect get-back for little Miss "New Employee of the Month". I can't believe Mr. Wilburn came up with that bogus shit," snared Lisa. Lisa was jealous that Mr. Wilburn rewarded Cierra and seemingly hadn't praised her work beyond "That's a good job." For three years, Lisa worked under his management. She felt that she deserved a whole lot more than his robotic acknowledgement of her efforts. She looked at herself in the mirror as she powered the shine off of her face and said, "I'll show her a thing or two."

"Word, girl," said Terri touching up her lipstick in the mirror as well. They discussed their plan and returned to Cierra's desk.

"Hey Cierra, we were just thinking about what you said and all. We think what you need to do is re-enter the dating game," said Lisa with Terri agreeing.

"Nah. I think I've had my fair share for a while," Cierra commented while waiting for a financial report to print from her new, laser printer that Mr. Wilburn authorized for installation in her office. Lisa tried to hide her envy. For the past six months, she asked Mr. Wilburn for a new printer and still she didn't have one. Lisa continued, "I could introduce you to my brother, Kyle. He's staying with a friend in the city and works as a plumber for Roto Rooter. I know he may not have a college degree like I'm sure your male friends have, but he is a really nice guy," she lied.

"Maybe some other time," remarked Cierra as she thought about how Kyle didn't sound like anything she was accustomed to or interested in.

Two weeks later, Lisa revisited her suggestion with Cierra.

"Oh, come on Cierra. How long has it been since you heard from your ex or your other friend?"

"Almost two weeks," Cierra recalled thinking of the last time she talked to Terrance. And she hadn't talked to Chris since early December.

"Girl, he's moved on. At least go out with Kyle just to have fun."

Cierra continued to show a disinterest, but Lisa was not bending. She insisted Cierra come to her place for dinner to meet her brother. Cierra agreed only to get Lisa off her back, but she wasn't excited about the whole setup.

"OK Lisa, fine. I'll come to your place for dinner," said Cierra.

Cierra arrived at Lisa's apartment that evening wishing she was at home working on a marketing proposal instead. When Lisa opened the door, she greeted Cierra with a warm welcome. Cierra entered scanning the small apartment. She looked around but didn't see Lisa's brother. Then she heard the toilet flush and the water run from the bathroom faucet. *That must be him.* The bathroom door opened and out walked Terri.

"Hey girl," she said rubbing her hands with lotion. They said their hellos. Then Cierra heard keys rattling at the door. The apartment door opened and in walked Kyle with a plastic grocery bag.

"Lisa, you need to get that lock fixed. The damn key won't turn right. Here's your bread," he announced not noticing that Cierra sat in the living room.

"Thanks. Kyle, we have a guest." Lisa pointed in Cierra's direction.

"Oh damn, my bad. Hi, I'm Kyle."

"Hi, Cierra."

"Yeah. Uh, Lisa told me a lot about you."

Cierra wondered what Lisa told him. She gave him a look over and found the nutmeg colored, slightly rugged guy to be nice looking after all.

Kyle was not at all shy about approaching her. He asked Cierra if they could go to the movies next weekend. She figured what the heck, "Sure." The three passed the evening eating a Lake Trout dinner that Lisa cooked. The meal tasted great and the company pleasant. At nine p.m., Cierra thanked Lisa for the dinner and returned home.

The week went by business as usual at the job with the exception of Lisa and Terri sending computer messages to Cierra about her upcoming outing with Kyle. They wanted to make sure that she didn't renege. Friday came and Kyle called Cierra to finalize their arrangements.

"So uh, you can pick me up at Lisa's at nine," Kyle informed.

"Pick you up?" Cierra questioned, a little baffled. *Didn't he ask me out?*

"Well, yeah. I don't have a car. I usually take the bus where I need to go. Surely, you don't want to ride the GRTC, do you?" He instantly deceived her, knowing his car was in town.

"No. Fine. I'll pick you up at nine," Cierra responded disgusted with the evening plan already.

"A'right," Kyle confirmed.

Cierra hung up the phone disturbed that Lisa nor Kyle told her that he didn't have a car.

At nine p.m., Cierra drove into the parking lot, walked up the short flight of steps to Lisa's apartment then knocked on the door. As she stood outside waiting, she saw a small flash of light coming from a parked car on the other side of the lot. As she tried to focus in the direction of the twinkled light, Kyle opened the door.

"Hey, what's up?" said Kyle as he exited the apartment.

"Ready?" Cierra asked, hoping she wouldn't regret her decision to go through with this so-called outing.

"Yeah. Which car is yours?" he asked scanning the parking lot. She pointed to her BMW.

"Oh, shit. Word," Kyle replied and walked passed her to the car. She followed with second thoughts about going out.

Across the parking lot, behind the steering wheel of a black, 1989 Ford Mustang sat Paul Phillips, the Drug Enforcement Agency's lead investigator in a Cuban cartel case known as Red Velvet. The skilled, handsome DEA agent monitored the activity of his suspect, Kyle.

Unbeknownst to Cierra, Kyle was a major drug dealer in the racketeering business of Carlos Rodriquez and Lawrence Turner. For over two years, Paul and his team infiltrated and monitored Carlos' illegal drug trafficking affairs in Cuba, and Lawrence's cocaine distribution activities in Brooklyn, NY. Paul wanted all three behind bars, the supplier, buyer, and dealer.

As Paul peered through his binoculars, he pressed the button on his two-way radio and said to the agent on the other end, "Subject is on the move and is accompanied by a black female. She appears to be in her twenties, about five foot seven, caramel complexion, has shoulder length dark brown hair, and is medium framed." He released the button and muttered to himself. *Fine as vintage wine. Sweetheart, what are you doing with this guy?* He watched them enter her car, and then pressed the radio button again. "Subjects are in a navy, 1984 318i BMW with local plates, Alpha, Eagle, Beta, 2, 4, 1. The female is driving. Over."

"Roger that. Running the plate now," replied the other agent.

"Roger. Let me know what you find. I'm tracking," said Paul, placing the binoculars and radio on the passenger seat and starting the car's engine. Ten minutes into his drive, the agent on the radio said, "Paul, I got the information on the girl."

"What'cha find?" asked Paul.

"Her name is Cierra Rae Sykes, born in Richmond, Virginia, age twenty-three, birth date is December 1, 1965. Her parents are Gregory and Brenda Sykes. They live at 1810 Berman Street. Cierra moved into a one-bedroom apartment in the West End on October 31, 1988. She is a graduate of Virginia Tech, class of 1988. She started working at Health First Insurance Company as an Assistant Product Manager in July 1988. She makes fifty thousand dollars annually and her bank records show no unusual activity. She has a savings of nine grand, some of which looks like she used towards her new apartment. Seven thousand still remains. She has no criminal record, no driving violations, and no credit problems. She's clean as a whistle."

"So, why is such a good girl hanging around Kyle Dexter? Over."

"Here's the connection. The apartment address you called in traces to a Lisa Dexter, Kyle's older sister who also works at Health First Insurance Company. Over."

"Mmm, interesting. I'll stay on him. You find out more about the girl," Paul ordered.

"What more do you think there is? Over."

"There's always more. I need to know what I'm dealing with here. Find out who are her friends, boyfriends, what she likes to eat, where she hangs out, does she have pets, what's her routine. I need everything you can find. I'm not letting this case be jeopardized in any kind of way. I must know everything about everyone that Kyle comes into contact with. Got me?"

"Roger, sir. I'll get on it. Over."

Paul followed Cierra and Kyle, parked the Mustang at the end of the movie theater parking lot, and discreetly tailed them. Looking closer at Cierra, he wondered again, *What's a fine girl like you doing with a major drug dealer like Kyle Dexter?*

Cierra and Kyle approached the ticket window while Paul pretended to read the upcoming flicks posted on the billboards.

"Yeah uh, two tickets for Nightmare on Elm Street: The Dream Master," Kyle ordered.

"That'll be eighteen dollars please."

Kyle pat his pants pockets then his jacket, then his pants again. "Damn! I must have left my wallet at Lisa's."

Cierra felt her flesh turn red with anger and embarrassment. She cut her eyes at Kyle and for a split second thought about walking away, getting in her car, and leaving his sorry, broke, no class ass at the ticket window. But she wanted to see the scary movie so she gave Kyle the eighteen dollars. The ticket window worker sucked her teeth and shook her head. Cierra looked at her and said, "I know. Ain't it sad." Kyle pulled one of the oldest tricks in the books then had the nerve to ask for popcorn. Regretfully, she bought one large bucket of popcorn to share and two drinks.

Paul watched intensely. *This girl can't know what Kyle's about if he just pulled that crap.* He sensed she was uninvolved with Kyle's activities but still wanted to be sure. He observed them for the remainder of the night.

When they arrived back at Lisa's place, Kyle leaned toward Cierra and said in a low tone, "Thanks for the movie and all. I'll pay you back when I get paid this week." Cierra, trying to be polite responded, "You're welcome." Kyle gave her an uninvited peck on the cheek that incensed her. He exited the car and walked toward the apartment entrance. Paul watched the quick peck and how Cierra wiped her cheek after Kyle got out of the car, confirming more in Paul's mind that she didn't know what she was getting herself into. Cierra put the beamer in gear then drove home, wondering, *What the hell happened tonight? This was awful.*

The next day Lisa called Cierra to apologize for her brother's lack of chivalry. Terri stood next to her listening into the earpiece as she and Lisa shared the receiver.

"Cierra, if I knew Kyle didn't have any money, I would've given him some. But I guess he was too proud to ask." Cierra didn't feel like discussing the matter any further and made up an excuse to get off the phone. Lisa and Terri burst into laughter about the ordeal after they hung up the phone.

Later that evening Cierra's phone rang again. "Thank the Lord for caller I.D.," she muttered as she read Lisa's number across the display. The answering machine picked up the call. Kyle gave his apologies again and promised to repay her. *Yeah right*, Cierra thought. She reached for the answering machine and pressed delete.

Anxious to redeem himself, Kyle caught up with Cierra at work the next week and asked her out again. She really didn't want to go and told him "no thank you" on more than one occasion, but he was extremely persistent and seemed sincerely sorry about the first outing. So, Cierra agreed and they went to the movies again. This time the outing went much better.

Kyle told Cierra that he enjoyed her company and wanted to go out again. However, he lied and said that his cash flow was tight and that going to the movies was the best he could do for now. He wasn't about to continue spending his drug money on her. She was cool with him but not really his type. He wanted her around for another purpose. The friendship with Kyle marked the first time Cierra hung out with a co-worker's brother and it felt somewhat strange to her. Nonetheless, she accepted his offer to the movies.

> *Well Lord, I prayed for someone to spend time with and You sent me Kyle. He's definitely not Chris or Terrance but he's available and could possibly be refined to be at least a good friend. After all, Lisa is a well-rounded person, so how bad can her brother be? I'll give this friendship a shot. Amen.*

Within a matter of two weeks, Kyle spent more and more time at Cierra's apartment just like he planned. She became uncomfortable about him being there so much. He was intruding on her personal space and his presence began to annoy her.

Paul continued to monitor Kyle's every movement, video taping his coming and going, and tailing him around the city in hopes of acquiring more leads for the Red Velvet case. He wanted to ensure that every charge against Carlos, Lawrence, and Kyle would stick in a court of law. There wasn't any room for mistakes. He provided his boss, Captain Tim Anderson, regular updates and reports regarding Kyle's activities and reminded Captain Anderson that he believed Cierra was not involved with Kyle's drug dealings and was innocent. Paul's superiors accepted his information but ordered him to keep Kyle and Cierra under surveillance. While on the phone, Captain Anderson informed Paul that the FBI was also after Kyle for witnessing a murder in the Gazotti case. He asked Paul to attend a meeting with him and the FBI in Washington, DC tomorrow. As requested, Paul left Richmond later that evening and traveled to DC.

At eight o'clock sharp the next morning, the two federal agencies met at the DEA's office in L'Enfant Plaza downtown. Paul discussed the work that the DEA had done thus far on Red Velvet. He acknowledged the FBI's efforts to bring Kyle in, but expressed the need to keep Kyle free for now. He explained, "Kyle is someone that Lawrence trusts and unfortunately, we need him. We have men undercover in their operation, one right next to Kyle and a female agent next to Carlos. We are this close to shuttin' this shit down. You simply can't arrest this guy. Besides, he can't possibly be your only witness. There's no way you would have a trial against Gazotti with only one witness. His attorney would laugh you out of court. Who do you think you're fooling? We can't afford to let anything disrupt our investigation. We've invested too many man-hours and have lost agents on this case. We won't stand by and let your agency screw this up for us."

"We have just as much right to this scum bag as you. He's involved with some major shit in New York. I want him off the streets and am prepared to take him in. You know damn well the FBI has precedence over the DEA," retorted an FBI detective.

"Paul, you're out of your jurisdiction on this one," said a second FBI detective.

Captain Anderson understood their concerns and tried to smooth things over.

"Look, it's obvious that both agencies have a need for Kyle Dexter and we all want him and his affiliates off the streets and locked away, but we also have to keep our eyes on the big picture, Red Velvet. Carlos Rodriquez is a notorious, crime lord who's trying to get a foothold in our backyard through Cuba. If he succeeds, the United States will be at a major risk of being involved in the largest drug trafficking scandal in the history of this country. Vincenzo Gazotti is a son of a bitch who reeks of bad politics, money laundering, and drugs. But he's on Carlos Rodriquez's payroll. If you wipe out Carlos, you wipe out Gazotti's drug money that he uses to operate his political and business ventures. As you know, Carlos is well connected in Europe, Central and South America. His next move is to start smuggling weapons to terrorists in the Middle East. If he's successful, we all will have a bigger problem to deal with. I think given these circumstances you can understand how important it is for us to use Kyle in our efforts to bring down Rodriquez's organization. All we need is one more major piece of evidence. Kyle Dexter is our ticket."

The FBI agreed to cooperate with the DEA but insisted on leaving one of their agents with them to monitor all activities involving Kyle.

"Do what you need to do. Just don't get in my way. Captain, if you need me, I'll be in Richmond," commented Paul, ending the typical turf battle between the two agencies. He departed DC and immediately returned to Virginia.

On Saturday, Kyle brought two big duffle bags to Cierra's place. "I just need these here for a few days. Don't touch 'em. I'll know if you do," he insisted. Cierra told him that overnight was fine but he could not keep his things at her place for a few days. Unbeknownst to her, one bag contained three hundred thousand dollars and the other bag, a large quantity of cocaine.

Sunday came and went without Kyle stopping by Cierra's place to pick up his stuff. She curiously wanted to peep inside the bags, but judging from the look on Kyle's face when he warned her, she believed that he would notice. She decided to leave the bags alone.

On Monday, Cierra came home from work and saw Kyle reclined in an unfamiliar car with New York tags. He sat idle on the passenger side next to his partner in crime, Jason Beckford. Engulfed in their conversation, they didn't see her pull into the parking lot.

"Man, you gotta get a Lexus like this one. The ride is unbelievable. This car hugs curves like a horny nigga on a woman's phat ass," Jason commented.

"Word. But I got my Benz up north. She's hooked and can fly too. You know this," said Kyle.

"Man, Lawrence is trippin'. I still can't believe he's got you down here driving a Ford Taurus, slinging the goods. He got your ass driving a family car around town," Jason laughed, shaking his head envisioning Kyle behind the steering wheel of the four-door Sudan. "Man, that's jacked up."

"Shut up, fool. I know driving that piece of shit is ridiculous but Lawrence said he don't want to draw any heat to our business here. I must agree that a brotha driving a flashy car around in Richmond ain't too cool when you're trying to establish a new territory. He thinks I should lay low, play it cool, and be a hard working blue-collar man, crazy shit like that. I say the hell with the heat. Man, I hate it down here. Ain't shit to do. I be glad when I can go home." Kyle looked out of his window wishing he was back in the urban vibe of New York City.

"I feel you on that one. I miss Brooklyn too," Jason agreed.

Cierra walked up to the car and tapped on Kyle's window. Surprised by her presence, Jason grabbed the handle of his nine tucked in his belt.

"Chill man. This is her," said Kyle.

"Damn, she's fine," Jason commented while covering his handgun with his shirt.

"Man, shut up," Kyle replied as he pressed the button to lower the window of the tricked out silver Lexus.

"Look, you need to be more careful. Don't creep up on people like that," Kyle warned.

"Oh, really, why? What'cha gonna do, shoot me?" Cierra

responded.

"Whatever. Look, this is my homeboy, Jason. Jason, this is Cierra."

She gave a quick, uninterested, "Hi" then focused her gaze on Kyle. "I thought you were coming to pick up your bags yesterday. We agreed on Sunday not today," she said irritated. Kyle ignored her comments and exited the car.

"Come on man," he signaled to Jason.

They went inside Cierra's apartment. She placed her briefcase in the closet by the front door then proceeded to the bathroom where she splashed warm water on her face to revive herself from a long day at the office. Meanwhile, Kyle and Jason watched TV in the living room. After Cierra touched up her makeup, she called Kyle to the kitchen and told him that he and Jason needed to go because she was going out. He demanded that they stay while she was gone but she refused his request. Kyle returned to the living room and told Jason to make himself at home that they would be there for a couple of hours. Cierra couldn't breathe, she was so furious.

"Kyle, what do you think you're doing? You can't invite people in my place and tell them they can stay here. This is my home."

Kyle walked up to Cierra with fury in his eyes and lied, "Look that's my boy. We go way back. He and his ol' lady had a fallen out. If he needs my help, I'm gonna give it to him no matter where the hell I am." Cierra, undeterred by his body language and hood like actions said, "Negro, please. Y'all need to leave." Kyle slapped her so quickly that she didn't see it coming.

"Nigga? Who the fuck do you think you're talkin' to?"

She instantly regretted using any form of the "n" word.

"I ain't going no goddamn where. Lisa and I had a big argument and I'm not going back there. So, I'm here and that's that," Kyle blurted.

This asshole is trippin'. Going out a few times to the movies with him was not worth all this for damn sure. She could tell Kyle and Jason had been drinking and she knew not to argue with a drunk. So, she left the matter alone for now. Regretfully, she phoned Kelly and told her she couldn't visit with Josi and her. Later that night after the alcohol wore off, Kyle approached Cierra and apologized for slapping her. She accepted his apology because she felt she provoked his actions by calling him a Negro. Kyle and Jason slept in the living room, one on the sofa and one on the loveseat with his legs hung over the side.

The next morning, they were gone before Cierra awoke but the duffle bags remained. She couldn't wait to catch Lisa at work to ask her about what Kyle said about them arguing. Lisa confessed that she and Kyle had an argument about how she disagreed with Kyle spending so much time with Cierra and that he should be concentrating on his wife.

"WIFE? You didn't tell me he has a wife," exclaimed Cierra.

Lisa explained that Kyle and his wife were separated and that's how he came to live with her.

"Lisa, you never told me this. You said that he lived with a friend cross town."

"I just thought the two of you could go out once or twice. I didn't know you would become close," said Lisa.

"We're not close. I mean Kyle is okay to hang out with every now and then, but I don't want a relationship with him. And I definitely don't want him and Jason thinking that they can camp out at my place. But more importantly, you should've told me he has a wife."

"I thought he'd tell you. Plus, he's not talking to me. So, I don't know what to tell you," Lisa commented.

"Look, you need to clear the air with him today because I'm not letting them stay at my place," Cierra said angrily.

Lisa just looked at her indicating she had nothing further to say. Cierra walked away mumbling. *That heifer lied to me. This is all a bunch of bullshit.* There was no way she could be productive today. When Mr. Wilburn passed by her office, he stopped and asked, "Cierra, are you ok? You look a little flushed." She took advantage of his comment and requested to go home early because she didn't feel well.

"Of course. Take tomorrow too if you need it," he offered.

"Thanks." Cierra packed her briefcase and headed toward the elevator. She saw Lisa and Terri snickering at the front desk. They looked at her, waved bye, and cracked up laughing. Cierra felt bamboozled.

Cierra arrived home glad to be away from the office. When she opened the door and saw that Kyle's duffle bags were still by the door, she realized that she forgot to take them to Lisa. *How could I be so stupid and forget to get this shit out of my apartment. Now, Kyle's ass will back. Damn.* The thought of seeing him again gave her a headache. She took some acetaminophen and lied down.

At six thirty p.m., her peaceful nap ended when she heard banging at her apartment door.

"Cierra, open the damn door," Kyle yelled from the outer hallway. She took her time approaching the door. Slowly, she unlocked and opened the door without speaking to Kyle and Jason. He brushed passed her, walked to the refrigerator grabbed two beers and gave one to Jason. They plopped on the sofa and chair, turned on the TV and surfed the cable sports channels. His hidden agenda to move into her place was clear as crystal. Cierra returned to her bedroom and slammed the door. She sat at the foot of her bed and thought about how to rid her apartment of the two hood rats that were obviously trying to move in. When Kyle and Jason were ready to leave, Kyle approached Cierra and asked her for her key in case he returned late.

"You must be out of your damn mind," she replied sharply. She stood her ground ready to block whatever blow he wanted to throw her way. He glared at her and grunted as he walked away. He knew before asking her that it was a gamble. But if the odds ruled in his favor, it was one less thing to worry about. She then heard the door slam behind him. Inside the Lexus, Jason asked, "Man, why are you being so nice to this chick? You should just bogart her like the others."

"Man, shut up. She works with my sister. I have to approach this differently. I'll get the spot don't worry."

"A'right. It's on you, Kyle. Don't piss off Lawrence."

Cierra watched them drive away. *Hallelujah.* When she turned around, the two duffle bags still remained in the corner by the door. *That fool didn't take his shit again?* She turned on the news, sat in the living room, and thought more about her plan to stop Kyle's unwelcome visits. She knew he was violent so she wanted to use the right words so there would be little to discuss about the matter. She wanted to be firm but delicate. The last thing she wanted was to get into a physical altercation.

At six thirty p.m., Kyle and Jason knocked on her door. Cierra opened the door and they entered smelling like beer and cigarettes. She despised their presence. She stood in the living room with her arms folded and watched them get the remainder of the beer out of the fridge. Then Kyle grabbed the duffle bags and they left. No words were exchanged. She looked out of the sliding glass door and watched them get into Lisa's car with Lisa in the driver's seat. *I guess they resolved their differences,* Cierra thought of Kyle and Lisa. When Lisa drove away, Paul followed in the black Mustang.

The next morning, Kyle called Cierra at work for what she didn't know. She thought things ended when they left yesterday. Nonetheless, she used the opportunity to ask about his wife and the other lies he and Lisa told. He didn't answer her. Instead, he asked if they could talk at her place later because he felt bad about how things went down and wanted to explain face-to-face. She hesitated and was about to say no but he quickly assured her that Jason wouldn't be with him and that nothing would happen, he just wanted to talk.

"Fine, whatever," she agreed. *I wish I never accepted Lisa's dinner invitation to meet her brother. All this craziness wouldn't have happened.* She said very little to Lisa and Terri throughout the course of the day. Cierra anxiously waited for quitting time at five p.m. to rush home and end this horrible mess. She planned to restore order in her life.

> *Lord, be with me as I talk with Kyle. I pray the conversation with him this evening puts an end to everything. But mostly Lord, please forgive me for going out with a married man. I didn't know. Amen.*

Cierra arrived home from work at five thirty p.m. waiting to confront Kyle. She looked out of the sliding glass door anticipating his arrival. Just when she thought he was a no show, she heard his footsteps outside her door around seven. Her adrenaline pumped as she walked to the door, turned the knob, and allowed the notorious man and his duffle bags into her home. The tension inside became as cold as the icy, January evening.

"Where's Jason?" Cierra asked.

"Gone. He said he didn't feel welcomed. So he left. I told you he wouldn't be here," Kyle replied as he dropped his duffle bags to the floor.

"Good riddance," she mumbled a little too loudly.

"What did you say?" Kyle asked.

"I said, 'good' 'cause he shouldn't have been all up in my home anyway."

The conversation turned ugly and she regretted agreeing to this meeting. Kyle charged her, stood in her face and yelled, "That's my friend! If I want him here, that's where he'll be! You don't tell me what the fuck to do! I do what I want, bitch!"

Cierra looked at Kyle and thought about her dad's cursing and his out of control behavior. *This can't be happening! And no he didn't just call me a bitch.* She shook off her déjà vu moment and proceeded to tell Kyle to leave.

"Kyle, you need to go, now! Get out of my home!" she yelled.

Paul watched through his binoculars as he monitored the confrontation from his car. With the curtains wide open and the apartment lights on, he had a perfect view of the dispute. He gripped his binoculars harder, detesting the sight before him.

Kyle charged Cierra again, grabbed her by her shirt collar with both hands, and backed her toward the wall. She tried to fight him off but her shoe heel broke and she lost her balance. He threw her to the floor. More bad memories of her dad clouded her thoughts as she remembered him doing the same. Rising from the carpet, Cierra pointed to the door and bellowed, "Get out, you bastard!"

Paul continued to watch, feeling helpless because he couldn't intervene and give Kyle the ass whipping he rightfully deserved. His breathing became heavy and shallow as he gripped the binoculars tighter, wishing he could do more.

Kyle charged Cierra a third time and flung her against the wall. Before she could move, he grabbed a fist full of her hair then slammed her head into the wall, leaving a gaping hole. He relished in her pain and arrogantly whispered, "I ain't going no damn where. So get use to me being here."

Cierra kneed him in his groin to get him off of her. He immediately doubled over in pain and released her. She grabbed her purse and keys and darted out of the door. Holding the back of her head, she ran frantically to her car. She didn't bargain for all this to happen.

"Shit!" Paul said in disgust as he tossed the binoculars aside. *I'm sorry I couldn't be there for you, Cierra.* He felt like he knew her a little, having watched her for so many days. Something in him ached as a result of watching her get hurt. He wanted to follow her and make sure she was okay but he knew that he had to stay with his subject, Kyle.

While driving down West Broad Street with her head throbbing, Cierra contemplated her next move. She drove directly to the police station. She filed an assault charge against Kyle and requested that Kyle be arrested and his belongings removed from her home. After the charges were filed an officer instructed her that she could return home but to wait for a patrol car before entering her apartment.

Cierra followed the officer's instructions. She returned home and sat in her car looking up at the four-story apartment building. She saw Kyle's silhouette pacing the living room through the sheer curtains. She remained in the car and thought about Chris and Terrance and how she wished she could be with one of them. She knew they would never treat her like this.

Kyle walked onto the balcony, lit a cigarette, and leaned on the rail. He noticed Cierra sitting in her car and raised his head like a dog listening to a strange sound. Just then, two police cruisers approached and parked in front of the building. One officer approached her, one went to cover the back of the building, and the other two officers walked up the steps to her apartment. Paul continued to watch from a distance. *Good for you, Cierra. I'm glad you did the right thing, most women don't.* As the cops escorted Kyle and his duffle bags away, Cierra heard them reading him his rights. He paid the officers no attention but tried to appeal to her with his poor excuses.

"Cierra, I'm sorry. I didn't mean to hurt you." She ignored him. "Are you listening to me? You don't have to do this."

After they placed Kyle in the police cruiser, two of the officers walked Cierra back into her apartment. One took a picture of the hole and the other told her what next steps to expect. They asked if she needed medical attention or needed to go to the hospital. She declined as she opened the freezer door, got an ice pack, and placed it in a kitchen towel then upon her head. The officers finished their report and left shortly thereafter. Cierra locked the sliding glass door, closed the outer curtains, and turned off the living room lights. She went to the kitchen and poured a glass of wine and ended the eventful evening. *Take care beautiful. I hope you're okay.* Paul started his engine and drove away to the precinct where Kyle was detained.

The DEA used Kyle's arrest to their advantage. They got a Search Warrant and confiscated his two duffle bags. Finally, they had the necessary evidence against him, but they also wanted Carlos Rodriquez and Lawrence Turner. Paul and some of his squad appeared at the county jail. Two DEA detectives interrogated Kyle, threatening him with so many federal offenses that he wouldn't see the light of day outside of a prison. After listening to the evidence piled against him, Kyle agreed to cooperate with the agency only if they dropped the assault charge. He didn't want anything to do with Cierra. One of the agents took his demand to Paul for further instructions.

"Paul, we got him but he won't cooperate unless we drop the assault charge."

"I heard his sorry ass. He doesn't have any bargaining power here. No deal. Ms. Sykes did the right thing. Make the assault charge stick."

"Alright. You got it."

At Paul's insistence, Kyle was still charged for the assault on Cierra. Paul observed Kyle's booking and interrogation from behind a two-way mirror. When he saw Kyle's outlandish reaction to his 'no deal' arrangement, he then walked into the interrogation room with two things on his mind, Red Velvet and Cierra.

"Who the hell are you?" asked Kyle as he eyed Paul from head to toe. Paul didn't answer.

"Tell me Kyle Dexter, does it make you feel like a man to hit a woman?" asked Paul as he walked around the grey, metal table where Kyle sat.

"Man, go to hell," Kyle snapped.

Paul abruptly approached Kyle and punched him in the jaw. "That's for hitting a female," said Paul as he watched Kyle's head swing swiftly to the left from the impact. Kyle tried to stand but Paul grabbed him and slammed him back into the metal chair.

"Sit your punk ass down," said Paul glaring at him.

"Guard, do something! You just can't stand there and let him get away with this shit!"

The guard stood motionless and did not make eye contact with either Kyle or Paul. Paul continued, "When I'm done with you, you will regret the day you met Carlos and Lawrence. I own your every move now, and don't you forget it, you pathetic piece of shit." Paul then looked at the guard and said, "I'm done. Get him out of here."

The guard escorted Kyle out of the room. Looking over his shoulder at Paul, Kyle yelled, "Fuck you! This shit ain't over. I'm gonna remember you."

"Yeah? You do that, you pussy!" Paul retorted.

The metal door closed behind a handcuffed Kyle Dexter and the escorting guard. Paul sat alone in the empty interrogation room thinking about his next move to bring down Carlos and Lawrence. Finally, he decided to call it a night and return to his Marriott hotel room. While cruising down West Broad Street, he decided to drive by Cierra's apartment to check whether she arrived home safely. He saw her parked car and felt strangely drawn to her. He wanted to see her one more time. He picked up his binoculars just in time to see her with the ice pack on her head as she closed the mini blinds to her bedroom. He was satisfied that she was okay. He then drove away wondering what she must be thinking and feeling.

She lied across the bed with an ice pack on her head, thinking about how her New Year was off to a rocky start. She deeply regretted ever listening to Lisa and Terri. *I should have known those bitches were no good. Like Rachel always says, 'You have to watch your back because people are scandalous.'* Then slowly she drifted to sleep.

She awoke the next morning stiff, sore, and bruised. Her head still ached but not as bad as last night. She managed to pull herself together and dressed in a skirt and long sleeve blouse to hide the bruises on her arms then drove to work.

Shortly following Kyle's arrest, Lisa and Terri sent nasty-grams over the instant message network to Cierra's computer at work. Cierra maintained her professionalism and tried not to let their messages, cat snares and glares disrupt her job performance. But the harassment made Cierra's workdays long and drawn out. She wanted to walk up to them and tell them exactly what she thought of them and let them know they could go straight to hell for all she cared. But that, of course, would be career suicide so she endured their snotty ways until their harassment got so bad she had no choice but to confront them and report them to Mr. Wilburn.

One day, Lisa and Terri entered the ladies' room laughing about how they tricked Cierra, not knowing that Cierra was already in one of the stalls.

"Girl, we got Miss Goody Two Shoes so good," Lisa chuckled.

"I know. Your brother did a number on her." They gave each other high-fives. Just then Cierra exited the stall, walked straight up them, and faced them head on undeterred that she was out numbered two to one.

"You got something you wanna say to me?" Cierra asked.

"Bitch, you better get out of my face," replied Lisa.

"Don't underestimate me, Lisa. I will mop this floor with your ignorant ass. I may have a face of a lamb, but I assure you, I have the heart of a lion. I warn you, don't keep fuckin' with me," Cierra said with conviction.

Terri wiggled her hands in the air and said, "Ooooo. We're so scared."

Cierra backed Terri against the sink, leaned into her, narrowed her eyes, and said, "You should be." Then Cierra walked out of the door. Terri looked at Lisa and said, "I can't believe you just stood there." Lisa sucked her teeth and commented, "Girl, please," as she fluffed her over processed hair. Disgusted, Terri returned to her desk.

Cierra drafted her complaint to Mr. Wilburn immediately following the restroom encounter. After reading her complaint, Mr. Wilburn met with Cierra. The following day, Cierra watched Lisa and Terri exit Mr. Wilburn's office. From that moment on, Cierra never received another instant message or even heard a peep out of either one of them. The office became a pleasant place for her to excel once more.

On February 7, 1989, Cierra went to court to witness Kyle's hearing. She had not seen him since January thirty-first, the day of his arrest. Paul sat in the rear of the courtroom to observe. He was glad that Cierra held Kyle accountable for his actions. He liked that about her.

After Cierra gave her account of what happened to the court, the judge reprimanded Kyle for striking her, fined him five hundred dollars, and ordered him to stay away from Cierra. The judge also ordered his return to New York due to outstanding warrants. This played right into the DEA's hand. Cierra sighed with relief upon the judge's decision and felt glad that she took action against Kyle's physical abuse, something she wished her mother had done a long time ago with her dad. Mostly, she was particularly glad that Kyle was leaving Richmond for good.

Paul exited the courtroom after the judge's decision, neither Cierra or Kyle saw him. Cierra made a pit stop in the restroom on her way out of the courthouse. Paul hung around to witness the U.S. Marshals escort Kyle into their vehicle to transport him immediately to NYC. On his way out of the courthouse, he saw Cierra walking down the corridor to the lobby doors. He desperately wanted to approach her and introduce himself, but he didn't. *If it's meant to be, I'll see her again.* As she walked away, he felt strangely odd because over the months, she somehow managed to carve out a special place within him. *This is crazy. All I did was surveillance her.* He tried to shake his feelings but it was no use, he was sprung.

Exhausted from the day's activity, Cierra went to bed early that evening.

> *Lord, thank you so much for delivering me from this horrible situation with Kyle. I knew Kyle was wrong from the moment I met him and yet I ignored the warning signs You sent me. Thank you for loving me in spite of myself. From now on, I will be patient and let You guide me to the man you desire in my life whether he is a friend or more than a friend. I have learned my lesson. Thank you. Amen.*

February

Fatigued from a day of meetings and conference calls, Cierra entered her apartment, flung her briefcase on the sofa and walked to the kitchen for a chilled glass of Sutter Home White Zinfandel. She pressed the answering machine button to check the four messages flickering on the display. Her mother, Josi, and Rachel called and left the first three messages. The fourth call took her by surprise.

"Hey, Ci. This is Chris. I know you're probably shocked at this call. You've been on my mind. I just wanted to talk with you and wish you Happy Valentine's Day. You can reach me at home. Miss you."

Cierra didn't know what to think. Her heart fluttered as she played the message over three times to repeatedly hear Chris' voice, but she wondered what he really wanted. She decided not to react on her first impulse to return his call right away. She decided to wait and think about whether to call him at all. After eating dinner and relaxing in a warm, Tiffany bubble bath, Cierra curled up in her bed, read an Essence magazine, and drifted to a peaceful place. Three hours later, the phone rang disturbing what felt like the best sleep in weeks.

"Hello," Cierra answered in a whisper.

"Hi, Ci. It's me, Chris."

"Oh, hey. How are you? I got your message. I would've called you back but it's been one of those days. I was gonna call you tomorrow."

"No problem. Like I mentioned on the message, you've been on my mind a lot and I just wanted to talk with you. I thought today being Valentine's Day, would be a good time to call."

"Did Damien and Rachel put you up to this?" Cierra questioned, wondering what initiated his call.

"No. They didn't have anything to do with me calling you. I didn't want anything in particular. I just wanted to hear your voice. We haven't talked in a long time that's all."

"I see. You're right. It's been almost three months," Cierra recalled.

"So, what's been up? How's the job?" he asked.

"Chris, how can you call here like nothing transpired? When we last saw each other in December on my birthday, you do remember that I asked you to get back together and you politely told me no because you have a girlfriend. So, why are you really calling me?"

"Ci, I've done a lot of reflecting and I handled that day all wrong. I could've and should've addressed you differently. I'm calling you because I want to let you know that I'm sorry for that day. Things didn't go quite like I wanted either."

"What do you mean?"

"I want us to be friends. It doesn't feel right not having you in my life at all."

Cierra remained silent and contemplated his request.

"Chris, I don't know. I'm tired of my heart being stepped on. All this back and forth with you is too much."

"Cierra, I know how you feel. We've been through a lot. But you gotta admit that it feels weird not talking to each other. It feels like a void in my life. You were right. We should at least be friends. So what do you say?"

"What exactly are you asking? Do you want to be just friends or try and get back together?" she asked still trying to figure him out.

"Ci, let's just go slow. Who knows what the future holds. I miss my best friend."

She sat silent thinking. *He's obviously taking the first step to reconcile. I'm glad he realizes his mistake. What the hell, why not?*

"Yeah, okay Chris, we can give our friendship a try."

"Cool. So, are you gonna tell me about your new job or not?"

"Oh, you don't want to know."

"That bad huh?"

"You have no idea. I mean the work is fine. But Lisa and Terri are off the chain," Cierra remarked.

"Who are Lisa and Terri?"

Glad that Chris expressed an interest, Cierra told him what happened with Kyle. Disturbed by the events she described, Chris felt somewhat guilty for not being there for her.

"Ci, I'm so sorry to hear that," he proclaimed.

"No need to be sorry. Plus, it's all behind me now," Cierra commented. For the next hour, their conversation flowed like they had just talked yesterday.

The next morning, Cierra promptly crossed the office door at eight a.m. She spun around in her office chair thinking about the wonderful conversation she had with Chris last night. Just then, Mr. Wilburn passed by with his cup of coffee and saw her in her happy state.

"Ms. Sykes how are you this morning?" he asked.

"Oh, Mr. Wilburn. I'm sorry. Forgive me," Cierra said as she straightened her chair to face the doorway.

Mr. Wilburn smiled, "No problem, Ms. Sykes. Continue to have a good day."

"Thank you, sir."

Cierra focused and organized the work on her desk. She started developing her new budget spreadsheet for the Senior Citizens new Medicare product when her office phone rang.

"Hello. Thank you for calling Health First Insurance Company. This is Cierra Sykes."

"Hey Ci. This is Rachel."

"Hey girl. How are you?"

"Fine."

"I was going to return your call last night but Chris called and we stayed on the phone for awhile."

"Oh? Do I hear reunited in the air?"

"Na girl. It's not even like that."

"Yeah right. You two are a trip."

"Seriously. It's been over two months since I've talked with him. The last time I talked to him was in December when I made my pathetic trip to Baltimore to ask him to get back together. Then out of the blue he called yesterday to talk."

"Whatever, Ci. You two kill me. You know you belong together. I don't know why you put each other through all these changes when you know you want to be together. He misses you. And that girlfriend of his, is not the one."

"Rachel, are you going to tell me why you called or not?"

"OK already. I wanted to tell you that Damien and I finally set a wedding date and planned the reception."

"Hallelujah! When and where? I'll be there."

"Well, I certainly hope so. You're my Maid of Honor."

"Really?"

"Yes, really."

"Cool. I'd love to be your Maid of Honor."

"Good. But I have to forewarn you that Damien asked Chris to be his Best Man and he accepted."

"That little sly devil. He didn't mention anything to me about the wedding when we talked last night. Now I know why he really called."

"Well, we asked him not to say anything until I talked with you. So, that wasn't his fault. You can blame me but he wanted to call you anyway."

"Y'all are always up to something. So, what's the date and venue?"

"We decided to get married in my home, St. Martin. The ceremony is on St. Patrick's Day, March 17, 1989, at the St. Catherine Cathedral and the reception will be outside in the Cathedral's rear garden.

"Rachel, that's only a month away."

"Yes, I realize it's short notice but that's the best we could do."

"I'm not questioning that. I just wonder if everyone you wanted to invite initially will be able to make it."

"Well, we downsized the guests list and cut back on some things. I know it's rather sudden. But as you know, this baby is not waiting to get here and we want to be married before it arrives. We only have a few months left. If folks can't make it, I understand. Is the date a problem with your schedule?"

"No, not at all. I'll be there with bells on. Don't worry about that. As long as everything is what you want and you're happy, then I'm happy."

The two finished discussing the high-level arrangements and made plans to talk in more detail at home after work. That evening when they talked, Rachel continued to describe the wedding, everything from determining the date to the food.

"I think Damien was so in tune with his first NFL season and the Pro Bowl that he didn't realize the growth rate of the baby until he went with me the other day to my last sonogram. Reality set in when he saw the size of the baby and watched it move its arms and legs. And then when he saw my entire stomach shift from one side to the other as the baby moved around, he looked at me and said, 'Baby, pick a date. Let's do this.' I already knew what day I wanted so I told him March seventeenth and it was a done deal."

"Oh that's so sweet. I'm glad you guys are together," Cierra said enjoying love vicariously through Rachel's experience.

"Are you going to find out the baby's gender?"

"At first we were but then we decided to enjoy God's gift to the fullest. We're looking forward to our little surprise. The doctor said the baby's development is normal and everything appears fine."

"That's wonderful. I'm so excited I can't wait to see her or him," Cierra said all giddy about holding and playing with the baby.

"You can't wait? Ci, I tell you, I'll be so glad when this pregnancy is over. You have no idea," said Rachel as she stirred her homemade spaghetti sauce for dinner. Damien walked into the kitchen and smelled the sauce over her shoulder as he wrapped his arms around her round belly. Rachel lifted the spoon to his mouth for him to taste.

"Mmm. That's good, baby," Damien commented.

"Well, I hear the man of the hour. Tell him hello," said Cierra.

"Here, you tell him." Rachel handed Damien the phone.

"Hey Ci, what's up? I haven't talked to you in a long time," he said.

"Hi superstar. Congratulations on everything, big papa. Man, you're doing it up, great season, baby on the way, wedding. You're the man."

"Thanks, Ci. On the real though, thanks for being around when Rachel needs a friend. We both appreciate your friendship."

"Don't mention it. I'll see you next month. I can't wait to go to St. Martin." Cierra envisioned herself sitting on a beautiful beach, swimming in the aqua colored water, and wondering how much would she and Chris see of each other while there.

"Yeah, me too. A'right, here's your girl." Damien handed Rachel the phone.

"Well, you better go feed all three of you," joked Cierra.

"I'll talk to you soon," said Rachel, preparing the dinner plates.

After talking with Rachel, Cierra took advantage of not having to complete any work from the job. She watched a movie then went to bed at a decent hour for a change.

Lord, I'm so excited. What an adventure this is going to be. I can't wait to board the plane and get away from here for a while. And would you believe Chris? He played like he didn't know anything. He could've given me a hint about the wedding date. But then again that would have spoiled Rachel's surprise. It was nice hearing his voice and talking with him again. And to be honest, I look forward to seeing him in St. Martin. But no matter what, I just hope I have a great time. I know if Bridget comes, I definitely will. Amen.

Spring 1989

March

The plane's hard landing at Richmond International Airport woke Cierra from her deep thoughts about the past. When the plane's wheels touched the ground with a final thump, the last images of Chris kissing her at the St. Martin airport jolted from her mind. As they taxied to the hangar, Cierra thought about her college friends. *Rachel is officially Mrs. Damien Hall now and will soon have their first child.* Visions of a similar fate pranced in her mind as she hoped for a union with Chris. Having thought about her parents, relationship with Chris, and friendships with Terrance and Kyle, she was thankful for the wonderful trip to the Caribbean. She hoped never to experience another year like 1988.

After exiting the plane and gathering her luggage from the turnstile, Cierra retrieved her car from the long-term parking and drove straight home to her apartment. She played the answering machine as she sorted a small batch of junk mail and bills. Kelly and Josi left most of the messages. A few calls were from her mother informing about the hellacious actions of her dad. She didn't want to talk to anyone at the moment and chose not to return the calls. She wanted to savor her March trip to St. Martin as long as possible and recount all the special moments Chris and she shared.

1989 is going to be our year. I just know it. She lounged on the sofa while memories of Chris and her kissing and embracing by the pool swarmed her mind. The recollection of his hands under her dress made her touch herself and want him all the more. She recalled the scent of his cologne and how it stimulated her senses. She felt her breast swell from the mere thought of being next to him. The sensations of his fingers in her made her fill her haven with her own. She squirmed as she thought about him making love to her on her sofa at Halloween last year. She wanted him again. She worked her fingers until she pleased herself to a satisfying climax.

Glancing at the clock across the room, she wished she could call him, but his flight to Baltimore wasn't scheduled to arrive until later. Time passed slowly as she showered, unpacked, fixed something to eat and lounged around in her sweats for the rest of the day waiting for nightfall to call Chris.

Damn just seven thirty. It's still too early to call. She made some microwave popcorn, started a movie and killed another two hours. Then finally the clock read nine thirty p.m. She picked up the phone and dialed Chris in Baltimore.

"Hi Chris,"

"Hey, what's up, Ci? I see you made it back to Richmond safely."

"Yeah. How was your flight?" she asked.

"That was the roughest plane ride I've ever been on. The turbulence was really bad. Let me just say that I'm glad to have my feet on the ground and be back home."

"Yeah, me too. But wasn't St. Martin absolutely beautiful? I had such a great time," said Cierra with a big smile upon her face.

"Yeah, me too," Chris replied as he unpacked the last of his clothes.

"Rachel and Damien are Mr. and Mrs. Hall now with a child on the way. It still seems like yesterday we were all at Virginia Tech," said Cierra remembering their college days.

"Yeah, time flies. That's for sure," Chris agreed.

"Sometimes, I wish I could freeze Father Time long enough to extend special moments, like the one we had walking on the beach when you kissed me, and out by the pool when we, well, you know, took things to another level," said Cierra, wondering what his reply would be.

"Word. That was special," remarked Chris.

Cierra continued, "And if Bridget's drunk behind hadn't come down the hall when you walked me to my hotel room, I know our night would've ended differently." She paused, giving him a chance to explain his hesitation at her door and decision to leave.

"Ci, you're probably right. But everything happens for a reason. Those extra moments made me think about Tonya. It wouldn't have been the right thing to do even though I wanted to be with you."

"Chris, if you want to be with me and I with you, why can't we? We dated for four years and I know you still love me."

"Ci, I do love you. But-"

"But what, Chris? You know I love you and you have my heart."

Chris searched his mind for the right words to try to explain his feelings. "Ci, time will tell. Maybe we just need to let things be and let time figure this all out."

"Fine, Chris. But you're only fooling yourself if you think your so-called girlfriend has your best interest at heart."

"Ci, you will always be my first real love. The four years we spent together were great. But I messed up with you at Tech and as a result we both ventured down different paths. I'm with Tonya now and even though you say you didn't date Terrance, he was diggin' you."

"Chris, I've told you a million times, he was just a friend. You know that. And I'm past your cheating with Amy at Tech. I want to move forward."

"I know, but Ci, I gotta see this relationship with Tonya through."

"Fine. But you're making a huge mistake."

His wanting to be with Tonya wasn't the answer she hoped for but she believed he would come to his senses.

"Ci, it's getting late and I need to catch some z's. I'll talk with you again soon."

"OK."

"Goodnight."

"Night, Chris."

After their phone call ended, Cierra grabbed her favorite pillow and embraced it as though it was Chris. *What a fool he is thinking Tonya cares about him.*

The next morning, Cierra awoke to Kelly's voice on the answering machine, "Ci, pick up. I know you're back. Pick up."

"Hello," Cierra said in a muffled morning voice.

"Hey girl, it's me, Kelly."

"I know. What time is it?"

"I know it's early but I couldn't wait to hear about your trip. Was Chris there?"

"Kelly. Not now. I need to sleep," Cierra pleaded.

"Yeah, okay. Well, look, Josi and I will be over around one today."

"OK. Can I go back to sleep now?"

"Yeah. See you later."

Kelly hung up the phone. Cierra looked at the clock, *Eight a.m. Sunday morning. Kelly must be out of her mind.* She placed a pillow atop her head and went back to sleep.

As promised, Kelly and Josi arrived at Cierra's doorstep at one. While having lunch, Cierra told her friends about her trip and encounters with Chris. By the time she finished, their mouths hung to the floor.

"So what are you going to do?" asked Kelly.

"Nothing. Play it cool," Cierra responded.

"This is like something you see in the movies," Josi said with her usual excitement.

"Josi, you're such the hopeless romantic. In my opinion, he still doesn't know what he wants. How can he still want to date Tenisha, TaTa or whatever her name is, after all that?" voiced Kelly.

"Oh hush, Kelly. Cierra, don't listen to her. You and Chris were meant to be together. You mark my words. He's gonna dump Tonya and get back with you," Josi foretold.

"We'll see," Cierra commented.

The three hung out at Cierra's place watching movies, eating popcorn, and drinking wine coolers. The evening rolled in and their fun came to an end. Kelly and Josi helped Cierra clean the mess they all created and then left.

Early Monday morning, Cierra returned to work vibrant and exhilarated ready to complete old projects and take on new challenges. Mr. Wilburn noticed her changed demeanor and commented that he needed a trip like hers. Due to the rollout of a new Senior Healthcare product, the remaining weeks in March passed quickly as Cierra stayed busy leading a team of twelve to an implementation date of April first. Cierra contributed her extra boost of dedication and energy to the inspiration Chris gave her as they kept in contact and talked twice a week, mostly during the day at work. She suspected evening calls were numbered because of Tonya but that didn't stop her from calling him at home from time to time and he didn't seem to mind. *Besides, he calls me in the evening sometimes, too. He's probably checking to see who's around my place.*

They continued to excel in their careers. Cierra encouraged Chris throughout his high profile architect project for Price Walters & Associates in Baltimore and he inspired her with the challenging HFIC marketing projects Mr. Wilburn assigned. Cierra felt completely at ease with their rekindled friendship. She loved how their conversations ebbed and flowed like the ocean tide. Their understanding of each other made their interactions effortless. Without question, the mental and emotional connection between them took root and thrived more intensely day-by-day. A special chemistry existed between them and the attraction fueled Cierra's belief that Chris' relationship with Tonya was just a whim.

> *Lord, Tonya or no Tonya, Chris is my piece of paradise on earth. I believe that You brought us back to each other for a reason. There's no way a kinship this deep can ever die. We were made for each other; he's my soul mate. I'm the only woman who has ever carried his baby and I know that means the world to him. It's been close to a year since Chris and I broke up. And now the time has come to set things straight. This thing with Tonya is far from over, far from over indeed. With your blessing, I want my man back. Amen.*

Epilogue

Life was a roller coaster ride for Cierra Sykes from the fall of 1987 to the spring of 1989, taking her to heights of joy and depths of despair. During that time, she endured the betrayal of her beloved Christopher Jackson, the miscarriage of their child, the relentless abuse of her father, and misunderstanding of her mother. Yet, when things were at there worse, Cierra took control of a bad situation and overcame the intentions of Kyle Dexter, who attempted to set up a drug trafficking ring in her home.

Smart, beautiful, and career oriented, she started to turn her life around. With a new job at a prestigious insurance company, she became more focused on the things she wanted.

She had shared a heart's journey with Chris and now that time had healed her heartache from his affair with Amy McKenzie, she knew that she wanted and needed him in her life. She wanted to pursue the dreams they shared, and explore what life held in store for them. Her love for Chris was as fresh and renewed as an early spring shower and she wasn't going to let anything or anyone stand in the way, especially Tonya Porter, his current fly by night, girlfriend.

One morning before starting her workday, Cierra looked at a photo Rachel took of Chris and her swimming in the ocean in St. Martin.

> *The Lord brought us back together for a reason. Like folks always say, if you let something go and it comes back to you, it was meant to be. I know this is the case with Chris and me. If only we can share another loving encounter like the one at my hotel room in St. Martin before Bridget interrupted us. I know he will be all mine, hands down.*

Cierra needed to sustain her inner peace and rekindled friendship with Chris. Love always seemed to remain in the midst of their circumstances. Every woman wants the man of her dreams and Cierra is no different. But what does a woman have to do to be complete? Cierra found the secret and experienced what most women only imagine.

Continue to take a journey with Cierra as the storyline unfolds her struggles and triumphs with her lovers, friends, and family. Read the next section for excerpts from the sequel, **Deep Waters: A Heart's Journey Part Two**.

Deep Waters

A Heart's Journey
Part Two

Janice N. Adams

Coming Soon

Chapter 1

(Excerpt)

May 1989

While nestled deep in her Egyptian cotton sheets, Cierra reluctantly answered the phone on its fifth ring, early that Spring morning.

"Hello," she muttered, placing the phone next to her ear.

"Ci!" Rachel screamed into the receiver, "I think I'm in labor and Damien is not here," she held her round belly, trying to control her breathing.

"Wait. What? I thought the baby was due in May not the middle of April," a shocked Cierra replied, suddenly sitting at attention, wondering what she could, being two hours away in Richmond, Virginia.

"It is but something is happening now and I'm scared," Rachel moaned in great pain.

"OK, stay calm. Where is Damien?"

"I don't know, practice maybe. He's not answering his phone. Ouuucchh! This hurts like hell," Rachel yelled.

"Oh my god, Rachel. Ok, stay calm," Cierra repeated, trying to keep Rachel and herself from panicking. "Breath Rachel, breathe," Cierra instructed as she paced the floor. She heard Rachel breathing how she was taught in birthing class. "Ok that's better. Have you called your doctor?" Cierra asked, concerned that the situation would escalate.

"No," answered Rachel, between breaths.

"No? Well, can you drive yourself to the hospital?"

"I don't know. I don't think so. It hurts real bad like cramps to the tenth power! Oh mon Dieu, mon Dieu," she cried in her French dialect. She leaned back against her headboard.

"Rachel, you need to hang up, call your doctor or drive to the hospital."

"I don't think I can drive."

"OK, can you call your neighbor? She told you that she could help if Damien's not around, right? See if she can take you because it sounds like you're having contractions."

"Oui," Rachel answered, crying in more agony. Cierra felt helpless being so far away from her friend. "Call me back and let me know what she says."

"OK," Rachel agreed as she tried to move to get her neighbor's phone number out of the nightstand drawer.

"If she doesn't answer, call your doctor or an ambulance if you need to."

"OK," Rachel moaned. They hung up.

Cierra looked at the digital clock, five-thirty a.m. *Where can Damien be?* She showered and dressed just in case she needed to travel to Reston to help Rachel. She made breakfast and paced the floor, waiting for Rachel's phone call. Forty-five minutes later, her phone rang.

"Hello," she answered, loading the last of the dishes into the dishwasher.

"Hey, Ci, it's me, Damien. We're at the hospital."

"Is Rachel and the baby OK?" Cierra asked concerned for her friend.

"I don't know. They're still examining her," commented Damien, truly worried about his queen and unborn child.

"I hope they are alright." She leaned against the counter wiping her hands with the dishtowel, debating whether to ask him about his whereabouts.

"Me too, Ci, me too. This wasn't suppose to happen this soon."

"Where were you, Damien? Rachel was going crazy looking for you."

Chapter 2

(Excerpt)

May 1989

Cierra stood in front of her foyer mirror, fanning her open palms vigorously toward her face, trying to remain cool. She took a deep breath and opened the door. There stood Chris with a warm smile. He quickly absorbed the sight before him, a sweet scented Cierra dressed in a pretty floral sundress and natural casual sandals. He walked into her apartment and hugged her liked he hadn't seen her in ages. At that moment, Cierra exhaled a sigh of relief, believing he had returned to reunite.

"Make yourself at home," she said, guiding him to the living room. He strolled in and walked around, checking out every room to see if anything had changed since his last visit in October last year, when he made passionate love to her throughout the apartment.

Cierra followed him trying to control her lustful thoughts and heart's desire as she watched his calf and thigh muscles flex with each step. She envisioned gripping and pulling his perfectly round, tight ass towards her pelvic once more. To stop her racy thoughts, she offered to make him breakfast but he declined stating that he already ate. She then offered something to drink and he accepted a glass of orange juice. They returned to the living room where Cierra sat on the sofa and gestured Chris to sit beside her. He drank the glass of juice as though it was a shot of liquor then took the glass to the kitchen. When he returned to the living room, he sat on the edge of the chair across the room from her.

"Chris, what's wrong? You're acting weird," she said becoming alarmed at his behavior.

"Cierra, this isn't going to be easy."

"What isn't?" she asked moving to the edge of the sofa.

"I have something to tell you."

"You're scaring me. What is it?"

Chris sat silently yielding that awkward moment Cierra detested.

"Chris, what is it?" she insisted.

"It's about Tonya."

"Dear God. She's pregnant," said Cierra as she threw her hands in the air disgusted.

"No. That's not it," remarked Chris.

Relieved Cierra asked again. "Well, what is it, Chris?"

"I asked Tonya to marry me."

"You what?" Cierra jumped to her feet and approached him. Chris stood trying to explain.

"Ci, don't make this any harder than it is."

"Chris, what the hell are you talking about? How could you ask Tonya to marry you after all that we've put back together? Did that bitch put you up to this?" Cierra's voice raised two octaves as angry, hurtful tears streamed down her face.

"Ci, please," pleaded Chris.

"Please what? I don't believe this shit." Cierra sat and cried with her face in her hands. Chris attempted to touch her shoulder.

"Don't touch me, Chris! Don't you dare touch me."

Chapter 3

(Excerpt)

June 1989

Cierra stared at the ceiling each night, wondering why things happened the way they did. Silent tears often crept out of the corner of her eyes as the memories of her last conversation with Chris orbited her mind. *How am I going to survive this Lord?* After weeks of sadness, Cierra felt her depression grow like wild ivy, taking over and smothering everything in its path. She avoided her mother and father as well as Kelly and Josi. She reported to work on time, but kept her door slightly closed; closing it completely would have offended Mr. Wilburn, and she didn't want that to happen. She didn't return personal phone calls, not even to Rachel, who frequently left messages about the baby. Cierra barely ate, couldn't sleep, and stopped exercising. She felt herself changing into a bitter person who didn't trust people, particularly men. She developed discontentment for relationships and vowed not to date anyone in the near or distant future. Her heart hardened as she recalled all the drama that had occurred in her life with her family, Chris, Terrance, and Kyle.

> *Lord, how can so much happen to one person in a year's time? I am mentally and emotionally drained and worn down. All this time, I thought that I was doing the right thing. Now I'm more insecure about my decisions than ever before. I feel like I don't know who I am anymore. I don't have a clue about who or what I should be. I'm so lost and feel as though I've traveled down a long road that has*

led to nowhere. Is this what You had in store for me? Don't I deserve better? I'm so angry and hurt. Why did You do this to me? Amen.

Chapter 4

(Excerpt)

September 1989

The Labor Day weekend brought above normal temperatures and clear skies, enabling Cierra, Kelly, and Josi to enjoy their usual weekend outing to the Underground Club in Shockoe Slip. Having danced most of the night, the three worked up a sensational appetite.

"Girls, let's go get something to eat. I'm starving," suggested Kelly.

"Me too," chimed Cierra.

"That's fine. Whatever you ladies want to do is ok with moi," slurred Josi.

They left the club and ventured to a twenty-four hour I-Hop on West Broad Street. Tipsy from one too many Long Island Ice Teas, Josi made a rowdy entrance into the restaurant as Cierra and Kelly tried to control her loud outbursts. People eyed the three young ladies as the hostess seated them at the closest available table.

"Hi, may I take your drink order?" asked the waitress, holding her pen and pad.

"Oh God. Please don't say that word," Josi instructed the waitress.

"What word," the waitress questioned, "I just asked for your drink order."

"Oh damn, she said it again. Where's the ladies' room?" Josi asked, holding her mouth and stomach. The waitress pointed to the left and Josi made a mad dash to the restroom.

"Pay her no mind. She's had too much to drink tonight," Kelly informed the waitress.

"Ohhh. That word. Well, that explains it. Now what would you ladies like?"

Cierra and Kelly placed their drink order. Shortly, the waitress returned with their orange juice, and fresh hot coffee for Josi. After waiting ten minutes for Josi to return from the restroom, Kelly grew impatient.

"Ci, forget about waiting for her. I'm starving and ready to eat. I'm placing our food order when the waitress returns."

"I'll go check on her," said Cierra as she scooted away from the table. She walked to the restroom and accidentally bumped into a six foot two tall, chestnut brown, handsome young man coming out of the men's restroom.

"Excuse me," he apologized.

"No, I'm sorry. I should watch where I'm going," Cierra remarked. *Damn, this brother is good-looking but is probably a dog like all the rest. In his case, I'm quite sure he's an atomic dog.*

Admiring Cierra's ensemble of makeup, hair, jewelry and stylish attire, the young man stared at her then commented, "If you don't mind me saying, you're breathtaking."

Yeah, right, whatever. If I had a dime for every time I heard that line, I'd be rich. "Thank you, but um-, I need to go check on my friend." She pointed to the ladies' room.

He wanted to move but his feet were frozen as thoughts of seeing her last year with Kyle Dexter consumed his mind. He felt strange standing before her. An urge within him wanted to apologize for not intervening when he witnessed Kyle slamming her into the wall of her apartment. He wanted to protect her but at the time he couldn't because he would've jeopardized the DEA Red Velvet operation. He stood there grateful that fate was now on his side.

"Forgive my manners. Hi, I'm Paul Phillips." He extended his hand.

"Look um- Paul, right," she shook his hand, "nice to meet you, but I really need to check on my friend."

"That's cool. I'll wait," he replied, smiling from ear to ear.

www.ingramcontent.com/pod-product-compliance
Lightning Source LLC
Chambersburg PA
CBHW022004010726
47494CB00003B/889